Back To Our Beginning

PROTECTOR'S OF JASPER CREEK
BOOK FOUR

CAITLYN O'LEARY

Thank you Marsha McDaniel for all of the support, help and laughter you have brought into my life these many years.

Authors Note

This book is Grady "Beau" Beaumont's story. His missing twin brother's story was recently released in Dreaming for Home. You do not have to read Dreaming for Home in order to enjoy this book. Both books are stand-alones. But reading Dreaming for Home might enhance your enjoyment of this book, no matter what order you read the books in.

Prologue

GRADY 'BEAU' BEAUMONT

The house wasn't just quiet—it was empty. A silence that wasn't just the absence of noise, it was the absence of life. My mother's life.

Mrs. Magill and Little Grandma had been the last ones to leave. I'd tried to be polite as I practically shoved them out the door, but now the house was quiet. Too quiet.

For the first time in over two years, I wasn't listening for Mom's voice to ask for water, or the rustle of sheets as she was getting out of bed to go to the bathroom. The silence should have come as a relief, but it didn't. Instead, it felt like a boulder pressing down on me, one I couldn't shake off.

I sat on our worn couch, staring at the darkened TV screen. My hands were clasped so tightly that my knuckles ached.

I barked out a sad laugh. Not a good thing for a wide receiver.

Fuck, how could I be laughing? My mother was gone. The woman who'd worked so hard to stay this side of sane and happy had finally lost her fight to brain cancer, and I was laughing.

What kind of asshole was I?

But tonight, I didn't feel any tears ready to choke me, instead I felt something much worse. I felt relief.

I shot up off the couch when I realized just how evil I was. My fist hit the wall beside the crucifix, plowing through the drywall. I didn't feel a thing. Pulling my hand out of the wall, I took deep breaths, trying to get my rage at myself under control. Trying to make sense of everything.

It was when I looked down at the picture that had crashed to the ground from my punch that I started to see sense. It was a picture of me and Brady. My twin brother.

I picked up the picture and looked at it. Brady and I had just turned three. One of us was sitting in a Radio Flyer red wagon, and the other was wearing red cowboy boots. My father had abducted my brother soon after that picture had been taken. I never saw either of them again.

When my dad took Brady, it was as if he'd taken all of the joy out of the house. My mom had been suffering every day since then, even before her cancer had struck. Every single day.

Year after year, my mom suffered, even before the cancer struck. Dragging me down as she leaned harder and harder on me, making no attempt to lift herself up, instead relying on me to be not one son, but two. Dooming me to failure.

I carefully set the picture of me and my brother on top of the mantle, next to my football trophy, and pressed my finger against Brady's face.

"I miss you, Brady. Why couldn't it have been me who got to leave? Why did I get stuck cleaning up all the shit?"

I caught sight of the trophy, and it reminded me of football and everything Coach Anderson and his wife had been doing for me. Hell, everything the whole town of Jasper Creek had been doing for me ever since Mom got diagnosed with cancer. She hadn't wanted any in-home care. Of course she hadn't. And there was never any thought of her leaving this house, so mostly, it had come down to me.

Except it hadn't.

Not this time.

The whole town of Jasper Creek had rallied around me. They made sure I had food in the fridge, that I didn't flunk out of high school, and that I still had a place on the football team. Coach Anderson and Maddie Avery were the two who pushed me the hardest. Okay, maybe Little Grandma too. They were the three who made sure I didn't lose myself in my mother's sickness. But it was Coach who told me that the best thing he ever did was not let his hometown keep him down. He told me that if I'd had the grades, he could have gotten me a football scholarship, but I didn't, so that was that. Instead, he told me to do like he did. Join the Marines.

As soon as he said it, I knew Coach Anderson was right. I could feel it deep in my bones, the need to get out, to escape like Brady had. Staying meant drowning in ghosts. Leaving meant a chance at something else. At something that wasn't an anchor.

There was only one problem, and it was a big one. I couldn't stand the thought of leaving my best friend. The thought of not having Maddie Avery down the street twisted my gut into knots. I'd had her in my life since kindergarten. When Coach talked about not letting my hometown holding me back, he didn't understand about Maddie being the one sure thing that had always lifted me up.

She always said we lifted each other up, and I guess maybe that was true. Her life at home was ugly, no matter how much her older sisters and brother tried to shield her. We'd clung to one another as my mother's depression got deeper and darker, year over year, and her daddy and ma got meaner and nastier every year. When it felt like we both had nothing, we had each other.

"But I'm free," I whispered to myself. I didn't need Maddie to lighten my load while I lifted her up, because Mom was dead. Now it would just be me helping Maddie...

"No!"

I stormed across the living room and yanked open the front door. I stared at the porch swing that we'd sat on thousands of times.

How was I supposed to walk away from her? I owed it to her to stay, didn't I? But what if I did stay and I ended up resenting her?

"Fuck!"

I wanted out of this damned town and away from these damned memories so bad. I wanted more than Jasper Creek—I had no idea what, but I wanted more than the whispers of pity and the constant reminders of all the people I'd lost. I needed a clean slate. A different life. Something that was all mine.

Graduation was in two weeks.

I sat down on the porch swing and slowly made my decision. Now I'd just have to tell Maddie. It was going to gut me. But she wouldn't cry. She'd pretend to be happy for me. That was who Maddie Avery was.

She was a much better person than me.

And after I left, I could never look back. Because if I did, I might forget why I left in the first place—and ruin everything we'd ever been to one another.

Chapter One

Fifteen years of almost absolute silence, and now he was here.

Again.

It was twice now he had taken leave and come back to Jasper Creek in the last eight months. Just to visit his twin, and both times he hadn't reached out to me.

I shoved open the door to Maverick's Bar and Grill, my pulse hammering in my ears, my stomach tied up in knots. Laughter, the crack of pool balls, and the scent of fried food washed over me, but none of it mattered. Because I was here for one reason.

Beau.

"Damn, it's crowded, Maddie. Good thing Michael said he saved a booth for us."

I looked over at my friend and gave her a wan smile. "Yeah, that's good," I said, then I went back to scanning the room. I'd called ahead and Vic, the bartender, had told me Beau had arrived half an hour ago, so now it was just a matter of finding him.

"Are you even listening to me?"

I looked at Fallon again. "What?"

"Michael texted. He's against the west wall. That means he's near the jukebox. Come on." Fallon grabbed my hand and started tugging me past the hostess stand and through the crowd.

"I see Michael," Fallon cried.

And that's when I saw him. And it was like the air got sucked straight out of my lungs.

It was Beau. Beau 'Grady' Beaumont. There, in the flesh. A man I hadn't seen in fifteen years. Someone I'd considered my best friend since kindergarten, and here he was in Jasper Creek. Where he'd been for the last week and a half, and he hadn't even reached out.

My stomach twisted.

Stop it! God knows this isn't the worst thing that's ever happened to me. Think of Mom and Dad.

I let out a harsh laugh.

Fallon grabbed my hand and pulled. "Come on, Michael's waving at us."

I stood my ground. "I see Beau. You go on ahead."

Beau was sitting at a high table next to people playing pool. He turned his head and his gaze zeroed in on mine like a heat-seeking missile. How was that even possible? But it was. Another set of silver-blue eyes looked at me, but I ignored him. It was Beau's identical twin brother, Brady. Everybody had thought he was dead, but here he was, alive.

Again, I didn't give a shit. My focus was on Beau. My best friend who I'd known down to my soul, a friend I thought I would never lose. The same man who had sent me only one letter during basic training, then never contacted me again, no matter how many times I had tried to get a hold of him.

Beau had been as much of a ghost as Brady.

Now he was back in town for the second time this year. Sitting at Maverick's, after being home for over a week. Eleven days he hadn't reached out to me. It cut deep. Deeper still because this was the second time he'd done this to me. How could I matter so little to him? What had I done wrong?

I blinked back tears.

Dammit, I will not cry.

This Beau was a stranger. He looked different. Broader, harder, with stronger edges in his face, but I could recognize his silver-blue eyes anywhere, anytime. His were sharper than Brady's. A little more silver. Yep, that was my man.

Still, he wasn't the teenager who'd left me with a gaping hole in my heart. Even though I'd agreed he needed to leave.

But what in the ever-loving hell gave him the right to ignore me like this? I deserved better!

"Maddie, let's just go sit down. You don't have to deal with this tonight," Fallon pleaded.

"Go sit down with Michael. I'll be there in just a minute."

I swallowed hard, straightened my shoulders, and forced my feet forward toward the pool area. Each step felt like I was walking through drying cement.

I stopped at their table and tilted my head, looking Beau in the eye. For just a moment I thought I saw shock, guilt, maybe even regret, flash in his eyes, but it was then covered with a mask of fake cheerfulness.

"Doesn't an old friend deserve a hug?" I asked.

His phony smile got bigger. Don't ask me how I knew it was phony, but I did, and I wanted to shrivel up and die, but there wasn't a chance in hell I was going to do any such thing.

"Maddie," he murmured, his voice like rough gravel.

I waited.

He stepped toward me and pushed his hands under my stiff arms, wrapping his bulging muscles around my waist. My eyes closed. It was as if every moment of my time with Beau came rushing back, and I circled my arms around his neck, pulling him closer.

Then I caught his scent—clean, crisp, with a hint of leather and something unmistakably Beau. A shockwave sizzled down my spine, hot and electric, leaving my knees weak.

I went stiff again, but this time it was for a different reason.

This wasn't a 'Beau' hug.

This was something else entirely.

Beau released me so fast, I thought I was going to fall. This time when I looked into his eyes, they were hot, penetrating, and slightly confused. But mostly hot.

I was sure mine were needy, and didn't that just suck donkey balls?

"You've changed." His voice was still low.

I only nodded. What could I say to such a stupid comment? After all, it had been fifteen years.

"You don't have anything to say?" he asked.

I shrugged. "What else is there? I got my hug. Now I'll go back and join my friends for dinner."

"Why don't you have dinner with Kai and me?" He motioned to his twin, who was watching the two of us with avid interest.

"No, I can't. I don't leave my friends hanging."

A direct hit. Beau winced, and I smiled sweetly.

"Maybe we can set up some other time to meet. How does that sound?"

I shrugged. "Sure." I turned to Kai and held out my hand. "It's nice to see you again. Say hello to Marlowe for me," I added, referring to his fiancée.

He looked between Beau and me, then shook my hand. Nope, not even a twinge of electricity. But I'd been pretty sure there wouldn't be. Still, it was always good to make sure. I turned back to Beau. "I'll see you around."

"Wait a minute. I need your number."

"Fallon and Michael are waiting to order. I've got to go."

He frowned down at me. It was a look I'd never seen before. He looked hard and commanding.

"Hand me your phone, Maddie," he ordered.

"Why in the hell should I?"

"Please?"

I wavered.

"I said the magic word." He smiled. Shit, it was the Beau smile I remembered. All teasing and coaxing.

I reluctantly pulled my phone out of my jacket pocket and handed it to him.

"What's your passcode?" he demanded.

I ripped my phone out of his hand, turned away from him, and keyed in my six-digit passcode. He was grinning when I turned back to him and slammed the phone in his hand. He keyed something into my phone and I heard a ring. It came from his back pocket.

"There, now I have your number, and you have mine."

"Gee, I feel so special." I yanked my phone out of his hand again. This time, I shoved it back into my jacket pocket.

I gave a little wave to Kai and didn't look at Beau as I hustled my way back to Michael and Fallon. I needed a drink. A double. I deserved it. I had successfully confronted my past, and it was finally a closed subject. I could move on.

"You, okay?" Fallon asked, as I slipped in beside her.

"I'm fine." My phone beeped with an incoming text, so I grabbed it in case it was from one of my sisters or one of my cases.

> UNKNOWN:What time should I pick you up tomorrow night?

I stared down at my phone in disbelief. The absolute audacity of that man.

"Is there a problem?" Michael asked.

I shook my head and continued to stare down at my phone as another message came in.

> UNKNOWN:I see you looking at your phone. If you won't answer, then I'll pick you up at seven.

> MADDIE:Am I supposed to be impressed that you know where I live, since you couldn't be bothered to stop by any sooner? So, no. Don't bother showing up. I won't answer the door.

> UNKNOWN:A Marine Raider never abandons a mission. I'll see you at seven.

> MADDIE:Do what you need to do

"Maddie? Everything okay?" Fallon asked again.

"Everything's fine now," I assured my friend. "And everything's going to be much better when I have a twenty-four-ounce beer in front of me."

Michael laughed.

Well, at least I fooled him. But Beau? He probably thought I'd won that round. But my hands were still shaking, and deep down, I knew the truth.

I hadn't won a damn thing.

I'd just kicked a hornet's nest, and the sting was coming.

I paced my living room. Usually it felt a lot bigger, but tonight it felt tiny. I felt trapped. I looked down at my smart watch. Twenty minutes to seven. Glancing over at my dining room table, I saw my laptop open with bills and piles of paperwork from work scattered around. Normally, I would have tidied that up, but I wasn't going to go to any extra effort for Beau. Nope, I didn't want him to think he was getting any special treatment.

I slid my hand down my curly hair and winced. The elixir I had put in to make my curls bouncy seemed to have lost its effect. I hustled to the bathroom and checked it out. I sprayed some more on my hair and applied another coat of pink lip gloss while I was at it. But it wasn't for Beau, it was for me. Sometimes I just liked to look nice when I was spending time at home.

I snorted.

Yeah sure.

At least I hadn't gone overboard on my clothes. It was just leggings and a pretty, off-the-shoulder sweater. Normal.

Kind of.

Anyway, he probably wasn't even going to show up. I marched back into the living room. My stomach was roiling with nerves. I grabbed the remote and started scrolling through possible options of things to watch. Maybe there would be some people searching for bigfoot. That would work.

My phone rang.

I rolled to my side and grabbed it out of my purse sitting on the coffee table. I saw it was Polly Owens.

It took me a couple of seconds to remember who that was. When I did, I got scared.

"Hello?"

"Ms. Avery? It's Polly. The Jacksons' neighbor."

My stomach clenched again. I knew exactly who she was. She and I had talked a couple of times since Eli Jackson had become one of my at-risk foster kids.

"What happened? Was it bad? Did you have to call the cops?"

"You got it in one."

I winced. Eli was six years old and his home was a nightmare. His mother, Colleen, had been in and out of rehab so often, she was due a free sandwich. For the last three months, she'd been living with some lowlife who had a history of domestic abuse.

"Are they still there?"

"No, they left. That's why I'm calling you. There was yelling and screaming. It was Colleen and Bruce. I even heard breaking glass. I waited for the cops in my front yard. I'm not afraid of Bruce. I have a gun. The police asked me questions, then they went and knocked on their door. Colleen talked to them. She must have said something good, because they said that they didn't have probable cause to search the place, and they were going to leave."

"What about Eli?" I asked Polly.

"That's the same question I had for the cops. They said that Colleen had told them he was with his grandmother for the night. I've lived here next to Colleen for two years. I ain't never heard tell of any grandmother. I told the cops that, but they said that wasn't enough reason to search the place."

"So, they're gone?" I asked.

"Yep. But I've got a bad feeling. You left your card with me after that time Eli was left at home by hisself for three days. I figured you might could do something about this."

"Thanks, Mrs. Owens. I'll be right there."

I shot to my feet and ran to my bedroom to get my socks and boots and put them on. I snatched my leather jacket and raced to the kitchen table where my files were. Eli's was on top. I grabbed it and threw it into my work satchel. I hefted that onto my shoulder along with my purse.

My heart pounded as I thought about the small boy in that house. It just wasn't fair.

Yeah, when was life ever fair?

I reached the door when a knock sounded. It was a sharp, firm rap against the wood.

Ahh shit. It's Beau.

I yanked the door open. "I've gotta go. We're going to have to do this dance some other night."

His brow furrowed as he looked down at me. "What are you talking about?"

"Don't have time." I turned and locked my door. "There's a kid in trouble who needs me." I jogged down my porch steps and headed to my carport.

"Hold up. What do you mean there's a kid in trouble?"

I hit my key fob and my Jeep unlocked. I got inside and shut the door. Beau stood at the bottom of my steps, hands on his hips, eyes narrowed. Not just pissed. Confused. Frustrated. Maybe even a little hurt. No; that last one I was just imagining.

Keep it together, Avery. Remember, we don't give a shit.

Only Eli mattered.

Chapter Two

I gripped my steering wheel so tightly my fingers ached. My teeth ground together as I followed Maddie's Jeep out of Jasper Creek, first on the highway, then through the back roads of Gatlinburg. She was driving too damn fast. Way too fast for these winding roads. I kept expecting her to lose control, for her tires to slide out on the gravel shoulders. That pissed me off even more.

What in the ever-loving hell had she been thinking, racing through town like that?

When she stopped in front of a house, I pulled up behind her, slammed my truck into park, and climbed out.

The house was just what I expected for this part of town. A shithole. Busted siding, sheets over the windows for drapes, dirt for a lawn, and two wooden steps missing from the front porch.

Maddie slammed out of her Jeep and stood in front of the house with her hands on her hips.

Silent.

Waiting.

She focused her entire attention on the house in front of her. How she'd missed my arrival was a mystery.

"Ms. Avery!"

We both turned our heads to look at the woman in the yard next door. She was holding a rifle. She was wearing a blue-and-gold Buccaneers jersey over pink-and-purple stretch pants. If I looked too long, I was afraid I might get dizzy. She started running toward us.

"Mrs. Owens, stay there," Maddie called out. She jogged over to the woman's yard with me following her. When I got close, I could hear Maddie talking.

"What's happened since you called me?" she asked.

"I heard Colleen scream again, but not like she'd been hit, more like she was pissed. Then I heard something shatter. Glass, I mean. Ya know?" She squinted through her thick glasses at Maddie to see if she was tracking, then looked at me. "Who's he?"

Maddie whirled around.

"What the fuck are you doing here?" Maddie demanded.

"We're on a date, don't you remember?"

"Beau, get the hell out of here. This is a volatile situation. I've got a six-year-old boy I'm worried about. I don't need you here fucking things up."

"How would he fuck things up?" Mrs. Owens asked as she eyed me up and down and smiled. "Looks to me like he might could do some good."

"Mrs. Owens, when was the last time you saw Eli?"

"Is Eli the kid in trouble?" I asked.

"Cute little kid," Mrs. Owens answered. "Kind of spindly. Might scared, but who could blame him with that bastard Bruce living there."

"Why haven't you called the cops?" I asked.

"Did. They left," she answered.

"What?"

"They followed procedure," Maddie sighed. "If Colleen, that's the mother, said there wasn't any problem, and they couldn't find any reason to enter, there was nothing they could do."

"But what about the boy?" I asked.

"I don't know." Maddie sounded defeated. She turned to look at the older woman, who was holding her rifle like she was ready to go to battle. "Mrs. Owens, when was the last time you saw Eli?"

"Not since yesterday. He was playing with that red fire engine truck of his. He runs it around the front yard. I ain't seen him since."

Maddie turned to me. "I gave that to him. It's still lying in the front of the house."

Of course she'd given it to him.

We both turned to look at the house in question.

"What are you going to do?" Mrs. Owens asked Maddie.

"I'm going to go check on Eli."

I nodded. "I'll go with you."

"No, you're not."

"Maddie—"

"I mean it, Beau." Her voice was steel. "I know what I'm doing. This is my job, and it's not the first time I've been in these kinds of situations."

"Situations where some abusive asshole might have a gun for all you know, and might blow your brains out? Those kinds of situations?" I was beyond pissed.

"There has been a time or two when I haven't known what I've been walking into, but I didn't have the probable cause for law enforcement. So, yes, I've gone in to check in on a child. That's my job, Beau. My job is to ensure the welfare of children who can't take care of themselves. I have the training to do this. I have met with Colleen and Bruce a few times. It's my job to make sure that Eli is okay."

"And I'll go with you." I kept my voice as reasonable as possible.

"Having you with me will just escalate things. It will ensure things turn into a shitshow."

She took a step toward the house. I touched her wrist and she turned around. "Eli Jackson's six years old. He's the smallest boy in his class, Beau."

Fuck. Suddenly, I could picture the kid.

I nodded. "You call out my name, and I'll break the door down to get to you. You got it?"

Her expression softened for half a second before she pulled free. "I'll be fine."

This wasn't the girl I'd left behind.

Nope.

This woman scared the hell out of me.

I watched as Maddie stepped over the broken step and knocked on the front door. I was vibrating with frustration that I couldn't be beside her. This whole situation sucked. But I needed to just think of her as another Marine.

She knocked on the door and a woman I assumed was Colleen Jackson opened it. I winced when I saw her black eye. She looked both pissed off and scared.

Maddie must have said something, but I couldn't hear her since she was facing away from me, but I could hear Colleen just fine.

"We don't need you here. Everything's fine. Anyways, Eli's not here. He ran away."

That set me off. This woman was saying her six-year-old son had run away, and she hadn't reported it?

I watched as Colleen listened to Maddie reply.

"Kid's always running off. What the hell am I supposed to do?"

I heard a man's voice bellow from inside the house and Colleen flinched. Damn, if she had any sense, she'd take this opportunity to get the hell out of there.

"You need to leave," Colleen whined.

Again, I didn't hear what Maddie said.

"Now. You need to leave *now*." Colleen was clearly agitated.

Another bellow sounded inside the house.

Colleen looked behind her, then looked back at Maddie. I could tell Maddie was saying something by the way Colleen's eyes were narrowing.

"Fine. Come on in. See for yourself."

Then, somehow, Maddie was slipping by Colleen, and then the door shut behind her.

My mouth went dry. This was not good, not good at all.

"Are you just going to stand here?" Mrs. Owens looked at me.

"No, ma'am."

"If you go through the backyard, watch out for the dog. Do you need my rifle?"

Her offer was the first thing in this whole nightmare that made me smile. "I think I'll be fine without it, but thank you, ma'am."

"Well, get going."

She turned around and stalked to her porch, then sat down on her rocking chair, her rifle lying over her lap.

I shook my head and turned back to the Jacksons' house. The fence to the backyard was busted in one section. It was wide enough for me to squeeze through.

As soon as I saw the backyard, I figured out that

they didn't bother to pay for trash collection. They just threw most of their garbage into it. It was disgusting. The smell was noxious. Buried in the dirt near the back fence was an old tractor tire with a chain attached.

Aw, shit.

A half-starved pitbull was connected to the chain and didn't even have the strength to lift his or her head. Hell, I couldn't even tell if the poor thing was a Staffordshire Bull Terrier or an American Staffordshire Terrier, it was so emaciated. What kind of people did this to a dog?

This place just got worse and worse.

I peered through one of the grimy windows. I could see it was a bedroom. The sheet that was supposed to be covering it was only tacked up with one nail, so I had a clear view. It looked like a kid's room or had been a kid's room at one time. There was one poster on the wall of a Disney character, and the same character on a dirty blanket, but there weren't any toys, and the carpet was half pulled up to show the concrete beneath. Hell, there were three spots where it was clear someone had punched holes in the sheetrock.

I went to the next window, and that one had the sheet covering the whole thing, so I couldn't look in. I listened intently, but I couldn't hear a sound.

Then I climbed up the five steps that led to the back porch. The screen door and the main door were cracked open. I turned to ice, just like I did on any mission. I put my ear up to it to see what I could hear. Murmurs. Voices too low to make out.

Then I heard a rustling sound. But not from inside. I listened closer and realized it was coming from below.

A raccoon under the porch?

I kept my ears open to what was going on inside, then I heard a whimper from down below.

Eli!

I jumped lightly from the porch, not making a sound, then peered under. I saw the whites of a scared little boy's eyes.

Another soft whimper.

He was curled up against the back stair, barely visible.

"Eli?" I whispered.

Now that my eyes had adjusted, I could make him out.

Another soft whimper.

I stretched my hand toward him.

This time it wasn't a whimper, it was a soft keening cry. He was more than scared, he was petrified.

"I'm a friend of Maddie's. I've come to help you."

He started to cry.

Dammit, I didn't want to crawl under there and force him out. That would call attention to us, and it would make things worse for the little tyke. "Do you know who Maddie is? Isn't she your friend?"

He shook his head.

That didn't make sense. Then it did.

"I'm a friend of Miss Avery's. She gave you the fire engine. She asked me to come get you."

That had him lifting his head and looking at me. One dirty hand swiped at his eyes.

"You know Miss Avery, right?"

I got a small nod.

"She wanted me to come and help you. Can you come out?"

He shook his head.

"Why not?"

"Bruce will be mad," he whispered. "He gets mad a lot."

Fury raced through my body, but I didn't let it show. "Bruce won't know. I'm going to take you to Miss Avery, and everything is going to be all right."

The boy didn't move.

"I promise."

"Cross your heart?" He whispered the question.

"Cross my heart." My heart ached as I said the words.

The boy moved really slowly. When he came close, even in the dim light of twilight, I could see that his face was bruised, just like his mother's. His small arms were covered with bruises, where a big hand had squeezed too tight.

Rage roared through me.

I kept my hands out, not trying to help him since I didn't know where else he might be hurt. He finally crawled into my waiting arms. There was nothing to him but bruises and heartbreak.

"You're safe now," I breathed into his damp hair. I scuttled backward, then stood up and started to carry him to the hole in the fence, when a bellow exploded from inside.

"Interfering bitch!"

I spun around, my heart slamming in my chest.

"I've got to go," I said as I laid Eli on the ground, propping him up against the fence, near some trash. I crouched down beside him, gripping Eli's hand gently. His whole body trembled under my hands. I felt bad, but I had to make this fast. "Stay put. No matter what you hear, don't move."

His swollen eyes locked onto mine. Fear and trust seemed to battle inside them. I squeezed his hand once more, then I turned and ran like my life depended on it.

I ran up the porch steps and flung the two doors open. I barreled through the back door and found myself in the middle of the kitchen. I immediately took stock of the scene in front of me.

Maddie was standing at one end of the kitchen, holding a softball bat at the ready. It looked like she was planning to swing to the fences. Colleen was cowering behind her, both arms covering her head.

On the far side of the kitchen was a huge, shirtless man with a belly so large he looked like he was pregnant. He was bald as a cue ball, but for all the missing hair on his head, he made up for it by having a pelt of hair everywhere else on his body. He was holding a cast iron frying pan.

"Come near her again, and I'll send you to Mars," Maddie yelled.

The furball crouched down, the pan over his head, and started across toward Maddie. How the hell he hadn't noticed me, I'll never know. He raised the pan higher, murder in his eyes. Maddie gripped the bat tighter, jaw clenched, ready to swing.

I stepped forward. He never saw me coming, the flea-brained oaf.

I slammed into him from behind, driving him face-first into the refrigerator with a crunch that rattled the condiments inside. He spun, wild-eyed, but I caught his throat in the crook of my elbow and squeezed until his knees buckled.

When he dropped the pan, I kicked it across the room, then hauled him around and slammed him to the tile floor so hard the cabinets rattled. He tried to lurch up. Big mistake. I punched him in the gut hard and fast, twice, until he wheezed and collapsed like the deflated bag of trash he was. Maddie turned to Colleen and dropped the bat.

"Colleen, are you—"

I stopped her. "Eli's outside, and he needs an ambulance."

Maddie's eyes went wide before she pushed past me as she sprinted out the door.

I heard the furball cough, and I looked at Colleen.

"You hurt him," she told me.

"No, I found him underneath the stairs. We're going to get both of you help."

She started to crawl across the floor toward the furball. "Are you okay, Bruce?"

"Are you shitting me?" I asked.

"You hurt him!" she shouted at me. "Get out of my house!"

I looked at the woman with the black eye and fingerprint bruises on her arms and wondered what was wrong with the world. "Lady, your kid needs an ambulance."

She wasn't looking at me, she had her cheek pressed against that asshole's face and I couldn't leave the house fast enough.

Maddie was exactly where I expected, sitting in a pile of trash, holding Eli in her arms. The boy was crying as she rocked him. Before I could get to them, Mrs. Owens stopped me. She had her phone in her hand. "The cops and an ambulance are on their way. You did good, kid," she smiled at me.

"Do me a favor. Can you call animal control? That poor dog doesn't look like it's been watered or fed in a week."

"I'm on it." She walked away.

I looked on as Maddie continued to soothe the little boy.

"It's going to be all right. I promise, honey," she said to Eli.

The boy kept crying, and Maddie kept on rocking him until he fell asleep against her. When the EMTs arrived, it looked like she was being asked to cut off her arm when they tried to take Eli out of her arms. It was the first time she looked at me with her big brown eyes since we'd left the house.

"Go in the ambulance with him. Give me your keys and I'll make sure your Jeep gets home."

She bit her lip. "Are you sure?"

I stepped up to her and cupped her cheek. "Trust me."

She let out a sigh. "Thank you, Beau. Thank you for all you did tonight."

I watched her get into the ambulance with Eli, then watched as the ambulance drove away. This was the exact reason I hadn't contacted her when I first got home. I knew I was going to get in too deep, and here I was, smack dab in the middle of the ocean.

Chapter Three

"That's what I said. He followed me to the scene. He was out of his mind."

It was the third time I had told my sister Evie what happened, and she still didn't seem to understand.

"I still don't see the problem."

"He followed me to the scene!" I screeched into my phone.

It was three days later, and I was still parked on my couch, one leg tucked under me, a carton of half-melted Chunky Monkey ice cream balanced on my thigh. Each bite was supposed to calm my nerves, but all it did was make me feel slightly nauseous.

"What else did you expect to happen? He's a Marine Raider, right? What do you think Drake would have done? What about Aiden?"

"Our brother and your husband are nuts. They have proven that over and over. I just figured that something was coded into their DNA and that's what made them become SEALs. Beau was always cautious."

I heard my sister snort.

"The guy stuck around even after Drake threatened to bury him in the woods. That should've been your first clue he wasn't cautious. It figures he turned out to be the same kind of man as the rest of them. Anyway, what's wrong with the SEAL types? Trenda and I are married to SEALs. Are you picking on our choices?"

I shoveled another big scoop of Chunky Monkey into my mouth, so I didn't have to answer.

"I can hear you eating. It's ice cream, isn't it?"

I continued to chew and avoided answering the most annoying sister I had. Why in the hell had I thought calling Evie would be a good idea?

Dammit! I sprang backward on my sofa when a plop of ice cream dripped onto my couch. I set down my phone and ice cream carton on the coffee table and ran to the kitchen for a wet paper towel.

By the time I had the stain wiped up, I could hear Evie yelling at me through the phone's speaker.

"I'm sorry," I said, cutting her off mid-rant. "I spilled some ice cream on the couch. I needed to blot it out before it stained."

"You're as bad as my boys."

I laughed. "Not even close. When are you, Holden, and Zephyr coming back for a visit?"

"Probably next month. Aiden has some leave

coming up next week, so we've got some family time coming up. Plus, Karen and Drake are going to take our two well-behaved sons for a long weekend, so Aiden and I can get away."

This time I snorted. "Well behaved, huh? Weren't you the one who told me that last year he got Rufus out of his dog crate in the middle of the night so he could do reconnaissance after he found his Easter basket beside his bed?"

"I didn't say reconnaissance. That was Aiden's term."

"Yeah, it was because Holden wanted to catch the Easter Bunny."

"I should have thought of that. Of course, Aiden's son would have been wigged out about a strange creature coming into his room in the middle of the night."

I laughed. "I still have to hand it to the kid for confronting you after he found all the chocolate candy wrappers in your office trash can."

"Shit, he was only four years old. Aiden is still mad that he wasn't home to see that. But I hope you understand now."

I scraped my spoon across the bottom of the carton of ice cream and came up empty.

"What do you mean, you hope I understand?"

"Some men are just wired that way. Holden is going to follow in his father's footsteps. He's a protector. Sounds like Beau is too."

"I had things handled," I protested.

"Yeah, like Chloe did all those years ago. Think of how you would have felt if you had bashed his head in. Trust me, it was better that Beau intervened."

I thought about that time at the lake, and I had to agree.

"Okay, so Beau's a protector. He's still the asshole who didn't call me after he came to town. He's also the asshole who never called or wrote after he left town."

"That's not true. He wrote you a letter," Evie protested.

"One letter in fifteen years. Be still my heart." I hated hearing the bitterness in my voice. But I couldn't help myself.

"It's a letter that is practically falling apart since you've read it so often. Don't you still carry it in your wallet?"

"Not that he wrote much," I grouched.

"Yeah, but you still have it, right?"

I flopped onto my couch with a groan, pressing the cold spoon to my forehead. "Evie, you're supposed to be helping me figure out how to get rid of him, not making it worse. He's still calling. He's left at least five messages. He said, and I quote, that our first date was a bust, and I owe him a do-over. He's delusional."

I got up and threw the empty carton in the trash and dispensed a big glass of water from the refrigerator.

"So, go on the date and tell him to stop bugging you. It's simple."

I set down the glass with a thump. "That's a shitty idea. I don't know why I called you. I expected something innovative, or at least sneaky."

"Okay, here's something else. Find out from Vic the next time he shows up at Maverick's and confront him, just like you did last time. Tell him you don't want to see him. How about that? Is that innovative?"

"Yeah, but I'll have to see him. I'll have to talk to him," I whined.

"Since when did my sister turn into a wimp?"

I sighed. She was right. I needed to do something. Beau was driving me batshit crazy. The problem was I was dying to spend time with him, but I was beyond hurt that he hadn't reached out to me as soon as he'd come home to Jasper Creek.

"Okay, that's not a terrible idea."

"See, aren't you glad you called?"

"Maybe," I admitted. "So, when are you guys coming to visit?"

"We're working it out, I think, next month."

"It'll be great to see you and the boys. I adore them, and I love you so much."

"We can't wait. Love you too, Maddie. Call me after you confront your Raider."

"He's not my Raider," I protested.

"Yeah, sure," Evie laughed, then hung up the phone.

I stuck my tongue out at the dark screen.

I saw I had a text that had come in during my

marathon call with Evie, so I opened it. It was from Fran Patterson. That woman was amazing. She and her husband had fostered Eli two times before this latest incident, and when I called from the hospital, they dropped everything and came to his side.

She'd sent a picture of Eli asleep, cuddled next to Nate Patterson on the couch. It made my heart melt. Maybe, just maybe, this time Eli had finally found a home worthy of him.

I sat back in the leather seat of my Jeep, glaring at the glowing sign of Maverick's Bar and Grill as if it personally offended me. Because tonight it kind of did.

"Damn it, I'm not nervous!" I yelled out as I wiped my sweaty palms along my jeans. I bit my lip. If this went wrong, I was going to kill my sister.

Evie. That's what I was going to do. I'll call Evie. I reached over and plucked my phone out of my purse. I started to push in Evie's number and then grimaced.

"No! I'm a grownup. If Holden can take on the Easter Bunny, I can take on Beau."

I grinned. Damn, I sure wished I'd seen that.

With that thought, I pushed open the door of my Jeep and jumped out, planting my boots firmly on the gravel. I smoothed my palms over the sexiest top I owned. It didn't show much cleavage, not that I had all that much compared to Trenda, but it was a crop top and showed off my belly button fake diamond stud. And that usually got a few male glances. Might as well let Beau know how much he'd fucked up by not calling me sooner.

"Dammit!"

We'd only been friends. It's not like we'd dated or anything. It shouldn't have mattered what I looked like. But I smiled anyway. He was a guy. It would matter.

My phone buzzed, and I fished it out of my purse. It was a message from Vic.

> VIC: Your boy's here. He's been playing pool for a while. I don't know how much longer he'll be here.

My boy. I rolled my eyes and started stomping across the parking lot toward the door of the bar. As soon as I flung it open, I realized my mistake as people turned to stare at me. Great, just the impression I didn't want to make.

"Hi Maddie," Ruby Miller shouted out.

"Why didn't you tell us you were coming?" Lacy yelled.

Lacy Cunningham had been doing my hair for eons, and Ruby was fairly new to town, and now worked at the Java Jolt. I usually hung out with them once a week. They were great girls.

"Come sit with us. We just ordered munchies," Ruby said.

I grimaced. I didn't want to be rude, but I needed to finish things with Beau and get the hell out of here.

STAT.

I walked past the hostess stand to their table. I grabbed a potato skin off their dish and took a big bite. As soon as I swallowed, I realized my mistake. My nervous stomach did not like greasy food. Ruby immediately noticed and handed me her ever-present Sprite. I sucked some of it down and felt better.

"What's going on?" Ruby asked softly.

Lacy was wonderful, but she couldn't read a room to save her life. Ruby, on the other hand, was extremely insightful and could pick up on everybody's emotions. The only thing she wasn't aware of was herself.

"Beau," I whispered back.

"He's here," she said. "He's playing pool with some woman."

"What are you two whispering about?" Lacy asked as she looked up from her phone and took a big sip of her margarita.

"Beau," I said.

"Oh, him again. I told you what to do. He's hot. Take him home and bang his brains out." She then went back to scrolling through her phone.

Ruby winced. "What's the plan?" she asked.

"He needs to quit calling me."

"Are you sure?" Ruby asked.

I bit my lip. Damn, how could she understand me so well?

"Why are you asking me that?"

She broke into a small smile, and her dimples showed. "Maybe because you switched out your normal belly button ring for a diamond stud?"

I blushed.

"I'm just here to tell him to stop calling, once and for all."

"Okay. Then I've got you're back." Ruby pushed out of the booth. I looked at her and saw she was once again wearing a tank top with a big flannel shirt that came down past her butt. On girls' night at one of our three houses, she'd get rid of that God-awful flannel shirt, and you could see just how great her curves were, but all she could say was that she was fat. There was no talking her out of it. My friend with her glorious red hair and her knock-out curves saw everything else clearly in the world, just not herself.

"Don't look at me like that," she shook her head. "I know what you're thinking, and tonight is about your demon, not my demons."

I sighed. She was right. "Okay, to the pool tables."

I reluctantly followed her. As we got close, she suddenly stopped and I almost bumped into her. I sidestepped her to see what she was looking at. As soon as I saw the situation, I knew why she had stopped.

There was Beau, his auburn hair gleaming under the pool light as he was lining up a shot, with a pretty, long-legged brunette leaning against a cue stick as she avidly studied his ass. It was clear that they were playing a game.

Beau made his shot.

She said something that I couldn't make out, and he laughed.

Bastard.

He roamed around the table, bent, aimed, and hit the cue ball against a solid ball that banked against the side and easily dropped into a corner pocket. All that was left was for him was to sink the eight ball. It was an easy shot.

I saw that there were a couple of guys watching the game, so I strode over to the table, Ruby following me. Before Beau bent over, he saw me, grinned, gave a chin tilt, then took his shot and sank the eight ball.

"I should have never bet money on this game," the brunette purred. "I should have thought of something else to bet if I lost."

The two men watching the game laughed. Her meaning was clear. She walked up so close to Beau that she was practically pressed up against him. "Are you sure you just want my money?" she asked.

"That was the bet," he said easily. He took a step back and held out his hand. She had to work hard to wiggle her fingers into the front pocket of her skin-tight jeans to pull out a twenty-dollar bill. I saw that she also slipped Beau her number.

"Let's do this again sometime," she purred.

He looked over his shoulder at the two men whose eyes were popping out of their heads. "I think Louie or Slim would be better bets for you next time. If you want, I can introduce you..."

The brunette gave him a considering look. "I think I'll pass. Just know, it's your loss."

Oh, for fuck's sake.

I looked over at Ruby and I knew she was thinking the same thing. This woman gave our sex a bad name.

The brunette had to push past Ruby and me to get to the bar, where I was sure Vic would flirt with her. So soon, all would be well in her world. Knowing Vic, he might even take her up on her blatant offer.

But still...ewww.

"Maddie, it's good to see you."

I'd been so busy watching the brunette sashay through the crowd, I hadn't noticed Beau coming toward me. I wouldn't have thought that was possible.

I looked up at him and realized he wasn't looking me in the eye. Instead, he was looking me up and down, his gaze lingering on my abdomen. When he did gaze back into my face, his blue-gray eyes were dark blue. I licked my lips, trying to figure out what that meant.

Finally, I got my shit together. "I came to talk to you."

"That's good news. I've been trying to get ahold of you."

"Can we go sit over there?" I said, pointing to a vacant top table at the back of the poolroom. It was covered with beer glasses and half-filled plates, but I didn't care.

Beau looked over his shoulder.

"I've got a better idea. How about we play a game of pool?"

Ruby let out a giggle snort, and I glared at her.

"I don't want to play pool, Beau. I want to talk." I needed to shut his shit down. I hadn't talked myself up for three days to confront him, to cave now.

"I'll talk if you beat me at pool. How about that?"

I squinted at him.

"I'll take that bet, as long as you agree to leave me alone if I win," I whispered.

His eyes narrowed as he assessed me. Out of the corner of my eye, I could see Ruby grinning. She'd seen me play pool. I didn't lose.

Beau thrust out his hand. "Deal."

I shook. "I'll rack 'em up. You break."

"Pretty confident," he teased.

I shrugged. I'd seen his bank shot. It wasn't anything to write home about.

Louie and Slim both put money on their table, and Louie whistled to get other people's attention.

Great.

Just great.

Beau looked over at them, then back at me. "Is there something I'm missing?"

"I worked here part time during the summer breaks to make money for college. I might have played some pool back then. How about you? You play much?"

I saw other people joining Louie and Slim, and soon more money was covering the table. I doubted anyone was betting against me. Louie was probably laying odds.

"From time to time," he said with an easy smile.

I stepped back from the table after I racked up the balls, and Beau let loose with a fierce break. Two solids and one stripe fell in. He studied the table.

"I'll take stripes."

He was smart. That's what I would have done.

He sank two stripes and missed the third. Then I was up. I smiled. I loved this part of the game. It wasn't just about making a shot, it was also about making sure you set up your next shot. I lined up my shot, exhaling slowly as I felt the cool wood of the cue slide between my fingers. The moment the ball struck, the crisp click of impact sent a thrill up my spine. Three solids sank in quick succession, smooth as butter, before I finally miscalculated my spin and cursed under my breath.

When I looked up, Beau had a grim smile on his face, because while I had set up my shots, I had also made sure to leave the stripes grouped together.

It soon became a battle. We both circled the table,

but I felt like Beau was still stalking me, like the predator he was. He was a good player.

But I was better.

I blocked out the chatter when Beau missed his shot, and I was left with two solids and the eight ball. The table was open, so I could knock one solid into a side pocket, and the other solid was an easy shot down the side into the corner pocket. I'd put some spin on the cue ball, so it didn't follow the solid into the pocket. Instead, it set me up with a pretty easy bank shot for the eight ball.

I straightened up and pretended to study the table, even though I knew what I was going to do.

Why wasn't I excited? Victory was literally in my grasp.

Beau caught my eye. He knew the shot I was going to take. I could see it in his eyes. He wasn't cocky anymore. No more teasing. He was just watching.

Waiting.

I hesitated. Dammit, why was I hesitating?

Didn't I want him to stop calling? Didn't I want him to stop looking at me like that? Stop making me feel like I was seventeen again, all breathless and reckless and stupidly hopeful?

I bent down and lined up my shot. My hands were steady. But my mind? It was all over the place. I pulled back my stick and hit the cue ball.

Chapter Four

She'd left the table wide open, and I'd finished the game in two shots.

"Dammit, Maddie! Do you know how much money I just lost?" Louie cried out.

"That's on you," Ruby shouted back at the man.

I gently took the pool cue out of Maddie's hand and put hers and mine up in the cue rack on the wall.

"It's early, only eight o'clock," I said to her softly. "Your house or mine?"

She bit her lip, and I could almost see what was going through her mind. She was debating whether she wanted home field advantage. I would want that, so I couldn't quite figure out why she would consider going to my house.

"Your house," she said, surprising me.

I shrugged. "Okay. Are you actually going to follow me, or are you going to ditch me?"

"I'll follow you. Unlike some people I know, I'm trustworthy."

My gut clenched as her verbal blow landed hard.

Little did she know she was right, because there wasn't a chance in hell that I would have stopped calling if she'd won the game. But I couldn't say that I wasn't fucking pleased that she'd lost.

I drove slowly to make extra sure that she wouldn't lose me. Not that it was necessary; it was my old house where she had spent half her childhood. When I pulled into my carport, she was right behind me. We turned off our engines at the same time, and she was out of her Jeep before I had a chance to open her door for her.

"Nice landscaping," she noted.

"Since I've been renting this out, Bernie's arranged landscaping to be done, so that the renters didn't need to be responsible."

"Makes sense."

She stood well behind me as I unlocked the door, but I held it open for her, forcing her to precede me into the house.

"Jeez, Beau, this place has really changed."

"Yeah," I agreed. "I'd tell Harvey want I wanted done, and he made sure it got done."

She nodded. "Yeah, Harvey and his company do good work. It's hard to believe this is the same house I used to come and play pinochle at."

I took a deep breath. I hadn't thought of that card game since I joined the Marines. Mom got such a kick teaching Maddie and me that game, and we'd play for hours when Mom was in a good mental place.

"Come see the kitchen."

"Okay."

I went to put my hand at the bottom of Maddie's back to guide her to the kitchen, and hesitated. She was wearing that crop top that had been driving me insane all evening. If I rested my hand where I intended, I'd be touching her smooth, bare skin.

Fuck it.

As soon as I touched her, she jerked, and I felt a jolt go through me like I had been too close to a mortar when it exploded. But I didn't move my hand. She felt too good.

She slid away from me and walked quickly to the kitchen on her own.

"This is amazing, Beau," she called out.

She was right about that.

She was opening the big stainless-steel fridge when I entered the kitchen. "This thing is huge. Do you rent to families?"

"Sometimes."

She shut the door and peered over at me. "And you have a double oven. Was that Harvey's idea, or yours?"

"Mine," I admitted.

Her smile fell. "Oh."

"Yeah. Mom always wanted one of those."

"I don't see any pictures of her."

"I rent this place, Maddie. Of course there's no

personal stuff. I have that shit stored in a box in the attic."

She gave a slow nod and leaned back against the quartz countertop and studied me. I could feel something big coming. I prayed she would not ask me why I hadn't kept in touch while I was in the Marines. I wanted to keep us in shallow water for now. But I knew it would not be my choice.

"You want to explain to me why I had to hear via the town grapevine that you were back again? Want to explain why you didn't pick up a phone and call me?"

Maddie had changed. A lot. She had a poker face now that could win her a lot of money. I couldn't tell if she was angry, sad, or just curious. Before I left, I could read her like an open book.

"I wanted to," I told her.

Shit, that sounded lame.

She lifted her right eyebrow. How many times had she done that same thing when I'd said something stupid?

I tried again. "I was caught up with spending time with Brady. I mean Kai."

She slowly nodded. It was regal, as if she were a queen and I was one of her peasants. "I see."

"No, you don't see. You can't see. Because *I* don't even understand it, Maddie." I rubbed the back of my neck.

"I call bullshit."

I looked at her again. She still looked like a queen,

but a queen with a poker face. I was so fucked. And she was right. I was spouting bullshit. Kind of.

I considered her for a long time, trying to think of the right thing to say. She pushed off the counter. "I'm outta here."

"Wait."

"No. I'm done. You're the one who wanted to talk. Apparently, you can't. So, I'm done. Don't bother calling again." She started to charge past me, and I reached out and grabbed her wrist. Not too hard, just with enough strength to halt her.

"What?" she snarled.

"I can explain."

She yanked her wrist out of my grip, but she stayed put. "You're doing a shit job of it."

"It wasn't bullshit. The first time I came back... Some months ago."

"*Eight* months ago."

I winced. "Yeah, eight months ago. I was in shock." I rubbed the back of my neck and looked down, then back up into eyes that used to be able to soothe my soul. Now they were shards of ice that cut. "Maddie, seeing Brady... Finding out he was alive... It didn't gut me, it turned my world upside down. I can't even begin to explain it. It was like everything I'd assumed, everything I'd ever known, was wrong, but everything I'd ever hoped for was there in front of me and I..."

She took one step forward and her eyes softened.

"It's okay, Beau. You can say it. You can say anything. I promise."

"For a moment I felt joy. A blinding moment of connection. But then a level of fear descended on me like a thunderbolt. I'd never felt anything like it, and I've been in life-and-death situations more times than I can count. Somehow, in my mind, I knew that having Brady back wouldn't last." I laughed. It sounded like nails on a chalkboard, and I saw Maddie cringe. "Yeah. Pretty fucked up, huh?"

She took two more steps and touched my hand. "Not fucked up. Real. It sounds real, Beau."

I smirked. "Yeah, really fucked up."

"You say potato, I say po-tah-toe."

I laughed. This time it sounded right.

"So how long did that last?" she asked.

"Who says I still don't feel like that?" I sighed.

"You must be feeling a little more put together if you're comfortable becoming my stalker."

"I'm not, though. I'm still fucked in the head. Eight months ago, everything was spinning. I did want to reach out to you, but for all the wrong reasons."

She frowned.

"I needed a safe place to land. Here I was, falling apart. Ten times worse than when I was dealing with the mom shit, and all I wanted to do was use you after fifteen years of no contact. That's the kind of bastard I was thinking about being."

"So why didn't you?"

Damn it. She was no longer angry, she looked hurt.

I grabbed both of her hands, my thumbs circling her palms. "Because then I would have been my mom. If I was going to come back to you, I was going to come back to you a whole person, not some needy bastard."

"And now?" she asked quietly.

"Now I believe in Brady. I mean, Kai. I figured out that life can just be shitty, and then it can be absolutely wonderful. And I can believe in it. Trust in it. It took the last eight months for that to become clear."

She nodded and pulled her hands out of mine. "I need to go." She started past me.

My heart jolted. "Hey, wait a minute. Why are you going?"

"You've explained things to me. I have my answers. I have my closure. So, thank you."

She was halfway to the front door before I had enough sense to get in front of her.

"Get out of my way, Beau."

"No. I want to know why you're leaving. I told you why I didn't contact you eight months ago. Why are you leaving?"

"Yeah. You explained what was going on eight months ago. Then you said you wanted to come back to me as a whole person. But for eleven days, you didn't call me. Not one word, Beau. You're either a liar or you need to see a psychiatrist. Either way, I'm not interested."

Panic slammed into me. Shit, she was right. Why

hadn't I contacted her? Why wasn't she the first call I'd made? What the fuck was my problem?

"Don't leave, Maddie. I'm begging you."

"Beau, eleven days."

"Does it count that I spent those eleven days finding out everything about you? I spent that time finding out everything you've been doing? What your job was? Whether you were in a relationship? Whether you had a pet? What books you checked out from the library? By the way, I think it is cool that you do so many do-it-yourself projects."

Oh fuck, I could see her cheeks turning red, and her eyes turning black. She was about to go ballistic on my ass.

"Eleven! Fucking! Days! Beaumont!" she screamed in my face. "Then you make me come to you! You are so out of your goddamn mind."

"Maddie, please."

"Don't you *Maddie please* me," she yelled.

Yelling was better than screaming.

"Don't you dare get me to almost cry for you about finding Brady, and how twisted up you were, and how you want to come to me whole, and then not... not... not... call me for eleven days!"

Oh shit, she was going to start crying. There was nothing worse than Maddie crying mad. Nothing.

"Oh, Baby, please, please, don't cry."

"I'm not fucking crying over you, Grady Beaumont."

Aw fuck, she was calling me Grady.

"Let me hold you, Maddie."

"No," she said as I pulled her into my arms.

"And you never returned my letters. And when I tried to call you after you left, you never returned my calls."

She was sobbing into my t-shirt. I choked up as I soaked up all the pain that I had caused my best friend. The best woman. The best person I have ever had in my life.

"I'm so sorry, Maddie. I know I didn't write to you. I know I didn't return your calls. Can you blame me for being scared to call you when I came back? It was better remembering us how we were than to have you reject me," I whispered into her hair.

She continued to cry for long minutes. Finally, she whispered "If that's your logic, then you really do need a psychiatrist."

Chapter Five

It had taken a lot of effort for me to put last night's conversation with Beau aside and concentrate on work, but I'd managed. And after the miserable day, I was bone tired by the time I made it home. I threw my satchel on the kitchen table and headed to the couch. I fell on it face first and finally mustered the energy to roll over.

It was after nine, and there wasn't one site visit I made that showed promise. The worst was the three Hollister kids living with the shittiest foster parents I'd ever met. The house was filthy, and when I checked the cupboards and fridge, there was hardly anything to eat. When I questioned the kids, it was clear they were too scared to say anything bad about the Farley family. How in the hell the Farleys ever made it through the screening, I'll never know.

What's worse, I couldn't say that the kids were in

imminent danger, so all I could do was go to my supervisor so that another arm of DCS could investigate and determine if the Farleys were truly unsuitable to be foster parents. This was the third time I had to report a foster family, but in the other two cases the kids were in imminent danger so I got to immediately pull them out. The fact that I had to leave them there was killing me.

I considered going to my freezer and pulling out my bottle of vodka to have a double shot, but walking over there would require too much energy.

I heard the faint sound of my phone buzzing. Rolling onto my side, I looked over at my purse and gave it the evil eye. I thought I'd put my phone on do not disturb.

Most of my cases called into my office phone, but I'd given the oldest Hollister boy, ten-year-old Bobby, my cell phone number. I had to answer it.

It was when I pushed myself to a sitting position that I realized I'd plopped down on my sofa—my beautiful sofa—with my muddy boots on.

"Fuck me!" What a perfect ending to a perfect day.

With that jolt of adrenaline, I shot to my purse to grab my phone out of its designated pocket and answered.

"This is Miss Avery."

"Hello Miss Avery. You haven't answered any of my texts this evening. I figure you had to work late. Bad day?" The sound of Beau's voice ran through my system like warm chocolate syrup, rich, sweet, and decadent.

"Yeah," I sighed. "I just got home."

"Did you ever have time to eat?"

"I found a package of Twinkies in my center console, so I was covered for lunch."

"Are Twinkies still a thing?"

I almost smiled. "That's blasphemy. You cannot ever speak badly about a Hostess product. I remember you partaking back in the day. I think your favorite were the cherry pies."

"At least they had fruit." He defended himself.

"Three cherries and unidentified red sugary filling does not constitute fruit." Since I was up, I walked into my kitchen, pulled out the vodka, and poured a generous shot.

"Just think about the names of your choices, HoHos, Ding Dongs, and Twinkies. Just the sound of those names should have told you they were bad choices. Kind of like that guy Ted you were engaged to. All bad choices."

I had the shot halfway to my mouth when Beau said that. Thank God I hadn't been in the process of swallowing. "There was nothing wrong with Ted. How did you know about him anyway? Now you're forbidden from talking for thirty seconds."

"Why?"

"Thirty seconds."

"Why?"

"If you talk, I'll hang up."

"Fine."

I swallowed the shot. "Good boy."

"You just had a shot of something, didn't you?"

I frowned. How had he known? I hadn't drunk hard liquor in front of him any of the times we had gone out with Kai and Marlowe. "I don't know what you're talking about."

"Let me come over with a pizza."

"I need to sleep."

"You might need to, but will you?"

I sighed, running my fingers through my hair. The smart thing would be to say no. To tell him I was too exhausted. But the idea of scrounging around for Ding Dongs and eating them alone sounded even worse.

"How soon can you get here?"

"I'll be there in twenty."

"No pineapple and no anchovies."

"Done."

"And no peppers."

"Got it."

"And no onions."

"So, meat only?"

I smiled. "Yeah. Meat only."

"Coming right up."

~

Twenty minutes gave me just enough time to shower, which I desperately needed to do. I thought about just unlocking the front door; this was Jasper Creek after all. But I'd seen too much in my line of work. I couldn't do it. I hustled into my bedroom, pulling clothes off as I went.

I heard a knock on the door after I was dressed, my hair still in a towel. I whipped off the towel and ran down the hall, finger-combing my hair. When I looked out the peephole, I saw it was the local pizza guy.

I giggled.

Great, I was going to have to pay for the pizza that Beau had promised to bring me. By the time I unlocked the door and opened it, I found Beau and the pizza delivery guy exchanging the pizza for money.

"You sure timed that right." I grinned at Beau as I opened the door further. He had a white plastic bag with him, along with some root beers. I snatched the pizza box out of his hands.

"Eager much?"

I scowled. "Starving is more like it." I turned and hustled toward my kitchen and had the box open by the time he got there. I was basking in the scent of meat and cheesy goodness. "What's in the bag?"

He set the sodas on my counter and dumped out a plethora of Hostess products onto my counter. "The cherry pie is mine. I need my fruit after all this meat and cheese."

"What did you do, rob the local Weigel's?"

"Bite your tongue. I have better taste in gas station pastries. I purchased this at Pilot Flying J."

I let out a laugh before I could stop myself. He helped himself to plates from my cupboard, and what was creepy was that he knew the exact right cupboard to look.

"You have forks, right? Or do you eat all your food like a feral racoon, with your fingers?"

"Hey, my car is better than a diner. Utensils are a luxury."

His expression softened a little, but thank God, he didn't give me any big brother or boyfriend type of hogwash. He just handed me a plate with two pieces of pizza and nudged me out of the kitchen toward the dining room. "Eat. You'll feel better."

I was too tired to argue. I pushed my satchel out of the way and sat down at the table. Beau came and set down silverware, root beer, and napkins. Then he took the chair across from me. His legs were so long, his feet touched mine.

My root beer was already open, so after I swallowed my first two bites of ambrosia, I took a long swallow and looked up to find Beau staring at me.

"What? Did I drip sauce on my chin?"

"Nope. Just watching you. Is that a crime?"

I shrugged and took a smaller bite and peered up at him under my lashes. He was looking at me as if I were some kind of puzzle. It was like we were on a date. It was too intimate. I needed to break the moment before I noticed how good his attention felt.

I pointed my slice at him.

"No deep thinking tonight. This is going to be one of the easy-breezy nights."

"Why?"

I frowned. "There doesn't have to be a reason for easy-breezy. They just are."

"I would be down with that. I really would, but I see the dark circles under your eyes. Despite your Twinkie jokes, I see pain in your eyes."

"You're making that shit up," I protested.

"And to top it off, one of your shirts and a bra are on your hallway floor."

I damn near tipped over my chair to go see if he was right. When I got to the hallway, I realized he was. I vaguely remembered pulling off my clothes on the way to my bedroom, but how in the ever-loving fuck had I walked over them on the way to my front door?

I scooped the clothes up off the floor and threw them into my bedroom, then slammed the door shut.

When I got back to the table, Beau had a shit-eating grin on his face.

I shoved my fists on my hips and glared at him.

"Really? You're going to laugh at me for that? I have one of the crappiest workdays of my life, and you're going to laugh at me?"

His expression changed to one of compassion. "Sit down and tell me about it."

I shook my head and sat down. I stared at my pizza.

"Come on, Maddie, eat. You know you want to."

"Yeah." I picked up my half-eaten slice and finished it off. I started to feel better.

"You want to tell me about it?"

"It started out great. I suppose that's why when it turned out so awful, it seemed really, really awful. Ya know?"

He nodded slowly. "I know exactly what you're saying."

Just looking at him, I could tell he did. I'd looked up Marine Raiders and realized he was in Special Operations. Kind of like a Navy SEAL. They did the really tough stuff. My guess was, he'd seen and done some really harrowing things. It probably made my stuff seem like small potatoes.

"Beau, you've been in war, right?"

His expression changed. Turned harder and a little bit cautious. He nodded.

"I don't intend to ask anything. I'm just saying, my shitty day doesn't probably even come close to your easiest day. So why should I vent?"

He reached over and covered my hand with his. "You matter, Maddie. What you do matters. The kids you work with matter, and I want to hear about your day."

Aw hell, he's making me melt.

"The good news? I started out with a quick visit to check on Eli."

"He's with those good foster parents you told me about, right? Nate and Fran Patterson."

I looked at him in awe. "You remember their names?"

"I remember what's important." Beau nodded. "So that was the good part of the day, then what?"

"I had to do some follow-ups. Those are where I see if a parent has cleaned up their act. Is the house dirty? Is there food? Sometimes I'll check in with the child's school. Things like that. I had five of those calls."

"Isn't that a lot?"

"No. The system is overloaded. Five follow-ups are normal. Then I had to check in on two foster families who were fostering some of my kids. One wasn't there, even though they were supposed to be. The yard had two cars up on blocks."

"The yard?"

"Yep, the yard. Not the driveway. The driveway was all torn up. Don't ask me why. All in all, this did not look good. I took pictures so I could ask the person who had originally certified this foster family, if this is how the house originally looked."

"Eat," Beau said. He pushed my plate closer.

I shook my head at him, but reluctantly grinned. I figured I better eat before I started talking about the Hollister kids.

When I'd finish a bite, he'd push my soda toward me.

I could get used to this.

When I was finished, he looked at me. "Now tell me."

"There are three kids. Bobby is ten, his two younger siblings are seven and six. They got placed with the Farleys three months ago. I just got assigned to them two days ago. I went for my first site visit today. Mrs. Farley didn't want to let me inside. She said that the children were at school."

"What time were you visiting?"

I scowled. "Six PM."

"So, she's a bright one."

"Yep. Anyway, I pointed that out to her, and she explained they were at a school function, but she couldn't remember what. I said I still needed to come in and inspect the place. I explained that was part of my job."

"The kids were there?"

"Boy, you're smart."

"I have my moments," Beau said bashfully.

"Yeah, she lets me in, and the place smells like cigarettes and booze. You'd think I was in a bar. I'm in the living room and there are four overflowing ashtrays. I explain to Mrs. Farley I have to do an inspection of the house. She told me none of the other Department of Children's Services ever did that."

"Do you go for the kitchen first or the bathroom?"

"Kitchen. I need to find out if there's food. There was hardly anything in the cupboard. Just some spaghetti noodles. When I looked in the fridge, there was mustard, ketchup and beer."

"Fuck."

"I took pictures of everything."

"Betcha that didn't make Mrs. Farley happy."

"You'd be right about that."

"I ask to see the children's bedrooms. She is jumpy as hell, and that's when I realize the kids are on the premises. Probably told not to make any noise. I demand to know where they are. She shows me their tiny bedroom with two beds. The ten-year-old, Bobby is huddled in the corner with his arms around his two sisters. The girls look scared as hell."

"Do you get to take them out of there?"

"I wish. I insist on talking to the kids alone. Even Bobby is afraid to talk to me. I recorded the session. I ask them when they last ate, and they can't remember."

"You must have been pissed."

"You can say that again. On my way to McDonald's, I call my supervisor. She says there's not enough cause for me to take them out of there. Which I knew, dammit. Hence the trip to McDonald's. Farleys are pissed, but I don't give a shit. I sit in the bedroom and eat with the kids. Bobby talks just a little more. He seems like a resourceful kid, so I gave him my cell number. I told him to call me if he has any problems."

"And?"

"What do you mean and?"

Beau smirked. I bit into my next slice of pizza

because his smirk irritated me. After four big bites, I set down the remaining crust and looked him in the eye. "Nobody likes a know-it-all."

"And?"

"Fine, I went to Publix and bought groceries. So, sue me."

Beau looked around my house. "Do you rent, or do you own?"

"That's none of your damned business."

"Just answer the damn question."

I lifted my chin. "I own." I still appreciated my zero percent loan I got from Evie and Aiden. It gave me the ability to do the job I love and not live hand to mouth.

"Well, that's good. I know teachers are constantly buying classroom supplies, hell, Marlowe talks about it. How often are you buying things for foster kids?"

"Not all that often," I lied. "The system has specific stipends for the kids and it's my job to make sure that the money is paid out for them. Trust me, I squeeze the county for every cent owed to these kids."

"You're still a liar." He got up and picked up our plates and took them into the kitchen. I followed him. When I started going through the Hostess treats, he caged me in and looked over my shoulder. "Choose carefully, Maddie," he whispered. His breath teased the drying hair at my temple.

I trembled. I quickly grabbed a package of Ho Hos and ducked under his arm.

"Scaredy cat."

"Smart cat," I refuted.

He picked up his cherry pie, and we stood there in silence as we ate our treats.

"What are your next steps with the Hollister kids?"

"With my photos and the little bit I got Bobby to admit, I'll take that into my supervisor. She's a good woman. A fighter. She'll take it over to the department in charge of reviewing and selecting foster families. They'll make a determination if the Farleys are unfit. In the meantime, I'll be making more unannounced visits."

"Is there anything I can do?"

I frowned. "Huh?"

"I know I can't kick the door in for you. But is there something I can do? Somebody I can pressure. Someone I can call?"

Words stuck in my throat. I've told my sisters and some of my friends about what goes on with my job, but nobody had ever asked if they could do something to help.

"I really appreciate that." I paused. Then swallowed. "You don't know how much. But there isn't anything anyone can do but wait."

"And buy groceries, and maybe something a little healthier than MacDonald's."

"Ding Dongs? Oh, I'm sorry, three cherry pies?"

"Brat."

He used to always call me that. And he used to always want to help me with whatever problem I had.

It didn't matter if it was a school problem or something going on at home. He always wanted to help. Sometimes when he couldn't or shouldn't. That's why I got in the habit of not telling him things. At least this situation wasn't nearly as bad as what went on when I was a kid and Dad lived at home.

"I am not a brat. You're a bully."

I turned back to the pile of Hostess products and picked up the package of Twinkies. He yanked them out of my hand.

"Hey, those are mine."

"If you have any more sugar before bedtime, you'll never sleep."

I sighed. He was right. But I didn't want to admit it.

"Don't you stick that bottom lip out at me."

"Why? Will it work? Will you give me back my Twinkies?"

"Nope."

I watched in horror as he scooped up all the treats back into the white bag. "What are you doing with those?"

"I'm taking these with me. I'll bring you a treat in the morning."

The morning? I perked up.

"What kind of treat?"

"Depends on how rested you look. If you get to the door all bleary-eyed, you'll get nothing. Now, if you come to the door like Little Maddie Sunshine, you'll get something really special."

Damn. It was like I was eleven years old again. I was practically bouncing on my toes.

"Promise?"

"Cross my heart. Now come lock up behind me, then go blow-dry your hair so you don't catch a cold."

"When in the hell did you get so pushy?"

"It comes with the job."

I followed him to the door, where he stopped and looked down at me. He tilted up my chin, then traced along my cheekbone with his thumb. "Remember, Maddie, I'll be looking you over. I want to see you rested," he whispered.

"Yes, Beau." I breathed out, wondering if he would kiss me. He let me go and then left.

I shuddered as I locked the door behind him and fell against it.

Damn.

My treat better include his lips on mine.

Chapter Six

My phone started to ring. It didn't make sense, because my alarm hadn't gone off, and I'd set my alarm for six-thirty. I rolled over and stretched for my nightstand where it was charging. I squinted and saw that it was Trenda calling.

What in the hell would she be calling for so early in the morning? Oh yeah. Something bad.

"Trenda, what's wrong?" I answered.

"Is he there?"

"Is who where?"

"Drake? Is he at your place yet?"

"What are you talking about? I haven't seen our big brother since last year. Why would he be at my house at the butt-crack of dawn?"

"Karen called me, and it's really early in California. Drake found out that Beau's back in town. He flew out late last night into Nashville, and he's driving here to talk to you...and probably Beau."

"Oh, for the love of God." I threw my arm over my eyes. There went my morning treat. "Is Drake out of his ever-loving mind?"

"Have you met him?"

I heard mumbling from the other end of the line and realized that Trenda's husband must be talking to her.

"Seriously, Trenda, why would Drake drop everything and come to Jasper Creek? This makes no sense."

"We all saw how you were when Beau left and didn't contact you."

"Not Drake. He was in California and on deployment all the damn time. He had no idea what I was like."

Trenda didn't respond.

"Unless... Unless my big sister spilled the beans. Is that what happened, Trenda? Did you tell our over-protective oaf of a brother that I was upset that my best friend blew me off?"

"Oh for goodness sakes, you were more than a little upset. You were devastated. You had no idea why he would have cut off all communication. Beau had been your lifeline for years. All through your childhood, and then poof, he was gone. You were a mess. It was like you'd lost a limb. So yeah, we might have mentioned it."

I shoved more pillows behind my back and sat up. "What do you mean, we? Are you saying it was more than just you?"

"I plead the fifth." I heard more mumbling. "Look, I've got to go. I need to clean the house. With Drake arriving, we're going to be having people over, and I want to get ready."

"We are not inviting people over because of your brother," I clearly heard Simon say over the line. "Today was a snow day for both of us. You agreed."

I giggled at the disgruntled tone in my brother-in-law's voice. Couple that with the term snow-day when it was the month of May and I was totally tickled.

"We are too having people over. I need to clean and cook." Trenda's voice was firm.

"I'll let you two figure things out. Thanks for giving me a heads-up, Trenda, but that doesn't get you off the hook for ratting me out. Did Karen give you any kind of ETA as to when Drake would be here?"

"She called fifteen minutes ago, and he was in Knoxville. Knowing how he drives, he'll be at your place in less than an hour."

"Got it. Again, thanks for the heads-up."

Simon's voice was rumbly when I hung up the phone. I figured that the first thing I needed to do was warn Beau not to come over. I scrolled down to his name and called him.

"Isn't this kind of early for you?" he asked.

"How would you know?" I scowled.

"Come on, Maddie, you were never a morning person. How many times were you late for school?"

I got out of bed and headed for the bathroom.

"I was late for school because I was getting Chloe and Zoe ready," I lied. I turned on the bathroom light and winced. I really should have dried my hair before going to sleep. It looked like a rat had slept in it.

Beau laughed. "Like Trenda would have allowed that to happen. She was always carping at you for being late. So was Evie, for that matter."

"Look, I didn't call for a walk down memory lane. This is important."

"You sound amped up. That doesn't sound rested to me. How did you sleep?"

"I was sleeping just fine until Trenda called. Now listen. Drake is going to be here in about an hour. He's got some kind of bug up his ass about you coming to town, so it's best that you don't come over."

Beau didn't say anything. "Are you still there?" I asked.

"I'm here, but what does Drake coming to your house have to do with me coming over?"

"According to Trenda, he's worried about my reaction to you being back in town."

"I guess I can understand that. I'll be there in a few." He hung up.

"What the ever-loving fuck!" I yelled.

All the men in my life were crazy!

I slammed the bathroom door shut and went about

my morning business, once again realizing I wouldn't have a lot of time to get myself together.

When the knock came at my door, I was halfway done blow-drying my hair. I marched to the door and flung it open.

"You're going to have to—"

"What the hell are you doing opening the door without seeing who it is?" Drake roared. He pulled me into his arms and lifted me off the floor in a rib-crushing hug.

I pounded on his shoulder. "I can't breathe."

He hugged me tighter, then set me down and looked me over. "Am I too early? Why isn't your hair dry?"

I shook my head as he walked past me into my house. "Do you have anything to eat? I'm starving."

"If you're so hungry, you should have stopped by Trenda's house, not mine," I grumbled. "Help yourself to whatever. I have to dry my hair and put on something besides pajama bottoms and a sleep shirt."

"I'm fine with what you're wearing," he said with his patented charming smile. "You look great, Maddie. Better than great."

I shook my head. "Just go scrounge something to eat and leave me alone." I grinned. God, it was good to see him.

I hustled back to my bathroom and continued to blow-dry my curls, trying to keep them in check. When I was done, I put on mascara and lip-gloss, then found my favorite pair of boot cut jeans and reached for another one of my crop tops but thought better of it. I didn't need any shit from big brother. So instead, I took out a Buccaneers t-shirt from the good old days at East Tennessee State University. It still kind of fit, even if I might have gained fifteen pounds since college and gone up a cup size.

Thank God.

"Get out here, Mads. Your waffle is ready," Drake hollered from the kitchen.

I hustled down the hall just as there was another knock at the door. I don't know how it was possible, since I was almost at the door, but Drake beat me to it. He looked through the peephole before opening it.

"Beaumont," he growled.

"Good to see you, Drake." Beau smiled.

They stood there, not moving. Drake didn't invite Beau in. He stayed in place, blocking the doorway.

"Drake, get out of the way and let Beau in," I admonished. I sniffed the air. "Do I smell a waffle burning?"

"Nope." Drake didn't bother turning around.

"Waffles?" Beau said. "Guess we don't need these," he said, holding up a pink box that I recognized from Down Home Diner. My mouth started salivating. I hip-checked my brother and grabbed the box from Beau.

"We most certainly do need these."

Drake looked down at me. "You don't even know what's in the box," he muttered.

"It's from Down Home," I countered. "Come on in, Beau. Maybe if we feed the beast, he'll be in a better mood when he starts to cross-examine you."

"Don't count on it," Drake muttered.

Drake followed me into the kitchen, where I took down three plates. "Here, take these into the dining room."

"I don't trust you with the pastries," my brother said.

"So, send Beau in to watch over me." I goaded him.

He plucked the pink box off the counter and grabbed the plates out of my hand. I grabbed three glasses down from another cupboard and turned around to find Beau behind me. He was smirking. "Seems to be going well."

I shook my head. "Just you wait," I warned him.

"I've already been through a Drake Avery talk once in my life, and that was when he was a senior in high school, and I was in seventh grade. I think I can handle anything he dishes out today."

My mouth fell open. "You never told me about that."

"There was no point. What's more, he did the right thing. He was worried about you. It was when he was leaving for the Navy. He wanted to make sure that I would treat you the way you deserved to be treated."

"But we were just friends," I protested.

"That's not the way it looked to him. He was worried, baby. Looking back, I can't blame him. If I had been in his shoes, I would have done the exact same thing."

"What's taking you two so long?" Drake bellowed from the dining room. "If you don't come out in the next two minutes, I'm eating all the cinnamon rolls and leaving you two with just the glazed donuts."

Beau raised his eyebrows.

"He's serious." I turned to the fridge and pulled out a carton of milk and a container of orange juice and pushed them at him. "Go protect our food. I'll bring glasses and silverware."

"Bossy."

I smirked. "You like bossy."

He bent close to my ear. "You can be bossy everyplace but one," he whispered.

I frowned in confusion. "Where's that?"

"My bed."

He turned before he could see the blush that suffused my face. Shit, that was hot. I stood there thinking of us in bed. Him holding my hands above my head. A slow shiver worked its way down my back, spiraling low in my stomach before I could stop it.

"Where are the glasses, Mads?" Drake hollered.

I grabbed the roll of paper towels and put that

under my arm, nabbed some silverware and picked up the glasses, and brought them into the dining room. The heavenly smell of sugar, cinnamon, and cream cheese pulled me into its orbit as I saw the plates on the table. The empty chair with a plate in front of it had two cinnamon rolls.

Score!

Beau and Drake just had one in front of them, along with muffins and glazed donuts. "Why did I make out?" I asked Beau.

"I'd already stopped at the diner before you called me. I'd gotten two cinnamon rolls for both of us, but with Drake here, I figured I'd share my second one. After all, he is here to give me shit. Right, big guy?"

Drake was in the middle of pouring himself a tall glass of milk.

"You've got it in one. You're still enlisted, right?"

Beau nodded.

"How much more time are you going to be spending here in Jasper Creek before you have to go back to Pendleton?"

"Where is Camp Pendleton?" I asked.

"It's in Southern California. About sixty miles north of me," Drake answered.

"How do you know he's stationed at Camp Pendleton?" I asked.

"You explain," Drake said as he looked at Beau. Then he picked up his cinnamon roll and took a big bite.

"Marine Raiders are based out of Camp Pendleton," Beau told me. "I've got a townhome near base."

"How often are you in the States?" I questioned.

"Depends." He took a bite out of his glazed donut. Not nearly as big as Drake's bite.

"That isn't an answer."

"The longest I've been home was for three and a half months," Beau admitted.

Beau was sometimes in the States for that long? I looked down at my plate. I was losing my taste for cinnamon rolls.

Drake looked over at me. "Aren't you going to eat that?" he asked.

"No."

He snatched one of the rolls off my plate.

Beau glared at Drake, then turned to me. "Maddie, I can explain."

"Maybe later," I whispered.

"You left her high and dry. You were a total prick." Drake took a long sip of milk to wash down half of the cinnamon roll he'd stolen from me.

"There's still stuff we need to talk about," Beau said softly. "Come on, Maddie. Eat your cinnamon roll. You know you love them," Beau coaxed.

I pushed my plate away and got up from the table. "Look, Beau. It's water under the bridge," I sighed. "We don't need to discuss your time away. But I do think that maybe we've been going a little too fast."

"You tell him, Maddie." Drake grinned at me, then glared at Beau, who had stood up as well. "She's kicking your ass to the curb. Are you hearing that, Beaumont?"

"Maddie, look at me."

I put a smile on my face. I knew it didn't reach my eyes, but at this moment, I didn't have it in me to care. "Seriously, Beau. It's all good. I'll save my cinnamon roll for later. Right now, I want to catch up with my big brother. You don't mind leaving, do you? It's family time."

"I'm coming back after he leaves."

"I'm not leaving. Maddie has a guest room. I'm staying here for the duration. We have a lot of catching up to do. Consider yourself gone." Drake didn't even get up, but he was still menacing.

Beau shot him a hard look. "I'll come over whenever I damn well feel like it."

At that point, Drake did get up. Beau might be six-foot-two, but my brother topped him by three inches. "Try it, and I'll have you up on stalking charges so fast, your head will spin. That won't go over well with your commanding officer, now, will it?"

I saw the look of frustration suffusing Beau's face.

I pointed at my brother. "Drake, cool it." Then I turned to Beau. "Don't listen to him, he's just being him. I agree, we have more talking we need to do. But we jumped fast, and I just need a couple of days, okay?" I looked into his eyes, aching for him to understand.

"You're right, honey. Anything you need."

Beau headed for the door and opened it, then he stopped. He dragged his hand through his hair and gave me a frustrated look. "Just know, Maddie, we're too important to throw away because of the past. Okay?" This time it was him who was pleading.

I nodded.

Then he left.

When I turned to Drake, he was seated again, but he wasn't eating. He was studying me.

"Is he right, Mads?"

"I don't know, Drake. I honestly don't know."

Chapter Seven

"You haven't been looking so good lately," Kai told me.

"Is it my hair, or is it my nail polish? Oh, let me guess, it's my make-up."

My brother chuckled. "Well, at least your sense of humor is still intact. Is it because Maddie hasn't been around?"

I took a long pull from my water bottle. Kai and I had been running off and on for over two hours. We kept on the trails. That way, he could keep a good pace and the ground was level.

It had taken a while for Kai to open up and tell me the extent of his injuries. Bullet fragments in the upper spine and a prognosis that he'd never walk the same again. But here was my brother. Running. He was one tough son-of-a-bitch.

Right now, we were resting at the base of an old hemlock tree.

"Yeah, it's Maddie. She's been keeping me at arm's length since she found out that I was based in California and was home for months at a time, and still didn't reach out to her."

"Ouch. You sure she's just mad about California? Or is she afraid of something else?"

"I'm ninety-nine percent sure it's California. But hell, maybe you're right. Maybe it is something else. Shit, now I have to think more. Thanks, Kai," I said sarcastically.

"You're welcome." He bowed his head to me. The little shit. After all, I was born four minutes before him. He should show his elder brother some respect.

"According to Lettie, you two were thick as thieves growing up. Is that true?" Kai asked me.

"Yeah, that's true. We've been friends since kindergarten, up until our senior year."

Kai gave me a sideways look. "Just friends?"

"I started to get other ideas at the end of our junior year, but Maddie wasn't thinking that way, so I tamped it down and started dating other girls. Maddie didn't mind. We stayed best friends."

Kai grabbed a granola bar out of his pack and offered me half. "That's hard to believe."

"How do you think I felt? But that's how it was. I think it was because I was dealing with my mom, and she was busy protecting her sisters from her mom's bad choices. Something romantic just wasn't on her radar." I ate the granola bar and washed it down with water.

"Huh. Are you thinking about changing that now?"

"Abso-fucking-lutely."

Kai chuckled. "That's how Marlowe and I saw it. I wasn't sure that Maddie was catching on, but Marlowe says that she is definitely interested in you."

"That's how I'm reading it."

"So why in the hell are you letting the past and her big brother stand in your way?"

"I'm just biding my time. I grew up with Maddie. When she's mad or sad or confused, she needs time to brood. If I go in too soon, I'll get my head bitten off. I need to wait for her to come to me."

"Are you sure about that?"

"Kindergarten to senior year. Yeah, I'm sure."

Was I? It had been three days. Maybe she had changed. Maybe I was wrong.

Dammit all to hell.

I stood up. "Is it time to head back?"

"I've got another half hour in me before heading back." Kai smiled as I held out my hand for him to grab.

"Let's hit it."

I was parked in the back left corner of her office parking lot. I watched as the delivery guy went in with the hundred-and fifty-dollar bouquet of flowers.

Whoever heard of spending that damn much money on flowers? Still, I was trying to make a statement. I knew she was in there, because I had spotted her Jeep.

She'd told me that Wednesdays were the days she tried to catch up on administrative stuff. I had the flowers delivered at four o'clock so that I could catch her in the parking lot as she left, in case the flowers didn't work, and she didn't call or text me.

After a half hour with no call or text, I tried to console myself with the thought that she was on a phone call or in a meeting.

"Yeah, sure."

Time for Plan B.

I'd driven to Nashville to pick up a five-pound sampler tin of Leon's candy. It had a mixture of homemade pralines, turtles, pecan rolls, and caramels. In my junior year, I had gotten her a one-pound tin, and I had received a hug and a kiss on my cheek that I still cherished to this very day. I was dying to find out what a five-pound tin would get me.

I tossed my phone on the passenger seat next to the chocolate tin and waited for five o'clock to roll around. After five, with no sight of Maddie, I turned on some music and listened to Linkin Park and Foo Fighters.

I kept my eyes open partway and focused on the back door where employees were coming out. At seven-thirty, I was getting damned pissed. Not because of no acknowledgement for the flowers, but because it was dusk and soon to be dark, and there was no sign of

Maddie. Only one of the two lonely parking lot lights came on, flickering weakly, while the other one didn't even bother lighting up. Neither light was close to Maddie's Jeep, not that it mattered since both were obviously broken. There was one spotlight over the employee entrance that practically screamed, 'Here I am, come get me'.

Since the only other vehicle in the parking lot was mine, I highly doubted she was coming out with someone, unless, pray God, there was security in the building who would be walking her out. I stewed and stewed and stewed as I waited for her. Finally at eight-thirty, the employee door opened. And it was worse than I imagined. Maddie was wearing a short trench coat and boots. I thought she must be wearing a skirt that ended, hopefully, right above her knees, because it wasn't showing below the trench coat.

Of course she was alone.

She rolled her shoulder to better haul her satchel and purse up higher. She had her keys in her hand. At least that was something. At least she wouldn't have to stop to and rummage through her purse when she got to her car.

That was all. That was the *one* thing she'd done right. Hell, she hadn't even looked around the parking lot to realize there was only one truck in it. Did the woman have any self-preservation instincts at all?

I watched as she crossed the parking lot. I got out of my truck. I didn't want to scare her, so I called out.

"Maddie, it's me, Beau."

She quickly did a quarter turn. "What the hell? You scared the hell out of me!"

"Better me than some random asshole," I continued to shout as I stalked over to her. "What in the hell are you doing leaving so late at night, without somebody to walk you out to your car?"

She dangled her car keys at me, and I saw a gray tube hanging from them. It was a can of pepper spray.

"If someone has a gun, that's not going to do you a whole hell of a lot of good."

"If someone has a gun, it's not going to do the two of us a whole hell of a lot of good, now is it?" she responded sarcastically.

"At least tell me you own a gun, considering the work you do." I begged.

"It's because of the work I do that I don't."

I ran my fingers through my hair. "You're driving me crazy here."

"What in the hell are you doing here, anyway?"

"I was waiting for you."

She rolled her eyes at me. "I got that part, but why? I told you I needed some time. But the flowers were nice. Amy loves them."

"Amy?"

"The girl I gave them to. She's a new employee. She's somebody that came out of the foster care system and is going to night school while she works for us. She's a great girl. Hard worker."

Of course. Of course, she gave away the flowers.

"Did you bother to read the card?"

"Thank you for not trying to write a poem."

Now I was getting mad. We'd been over this shit. I'd spilled my guts.

"Jesus, Maddie, aren't you going to cut me any slack?"

"I guess we'll never know, because you didn't give me the time I asked for."

"Think about it, I've laid it all on the line for you ever since I saw you. I even went easy on you when we played pool."

Her eyes sparkled and she took a step toward me. "You did not go easy on me. You're not that great of a player."

That got her motor revving. This was good.

I slowly smiled. "Yes, I am. I could have cleared the table at any time."

She shoved a finger into my chest. "That is total bullshit. I let you win because I felt sorry for your pathetic ass."

"I call bullshit. I handed that last shot to you on a golden platter. You screwed it up because you wanted to spend time with me."

"That is not true. Take it back!"

I was clearly saying I had thrown the game and it was driving her nuts. Served her right; now that I saw how late she left the building every night, that was going to drive *me* nuts.

"I won fair and square." I said. "You choked."

Even in the dim light, I could see her face getting red. I hadn't seen her like this in ages. I'd forgotten just how much fun it was to wind Maddie up.

"Come over to my place tonight. I have a guest room and an extra toothbrush," I cajoled.

"You are not the better player," she pouted. "Anyway, I really need to go home. I still have paperwork I need to get done."

I eased her satchel off her shoulder. "I'm stealing this for the night. You're going to be of no use to your kids tomorrow if you stay up all night going over cases."

She frowned. "How do you know?"

I brushed back a lock of her dark curly hair that had slipped out of her ponytail, then cupped her cheek. "I know because you would always knock yourself out helping me all night on some test or with some paper at a cost to you. It wasn't til our junior year that I stopped doing that shit to you."

"I liked helping you."

"To your detriment."

Maddie's bottom lip stuck out in a pout. She had such kissable lips. I was so hungry for her, but I had to get past all the hurdles we had before I could get to that point. And hell, even if I got through all the hurdles, would she ever un-friend-zone me?

She let out a frustrated sigh. "Jesus, Beau. Do you think I don't know how to take care of myself?"

"I think you work so damn hard taking care of everyone else that you forget to watch your own back."

Her breath hitched, but she covered it fast.

"Go home," I said, softer now. "Eat. Sleep. Let your brother make you laugh because he's an idiot. But don't think for a second that I'm done, because I'm not."

"You're impossible."

"No, I'm determined."

I grinned. I'd forgotten my ace in the hole. I turned and raced to my truck. Even as I ran, a voice in my head wondered if I should let go.

I ignored it.

Yeah. Like I was ever going to give up. That wasn't what a Marine Raider did.

I grabbed the tin and turned back around. I saw Maddie still standing where I'd left her, watching me. I looked her dead in the eye and stalked her way. She started backing up toward her Jeep. Yep, she was catching on. There was no way this was over.

When we both reached her Jeep, she looked up at me, her chin jutting out.

"What now, Beaumont?" she asked belligerently.

I thrust out the big tin of Leon's candy.

She eyed it with suspicion, then looked back up at me.

"It's not going to bite."

"Yeah, but you might," she muttered.

"At least you've got that right." I grinned. "Here, take it."

Her eyes flicked back to the tin, then back to me, her expression guarded.

I rolled my eyes. "Come on Maddie, it's not a bomb. It's just candy."

She bit her lip.

"You remember, honey, it's the good stuff."

She took it reluctantly, turning it over in her hands. When she saw the weight of it written on the cover, her eyes narrowed. "Five pounds. Are you trying to bribe me with chocolate, sugar, and, hopefully caramel?"

"Would I do that?"

She caressed the tin like a lover and I felt my body heat up. "I'm just reminding you of the one time in your life that you actually liked me," I said desperately.

Her lips twitched as she looked up at me. "One time, huh?"

I took a step closer so we were toe to toe. "Maybe two times."

She swallowed and licked her bottom lip again. Fuck, she was killing me. She looked down at the tin that she had continued to caress. I could tell she wanted to open it. I remembered how she had dived in and glutted on the pralines back in high school. She'd only saved one for me.

She looked up at me from under her lashes. "You're not fighting fair," she whispered.

"Never intended to."

She looked back down at the tin, then her clear green eyes looked into mine. "This doesn't mean I forgive you. You know that, don't you?"

I chuckled. "It wouldn't be any fun if you did."

She let out a small huff, then turned to her Jeep and pressed the alarm. I heard her mumble something about big, cocky men. Or maybe it was something about big cocks. A man could only hope.

I watched as she slid inside her vehicle and started her Jeep.

She rolled down her window. "Drake's last night here is tomorrow. Trenda's throwing a party. She invited Kai and Marlowe and asked me to invite you."

"Does this mean you're inviting me?"

"I suppose it is."

"What time and what can I bring?"

"Seven o'clock. No need to bring anything. Trenda will have too much as it is. And quit being so polite, it's fucking annoying."

I grinned.

"What are you going to wear?"

"Bite me, Beaumont," she said as she pulled on her seatbelt.

"With pleasure," I murmured. "With pleasure."

I caught her opening up the tin and popping a caramel into her mouth just before she drove away.

I took my time walking back to my truck and looked up at the broken parking lot lights. First thing tomorrow I'd be having a few words with the property management company.

Chapter Eight

I barely stepped foot into Trenda's house, when I was almost tackled to the ground by a nine-year-old tornado of energy.

"Aunt Maddie, Aunt Maddie. What took you so long? Everybody's been talking about you, and I've already made fourteen dollars for my swear jar."

I looked down at my precocious niece and smiled. "Only fourteen dollars? But Uncle Drake is here. How come you haven't made more?"

"He keeps going to the back porch to talk with Dad and Mr. Roan, Mr. Kai and Mr. Jase." She gave a put-upon sigh. "Dad gave me the look when I tried to go with them. You know the one."

I laughed. "Yep, I've seen that look. Men do that sometimes."

"Is it true that you have a boyfriend?"

Aw, hell, even Bella knew about Beau. For the love

of God, didn't anybody in Jasper Creek have anything better to do than gossip about my life?

"No, Sweetpea, I don't. I have a very good friend who is on leave. His name is Beau, and he's Kai's twin brother."

Bella bounced up and down. "Do they look alike?"

"Yep."

"Is he coming to the party?"

"I think so. He was invited."

She clapped her hands. "This is going to be so cool."

Trenda came over and put her hand on her daughter's head. "Are you bothering your Aunt Maddie before she's even had a chance to put down her purse?"

Bella frowned. "Oh yeah. I'm supposed to welcome people and show them where they can put their things. It's in the guest room. I can put your purse there if you want. But we have to be real quiet, because baby Drake's room is right beside it. He's asleep now. Mom said we don't want him to wake up. Right, Mom?" Bella looked up at Trenda.

"Right," Trenda agreed.

I wanted to pout. Getting to hold my nephew was one of my favorite things in the world.

"Hey, you can come over anytime and play with my son," Trenda promised. "All you have to do is leave work at a reasonable hour."

I heaved a big sigh. "Okay."

"Give me your purse, Aunt Maddie. I'll put it away," Bella said with a grin.

"Am I going to owe you any money?"

Bella giggled.

God, I loved her giggle.

"No, don't be silly. I only collect money for swears. So be careful, I'll be listening," she said as she skipped off with my purse.

"Your daughter is amazing," Ruby Miller said as she came up behind Trenda.

"That's one way of putting it," Trenda said. "I would go with terrifying."

"I think she's going to run the world one day," I chimed in.

"The kitchen is empty," Ruby told Trenda. "Let's take our little friend in there so we can figure out the lay of the land."

"I think that's an excellent idea."

Ruby hooked one arm through my right elbow, and Trenda hooked my left elbow and they shoved their way through the crowd with me sandwiched in the middle.

"There better be food if this is an interrogation. And you better have little smokies wrapped in dough," I warned my sister.

"It wouldn't be a party without little smokies," she said as we entered the kitchen.

I untangled myself and headed for the cookie sheet on top of the stove and grabbed a plate to fill it up with some of the little treats. Okay, a lot of the little treats, like a whole pile of them.

"You better be sharing," Ruby grumped.

"It depends how mean you two are going to be."

"Beau. I want to know if you invited Beau," Ruby commanded.

"Okay, now I know," I said as I dipped my smokie in hot mustard. "You don't get any, Miss Miller."

"Fine. I'll fix my own plate." And she proceeded to do so while I bit into my food.

"I can answer if she invited Beau," Trenda interrupted. "Since I invited Kai and Marlowe, I told her to invite Beau. It took some arm-twisting...not," my sister laughed. "So, he should show up anytime. He's such a gentleman. He called to see if there was anything he could bring."

Ruby's eyes widened. "Impressive."

"That's what I thought," Trenda agreed.

"So, it didn't take any arm twisting, huh?" Ruby said with interest.

I shoved a whole little smokie into my mouth and shrugged.

"Do you notice what she's wearing, Trenda?"

"Oh, I noticed. It's warm tonight, but little sis is wearing a clingy sweater. And if I'm not mistaken, she has a tank underneath, and as the party goes on, she's going to get hotter and hotter, and be forced to take off the sweater."

"Isn't she the little minx," Ruby cooed.

I swallowed my food and grabbed for a bottle of water and drank some down. "I will not be taking off my sweater. What's more, it's lightweight cotton, so it's really cool. Not hot at all. So, your supposition is all wrong."

Ruby shoved a margarita at me. "Here, you know you love Trenda's strawberry margaritas. She made them weak, so they won't get you hot. You'll be fine."

I took a sip and coughed. "Jesus, Trenda, just how much tequila did you put in this, the entire bottle?"

Trenda looked innocent as she sipped from a bottle of water.

Smart woman.

"Ruby, don't you think it's time we give Maddie some advice? She's used to milquetoast men like Ted. She needs to know how to handle a live one."

Ruby gave Trenda a surprised look. "Trenda, I might have lived in LA most of my life, but I don't have the slightest idea about how to deal with a live one. Hell, look at me, like anyone as hot and impressive as Beau would ever be interested." She held out her arms to show off her voluptuous figure.

"You need to stop doing that, Ruby," I said seriously. "Half the guys who show up at Java Jolt in the morning are not there for the coffee. They're there for the view."

Ruby gave me a hurt look. "Give it a rest, Maddie. I don't need you blowing smoke up my ass. I know who I am. I've come to terms with it. Okay?"

Aw shit. I'd fucked up. I didn't mean to hurt her feelings.

I glanced over at my sister and she gave me the 'shut it' sign. Still, it killed me that Ruby had such a skewed perception of herself. If I ever got ahold of the people who hurt her in LA, I would let loose a full can of whoop ass out on them.

"Ignore me, Ruby. I'm just nervous about Beau," I apologized.

"Now, that I believe." She smiled. "So, Trenda, you snagged Simon. What advice do you have for Maddie?"

Before my sister could answer, I said, "I don't want to snag Beau. He's my friend. That's all he's ever been and ever will be."

"Sure. And that's why you let him win that game of pool," Ruby scoffed.

"I heard about that," Trenda laughed. "Maddie always wins. I wish I could have seen that."

"Maddie, in real life, aren't you the teeniest, eeniest interested in Beau, not as a friend, but as more? Maybe as a lover?"

I started coughing. I should have known better than to be sipping the red-dyed tequila when Ruby started to talk. Trenda patted my back.

"I don't know," I wailed. "That's the problem."

"Well, I know," Trenda said. "I recognize the symptoms. You have the same Avery girl sickness that has assailed Evie, Chloe, and me. The dazed look, the confusion, too much ice cream, longing looks and feeling like you're a planet orbiting around the sun."

"Orbiting around the sun? Are you kidding me? Where in the hell do you get this hooey?" I demanded.

Ruby looked at Trenda like she was some sort of oracle. "I've seen the longing looks and the confusion. Let's not forget the panic attacks."

"Oh yeah, there's those, too," Trenda nodded.

"Are you talking about Maddie's infatuation with Beau? I think he might be okay."

I turned around so fast at the sound of my big brother's voice, one of my little smokies shot off the plate and rocketed toward Drake. He caught it and popped it into his mouth.

"You like him?" I asked.

He swallowed the smokie, then grabbed the margarita out of my hand and took a swig. "I said I *might* like him. Still thinking about it. But I did a little digging with some of my buddies in California. He checks out."

"What in the hell does 'checks out' mean?" I demanded to know.

"He's solid. I'd trust him to have your back. Doesn't mean I like him yet." Drake plucked another little smokie off my plate and dipped it in mustard. "Nice sweater." He smirked.

"God, can you all just stay out of my business?" I cried.

They all laughed.

"At least he's a major improvement over Ted what's his face. The man with the most boring Netflix queue ever," Drake laughed.

"Yeah, what was he like in bed?" Ruby asked. "Was it ever anything besides missionary?"

Drake threw up his hands. "For the love of God, I am so out of here," Drake groaned. He turned around and left the kitchen, only after grabbing two more smokies off my plate.

I smiled at Ruby. "Thanks."

She curtsied. "You're welcome."

"Auntie Maddie, he does look exactly like Mr. Kai. I thought he was Mr. Kai, but I checked outside and Mr. Kai was still outside. When I called him Mr. Kai, he said his name was Beau. I think he's even cuter than Mr. Kai, even though they look exactly alike. He asked where you were. I told him you were in here. So be ready. He's coming in here." She peeked over her shoulder. "He's coming. He's coming." Bella was jumping up and down.

"Actually, I'm here," Beau said, as he gave me a heated smile.

Oh hell.

Chapter Nine

As soon as I walked into the kitchen, Ruby, Trenda, and the little girl hustled out, leaving me with an open-mouthed Maddie.

She stood in the nook where the two counters met, balancing a plate of food in one hand and a drink in the other. Her cheeks were flushed. I wondered how long she'd been here and if she'd been drinking much, but then decided no. There was no way that Maddie would drink too much, not if she was driving.

I closed the gap between us. I pulled the dishes out of her hands and put them on the counter behind her. I reached out and brushed a strand of hair off her cheek and tucked it behind her ear. "I meant what I said the other night, Maddie. I'm not giving up."

Her eyes darkened, but she didn't say anything. That was fine. I wasn't done.

"I've wanted you since forever. Since our junior year."

"You asked Mary Slaughter out," she whispered.

"I was a dumbass. I was confused back then, but I'm not now. I know what I want. I know who I want."

"You don't live here."

"We'll cross that bridge when we come to it. Right now, we have time to make up for."

Her breathing hitched.

Her eyes widened.

I leaned in and put my hands on the counter on either side of her, boxing her in. I pressed my cheek against hers. "I don't want to be just your friend. I want to be the man who hears your laugh first thing every morning and the man who makes you scream his name every single night."

A soft gasp left her lips, and she clutched my waist.

I leaned back so I could look her in the eye. "Unless you tell me to stop, I'm going to kiss you."

She didn't say a word.

I touched my lips to hers, and the world ceased to exist. There was only Maddie. She tasted like strawberries and heat. Like passion, fire and want. She moved her hands so that they were twisting in the front of my shirt, dragging me closer. Our kiss turned carnal. Soon there was nothing between us but years and need.

I wasn't kissing her. I was finally claiming her, like I should have done so many years ago. She melted into me, then surged upwards, opening her mouth with a ferocious taking that set me on fire. I let go of the counter and slid one hand to the small of her back, pulling her tight against me, never wanting to let her go.

I could kiss Maddie forever. She was more necessary than air.

A distant voice broke through the haze.

"...Kai, don't go in there. Just wait—Kai, I'm serious—"

Ruby. Damn.

I pulled back just as the kitchen door creaked open. Maddie swayed slightly, lips parted, cheeks flushed. I turned around, keeping her behind me, shielding her from view.

Kai walked in, eyes sharp and curious. "Beau. You got a minute?"

"Now's not a good time."

"This won't take long, and Jase has to leave. So, it'd be great if you could give me five minutes."

Fuck! Could the timing be any worse?

I looked over my shoulder at Maddie. She looked pale. I'd come on too strong, and she was going to run. Talking about the long-term was too much for her.

Dammit!

I nodded. "Yeah. Just give us a sec."

He looked past me, probably trying to see Maddie.

"Great, we're out on the patio."

"I'll be right there."

Kai left the kitchen, and I turned to Maddie.

Dammit, I could practically see her building the walls, brick by brick.

"Don't leave. I'll be right back."

"Go do what you have to do."

"Shit, you're going to leave, aren't you?"

She shrugged her shoulders. "Just go talk to Kai and whoever else is on the patio."

"Maddie, if you run, I'm just going to follow you."

"Go talk to Kai."

I opened the sliding glass door and stepped out onto a newly built cedar deck. Somebody had spent some serious coin on high-end patio furniture that five men weren't bothering to use.

Figured.

Instead, they were all standing around the built-in grill or leaning over the railing that looked over open land. Most of them had a beer in their hands.

"Hey. Let me introduce you," Kai said as he came up to me. "You know Drake and Simon, right?"

I nodded.

"This is Roan Thatcher," he said as a tall man who had been standing next to Simon stepped forward.

"Beau, I've been waiting to see you again. At least the real Beau Beaumont." Roan chuckled as he held out his hand.

"Roan, you old bastard. How are you doing? Last I heard, you were at Walter Reed and kicking ass."

"Damn right I was," Roan grinned. "They told me I wouldn't walk again. Nobody should bet against a Marine Raider."

"Damn straight." I looked over at my twin, then at Roan. "So, you saw Kai and mistook him for me, did you?"

Roan nodded.

"When he explained, I was excited to know you were in town. It's really good to see you, brother. I thought you were never going to step foot in Jasper Creek again."

"It's good to see you again, too." And it really was. It was good to see him upright, and it was good to see him here in our hometown. "When I found out about Kai, i.e. Brady, nothing would have stopped me from coming home."

"I imagine. So, are you here to stay?" Roan asked me.

"No, I'm going back in a couple of weeks. Are you running your dad's place?"

"Nope. I work with Simon. We own Onyx Security here in town. I sometimes turn a wrench at the shop when they're backed up, only because I like the management."

Kai came over and chuckled. "He makes it sound like they handle all the jaywalkers here in Jasper Creek. They actually work nationally to—"

"Regionally," Simon interrupted. "We currently work regionally to handle a few things that fall under the arm of security."

I looked over all the men on the deck. "Are you all former military? Except for Drake?"

"The men who work with Onyx are," Simon answered.

"The last man in our group here is Jase Drakos. He recently transitioned out of his SEAL team in Little Creek and settled here."

Jase was the biggest man in the group, even bigger than Drake. He'd winced when Simon said he'd left his team. I knew what that meant. He'd been discharged against his will, just like my brother Kai, most likely due to an injury.

Jase stepped forward to shake my hand and give a half smile. "Good to meet you, Beau. I think I've seen you somewhere before."

"Lame joke," Kai and I said at the same time. We turned to one another and laughed. Shit, we were acting like twins who had grown up together.

How fucking cool was that?

"So why am I out here?" I asked Simon. I instinctively knew it was his idea to have Kai drag me out to the deck.

"Could just be a military circle jerk," Drake offered.

"Shut it, Drake," Simon ordered. It was then I remembered Simon used to be a Lieutenant

Commander of SEALs. He'd probably been Drake's boss's boss. It didn't stop Drake from rolling his eyes at his brother-in-law, but Drake stopped talking.

"You're here because I wanted to let you know that there would be a place for you here at Onyx if you were thinking about leaving early and settling down here in Jasper Creek."

Now this I hadn't been expecting.

"So, what is it again that Onyx does?" I asked.

Simon nodded to Roan, who was leaning against the grill. "About three years ago, when I came back home, Simon had already started Onyx Security." Roan explained. "Simon had done a couple of jobs. When we got together, we thought we might do some low-key consulting, maybe a few high-end protection gigs. But it didn't stay small for long. Word got out after a couple of tough rescues, situations that needed creative problem-solving and quiet extractions, not red tape. Most of our work comes through referrals now, former clients, law firms and private security networks. It got out of hand fast."

"Like what?" I asked.

Roan turned to Simon, who nodded.

"Our latest was such a pain in the ass. We had to go after a guy."

"You take skips?" I was surprised they went after people who didn't show up to their court dates.

Simon shook his head. "No, we'd been hired by a corporation to check into why they were leaking money like a sieve. It took some time. Needed to bring in an expert, because that's not Roan or me."

I frowned. "A military asset?"

"Fuck no." Simon was aghast. "We would never pull in one of my old military subordinates on something like this."

Drake chuckled. "He doesn't have to, not when he can pull in one of their wives."

I was confused. "Wives?"

"Two of my teammates are married to superb hackers. These ladies give our computer tech a run for his money. So did you pull in Lydia or Rylie?" Drake asked Simon.

"Rylie," Simon answered. "She was able to narrow it down to one woman. She was siphoning off everything to a Swiss bank account. Turns out her brother was a member of the Blood Ravens, a motorcycle gang out of Chicago. He was the one pulling her strings. She had no priors. We should be able to scoop him up the day after tomorrow."

I was impressed. It would be damn tough to separate a brother from his gang and have him arrested.

"How are you going to do that?" I asked.

"Let's just say it's going to be tricky, and leave it at that," Roan answered.

"Gotcha."

"So, you see why we need to expand," Roan said to me. "We are getting more and more cases, and we need experienced men."

"It's a nice problem to have," Simon said as he tipped back his beer.

"About that time, Nolan O'Roarke—"

"A former SEAL out of Little Creek," Simon interrupted Roan.

"Yeah," Roan agreed. "Nolan came to live here in Jasper Creek with his wife and adopted daughter. Simon talked him into joining us, so we could cover the jobs we wanted to take."

"Then they recruited me," Jase spoke up.

"And me," Kai grinned.

I held up both my hands. "I see where this is going, gentlemen. But I'm not interested. I've got five more years to serve before I hit my twenty. I intend to serve it."

Drake took a step toward me, his expression flinty. "Then what are you doing with Mads?"

"That's between her and me."

"That's where you're wrong," Drake said as he pushed into my personal space. "You've already pulled a runner on her before, and I sure as hell won't stand for you breaking her heart again."

"Again. It's between her and me."

"Beaumont—"

"Leave it." Simon settled his hand on Drake's shoulder. "All of your sisters are grown women. They appreciate the fact that you care about them, but there is a line you can't cross."

Drake glared over his shoulder at his brother-in-law. "I don't want to see Maddie hurt."

"She's a smart woman. She can handle herself," Simon assured Drake.

"Drake, I care too much about her to lead her on."

"That better be true." Drake glowered at me.

"So, you're heading back to California?" Kai asked. "When?"

"I talked to my commander. A little less than two weeks."

"Understood," Kai nodded.

"Just know that if you decide to change your mind, I have made some phone calls, and you come highly recommended. It would be a pleasure to have you join us," Simon said with a firm nod.

"I appreciate that."

"You should," Drake growled.

"You still staying at Maddie's place?" I asked.

"I'm thinking about bunking here tonight," Drake responded, shaking his head in disgust.

"Good thinking."

I headed back into the house, knowing that the odds were I was going to have to hunt down my prey, which was fine by me. It was about time Maddie and I got some things straightened out.

Chapter Ten

I ran.

Of course I ran. What else could I have done after Beau kissed me like he had? After what he had said. Telling me he wanted to wake up to me every morning. He couldn't possibly mean it. But it was exactly what I wanted him to say, and it hurt too much to have him say those words and know they weren't true.

So, fuck yeah, I'd run.

I was curled up on my couch, my knees tucked under my chin and my arms wrapped around my shins, when I saw Beau's headlights pull into my drive. They had to be Beau's headlights. Who else would they be?

I pulled my legs even tighter. I didn't even know if I was going to let him in.

I was a mess.

How dare he talk like we had some kind of damn future!

How dare he!

"Open up, Maddie!" Beau's shout was coupled with his fist pounding on my door.

I started to rock. I couldn't figure out what to do. I couldn't.

"Maddie, we need to talk."

What should I do?

More pounding.

None of the lights were on in the house. Maybe he would think I'd gone to bed.

"I know you're up. Answer the door," he yelled.

I stared at my front door, trying to think of what to do. One thing I did know is that Beau and I couldn't have a future together. I knew that. I'd resigned myself to that years and years ago. Opening myself up to hope would kill me.

More pounding.

This time, he wasn't as loud, but I could still hear him. "If you don't answer the door, I'm going to start yelling about how good you feel in my arms. What a fantastic kisser you are. How you set me on fire. How I can't wait to fuck you."

I don't even remember getting off my sofa. I was just in front of the door and flinging it open, then Beau was standing in front of me with a smug expression on his face.

"Are you going to let me in? Cause if you don't, I'll start yelling..."

I yanked his arm and pulled him inside. He

immediately turned on a light, and I blinked a few times so I could get a better look at him. I could see that he had been running his fingers through his hair, a sure sign that he had been agitated.

"Why are you here?"

"I told you we needed to talk. We need to work out everything. Us. Everything."

"I hate talking," I whined. Then, when I heard my whiny tone, I slapped my hand over my mouth.

Beau grinned. "You do not hate talking. You love to talk. Just not about your emotions."

"You're a man. You're not supposed to like to talk about *your* emotions."

"But I did," he whispered.

Damn, he was right.

He tugged me into the armchair and pulled me into his lap.

I sagged against him, my forehead dropping against his chest. "You're saying all the right things. I hate it when you do that. How do you do that?"

"I do it because I know you. I do it because they come from my heart and my heart belongs to you. Haven't you figured it out, Maddie? We're still it for one another."

I looked up at him. I felt a hitch in my breath. The one I couldn't seem to control. He saw it. Probably felt it, too.

"You're just..." I looked away, hating the crack in my voice. "You're just so good at this. I'm only good at talking out feelings with my kids. Not my own." I looked up into his beautiful, compassionate gaze. "You say things that make it impossible for me to keep my guard up."

"That's because what I'm saying is true." He gathered me closer. His voice lowered. "You remember that time in eighth grade? Your sisters were at your Granny's for the weekend, but you stayed back because of dress rehearsal for the school play. Remember?"

I frowned. Then my eyes opened wide. Everything came flooding back.

"Yeah, you remember. I remember it like it was yesterday. You were so cute and excited. You were playing a girl named Emily in Our Town."

I smiled, but then grimaced, as I remembered what happened the evening he walked me home. "I don't know what I would have done if you hadn't been there," I said softly.

"I hated your mom. She never gave a shit about you or any of your sisters. I could hear the music and the voices from outside the door of your house. I should never have let you open it."

I couldn't look into his eyes. I stared at the front of his shirt.

"I couldn't believe it when that drunk snatched your arm and tried to grab your breast. I lost my mind."

I could see it in my head. Beau had yanked me back out on the porch so fast I'd almost fallen, and he shoved at the big man who was so much bigger. But he was drunk, so he'd staggered back. We'd taken off running for Beau's house.

"You were wonderful," I murmured.

"You were so strong." He put his knuckles underneath my chin and tipped my head back so he could see my face. "Mom made you hot chocolate, and you crashed on the couch. I stayed up all night just to make sure you were okay."

"You did?"

Beau nodded.

Tears burned the backs of my eyes. I hadn't thought about that night in years. But now I remembered everything. Not the fear—though, that was there—but the safety.

Beau.

Always Beau.

"Maddie, I've been showing up for you since we were kids," he said. "I don't plan to stop now."

I shook my head, whispering. "This isn't forever, Beau. You're leaving. We both know it."

"I've got two weeks."

My mouth opened, but no words came.

"Maddie..." His hand cupped my cheek, his thumb brushing lightly. "Say something."

I didn't. I reached up and pulled down his head and kissed him instead.

It wasn't a soft kiss. It was desperate. Demanding. Fierce. Every moment of yearning, every ache and want crashed into me all at once. I pulled at the hem of his shirt, tugging it upward, but it didn't work, not with me sitting on top of him. I stopped trying. Instead, I let myself slip deeper into the kiss, forgetting everything else but the essence of Beau.

I don't know how long it was before I felt him tug at my hair, pulling us apart.

"What?" I asked. My voice sounded dazed.

"Not like this."

"I want you. Now," I protested fiercely.

He pressed his forehead to mine. "We're not doing this like it's a goodbye."

"It might be," I said, my voice breaking. My hands fisted in the front of his shirt. "But I don't care. I've spent years guarding my heart. Letting no one in." As soon as those words came out of my mouth, I realized how true they were. All these years I'd been waiting for Beau.

He closed his eyes, like he was struggling with himself. "No, Maddie. Not like this."

"Yes, exactly like this."

He shook his head.

"Why?"

"Because this isn't a one-night stand for me. It never was." He kissed my forehead, my cheek, the edge of my mouth. Each kiss made me want more. Ache more. "You're not someone I just want. You're someone I've always wanted. And when I finally have you, Maddie, it's not going to be fast or frantic... It's going to be everything."

I said nothing. I couldn't. I just held on to him like I was afraid he might vanish. And maybe he would. But it was too far to turn back now. And for the first time in years, my heart was in charge, and I was going to listen to it.

I don't know how long I sat on his lap, my head on his chest, listening to the steady rhythm of his heartbeat. What I did know is that I hadn't felt this safe and cared for since forever. I allowed all of his words, the ones that had been tipped with gold dust, to weave their way through my soul. I replayed them again and again.

You're someone I've always wanted.

Yes. Gold dust.

Somehow, I needed him to understand that I wanted him more than just on a physical level, or a friend level. But the right words? I love you. They caught in my throat. Were they true?

Maddie, stop it!

I placed a kiss over his heart and heard him sigh. Then I pressed up and looked into his light blue eyes that gleamed almost silver in the moonlight. He grinned down at me.

"Why are you grinning?" I asked.

"Because I think I know what's coming." He smirked.

"You do, do you?"

He kissed the corner of my lips, then pulled back and looked at me and nodded. "Yep, I do."

"I intend to give you a talking to."

"That's what I thought," he grinned wider.

"You're not the only one who's involved at the heart level. You know that, don't you, Beaumont?"

He nodded. "I've just been waiting for you to catch up, Avery."

"Asshole," I muttered.

He chuckled.

I smoothed my hands up his chest and rested them on his wide shoulders. He felt so good beneath my palms. Hard, hot, and masculine.

"So, now that you've figured out you're involved at the heart level, are you going to give me a massage?"

"I repeat...asshole."

This time, he threw back his head and laughed. Then he pulled me in and kissed me.

His kisses were decadent. Better than any dessert or alcohol, better even than a Leon's praline. I gorged myself for long minutes until I finally pushed at his chest.

"Do you know what I've been waiting for?" I asked. I was slightly out of breath. His eyes were sparkling.

"No, what?" He sounded out of breath, too.

"I've been waiting to feel like myself again, you know?" I glanced up at him through my lashes. "Not the social worker. Not the sister. Not the fixer. Not the one who has to hold things together. Just to feel like me."

He sobered immediately, and one of his hands cupped my cheek like I was something precious. "You are you. You've always been just Maddie. At least to me you are. You're just my precious Maddie."

"No," I whispered. "I've been pieces of me. Broken off bits I show to people. I'm whatever they need to see. But now I realize I've always felt whole with you." I sucked in a deep breath. "That scares the hell out of me, Beau."

His thumb grazed my lower lip. "It doesn't scare me. Not even a little bit. Like I said, the real Maddie, the whole Maddie, she's precious. She's a gift."

"Ah God, you better not make me cry, you jerk." I sucked in another deep breath. I kissed him again, slow and deep this time. When we pulled apart, my smile was shaky. Maybe a little watery, but oh so happy.

His smile was more of a smirk.

"You're annoying," I grumbled as I smiled.

"You're still bossy," he said, as his smirk changed into a bright smile.

"If I'm still bossy, I might as well run with it." I pushed out of his arms and stood by the chair. I held out my hand. "Come to bed with me."

He hesitated.

"It's not what you think. At least not yet. I just... want you there. I want to fall asleep next to you. I want to wake up with your stubble scraping my shoulder. I want to know what it's like to have your arms around me in the middle of the night and not feel so alone."

Something flickered in his eyes. Heat, yes, but more than that. Something almost reverent.

"I can do that," he whispered as he took my hand. The jerk made me really tug to get him out of the chair, and I found myself laughing again.

I led him down the hallway. "Come on, Beaumont, let's see if you snore as loudly as I've always suspected you do."

"You've dreamed about me snoring?"

"Vividly."

He followed me to the bedroom, our fingers laced, and for the first time in years, I didn't feel like I was walking toward an ending.

I felt like I was walking towards home.

Chapter Eleven

It was barely dawn, but how in the hell could I sleep with Maddie's ass snuggled tight against my cock? That's not true. I'd slept fine to begin with. Falling asleep with Maddie in my arms had been a dream come true. Of course, then there had been the half-hour of her snoring. That had been funnier than hell. It had been ladylike snoring but snoring nonetheless.

But now it was dawn, and she was sleeping quietly, peacefully in my arms, and torturing me, and I was loving and hating every minute of it.

Maddie stretched, her ass pushing against me even harder.

"Beau?"

"You were expecting someone else?"

She gave a soft chuckle before rolling over.

"I wasn't quite sure if I was dreaming or not."

I circled her around in my arms then pulled her

close so that we were face to face. "You're not dreaming."

"I'm still not convinced."

"Hmmm." I reached down and squeezed her butt and arched into her pelvis.

"Ahhh." Her eyes lit up as she shimmied against my morning wood. "You're beginning to convince me."

I shoved harder and her eyes gleamed. "Only beginning to?" I asked.

She shifted her leg and wrapped it around my waist, bringing her core against my cock. I was suddenly pissed at myself for insisting that we kept our underwear on in bed. At least I'd had the foresight to pull out the one condom I had in my wallet and put it on the nightstand.

"Would you think I was going too fast if I told you I really want to get to know you a whole hell of a lot better than I ever had before?" she asked.

I didn't answer her right away, instead I searched her eyes. I saw both vulnerability and need. The need I liked, the vulnerability, not so much. I threaded my fingers through her hair. Her eyes searched mine, as if I would have the answers to all the world's mysteries.

"No. This morning, I wouldn't think we're going too fast," I promised.

A slow smile spread across her face. "Are you just saying that because your mammoth cock is about ready to tear through your briefs?"

I laughed. She always made me laugh. No wonder I

was in love with her. She made me feel every emotion in the rainbow.

I bit her bottom lip for her sass, then kissed her softly, slowly, letting my lips tell her all the things she wasn't quite ready to hear. She answered with a sweetness that was all Maddie, and it stole my breath. Then she opened her mouth and gave me her heat.

My hand slid under tank, finding her soft skin, then I moved upward, and gently squeezed her perfectly formed breast. She gasped against my mouth, her nails dug into my shoulder. I took my time, lazily exploring her body until I couldn't stand it anymore.

I pulled her into a sitting position and snatched her tank over her head, then feasted my eyes on the glory that was Maddie.

"God, you're gorgeous."

"Right back at you, handsome." Her hands threaded through my chest hair, then tugged lightly, before she lightly licked my nipple. I had her flat on her back in under a second, not caring that I lost a few chest hairs for my trouble.

"I was busy doing something," she grumbled.

"I noticed," I grinned. "Now I want to do something." I licked around her right nipple, teasing her mercilessly, while my other hand plucked the nub of her left breast. For once, she didn't say a word. Instead, she just gasped. Then, as I took her nipple into my mouth and sucked deeply, she moaned.

I let my hands wander, as I continued to torture her breast. Or was I torturing myself?

I slipped my hand under her cotton panties and slid my fingers between the wet folds of her sex. She was as drenched as I was hard.

Perfect.

I circled the entrance of her body, slowly. Taking my time.

Maddie whimpered.

"Beau, quit your teasing," she finally pleaded. I pushed one finger deep inside her tight depths and she moaned. "That's a good start."

"So bossy," I whispered against her breast.

"You like bossy."

I liked Maddie's brand of bossy. I slid a second finger inside her body, and I saw a quick grimace. Fuck. How long had it been for her? I pulled my fingers out, and she whined.

"Who told you to stop?"

I reared up and kissed her smart mouth as I circled her clit with my wet finger. Maddie arched against me and quivered. Our kiss became carnal, all tongues, teeth and passion. I continued to torment her swelling clit, ignoring her whimpers. I listened to her body instead.

She was writhing against my finger, trying to get closer. Her fingers were scraping through my hair. Then I felt her nails digging into my scalp as she arched up so high, only her shoulders and heels touched the bed.

She wrenched her mouth from mine and yelled my name as her body shook, and she reached her peak.

I rolled us over so that she was lying on top of me. I wanted to cuddle her. Shit, when had I become a cuddler? She settled against me, soft and quiet, like she finally felt safe, and didn't that feel damn good?

Okay, I was a cuddler.

"Beau," Maddie whispered. Her voice was low and seductive.

"Yeah?"

"Can you grab that condom?"

I looked at her. "Are you sure?"

She punched me in the ribs.

"Ow, that hurt."

"Suck it up, Marine Boy. Lose the shorts and armor up."

Instead of obeying her, I took my time pulling down her panties and tossing them over my shoulder. "You're gorgeous," I said.

"You've already said that."

I slid my hand from the bottom of her foot, up her calf, to the inside of her thigh and then pushed her leg outward so I could see the flushed, wet pussy I had just made love to. I slid my thumb through the silky liquid, then circled her clit a couple of times. I watched as she shivered again.

"Enough playing a-a-round," she stuttered.

"I love how you respond to me. I love your passion,

Maddie. You were meant to be mine." Her brown eyes turned black.

"Condom." She squeaked out the word.

I got up and stood next to the bed and shucked off my briefs. I grabbed the condom and rolled it on without taking my eyes off Maddie. As soon as I was done, she held out her arms. I got on the bed and settled between her legs, my arms around her head. I opened my mouth to ask—

"If you ask me if I'm sure again, I'll kick you the hell out of my house," she growled.

I laughed. She knew me too well.

I leaned all my weight onto my forearms, then kissed her as if it was the last kiss we were ever going to share. I was determined to take this slow. Maddie had other plans in mind. She reached between us, and smoothed her palm over my sensitive dick, then gently squeezed.

I groaned.

She grinned against my lips.

"Maddie," I admonished.

"I found something new to play with."

"Let go."

"Either you put it to its intended use, or I'll continue to take matters into my own hands."

I dropped my forehead against hers and groaned. "You play dirty."

"You're going to like that about me," she whispered against my lips.

She was probably right.

I pulled both of her arms up and took each hand in mine, then twined our fingers together beside her head. I nudged the head of my cock against the entry of her body. Of course, Maddie didn't let me take my time. Why did I think she would? Nope, she thrust upwards, wrapping her legs around my waist.

"Jesus, Beaumont, you're a monster," she moaned.

I checked out her face and saw a grimace spread across her face, followed by a smile that could outshine the sun. I pushed further into her welcoming heat. Nothing had ever felt better than looking into Maddie Avery's eyes as she welcomed me into her body.

I strung kisses along her jaw as I started a slow rhythm, a dance, locking and unlocking my body with hers. Each time I almost left, her heels would dig into my ass, and I would push back in.

"Faster," she insisted.

"I like taking it slow." I continued my slow strokes, even though it was just about killing me. In all my thirty-three years on this earth, I had never felt anything better than the hot, tight clasp of Maddie's body, clutching mine like she never wanted to let me go.

She wrenched her hands out of my grip and dug her nails deep into the cheeks of my ass.

"Start. Going. Fast."

By the look on her face, I knew if I laughed, her nails would draw blood. What the fuck, my body was clamoring for me to go fast, to go hard, to go deep. Exactly what I wanted, what I needed to do. I drove in deep and twisted my hips. She cried out my name, her heels and nails digging in harder.

"That feels so good," she panted.

She was right about that.

Again, and again and again, I teased us both. Leading us upward to that glorious pinnacle of pleasure. I felt heat streak down my lower spine and my balls tighten up. I was so close. "Come on, baby," I encouraged. I worked my hand between our bodies and found her swollen clit. I thrust in one more time as I pinched her clit. She screamed out my name as I shuddered my release. It was unlike anything I'd ever experienced before. Of course it was. I was with Maddie.

My Maddie.

My dream come true.

Chapter Twelve

Early this morning had lasted a long time, and falling back asleep in Beau's arms had been magic. Now that the sun was really bright, it seemed that my man was intent on using all that he had learned for another round. He licked the sweet spot under my jaw and my toes curled as he blew over it.

"Are you done playing possum?" he asked.

"I don't know. Will you stop if I tell you I'm awake?"

"No," he assured me.

"Then I'm awake."

He trailed kisses along my jaw until he found my mouth and took control. He started slow, but soon it was the kind of kiss that could power a city block. When he broke our kiss, I whimpered my displeasure. But then he was sliding down my body, kissing and licking, touching and praising, driving me out of my mind.

Eventually Beau hit his target as he spread my legs and kissed and licked my needy sex.

"You taste so good, Maddie."

I had nothing to say. All I could do was feel, as his tongue delved deep and began to fuck me. My arms were limp, I had no strength to touch his head. I wanted to. I wanted to grab his hair and insist he fuck me properly.

"I don't want to come this way," I whined.

His tongue swirled around my clit, then he sucked it into his mouth, and I about died.

"No. Cock." I demanded.

He lifted his head. "Do you have condoms?"

I frowned. What was he talking about?

For a second, the shift in tone hit me sideways. One minute I was floating, seconds from falling apart in his mouth, and the next minute he was asking me questions.

Oh yeah. Condoms. I remembered those things.

"Maddie, I only had the one condom. Unless you have any, you're stuck with this."

"Dammit. I thought soldiers were supposed to be all prepared and stuff."

"I'm a Marine, not a soldier."

"Soldier. Marine. Whatever. You should have been prepared."

He shook his head, then slid even deeper into my bed and parted my folds again. There was no teasing this time. He thrust at least two fingers inside of me and sucked my clit into his mouth. His fingers moved like they were searching for something. Then I cried out and trembled.

"W-w-what?"

His tongue swirled around my clitoris as he continued to suck. His fingers continued to brush against that magical spot inside me. I was going insane. I was so close. So desperately close to shattering.

"Beau," I gasped, but I didn't know if it was a plea or a prayer.

He didn't answer, just groaned against me, his mouth working me like I was the only thing that mattered in his world. His curved fingers continued to stroke that place inside me that made everything unravel.

The pressure coiled tighter and tighter and then, and then...

I came apart with a cry, my back bowing off the bed, my hands fisting in his hair, everything in me pulsing with pleasure until I saw stars.

Somehow, he held onto me, but he never stopped. He continued his endeavors, letting me ride out my pleasure. When I finally slumped back against the mattress, dazed and trembling, he looked up at me like I was his own personal miracle.

Which was only right, because he was mine.

Beau opened my car door and held out his hand so I could more easily step on the running board to get out of his truck. For God's sake, it was about the same height as my Jeep, and I constantly jumped in and jumped out of my vehicle all the time. Hell, it wasn't like I was wearing a dress or skirt. I wasn't even wearing sandals. I was in jeans, a crop top, and my boots. But if Beau wanted to be all mannerly, I wasn't going to complain.

It'd been my suggestion to grab coffee at Java Jolt. Not only was I dying for a vanilla chai with whipped cream, but I had my fingers crossed that they'd baked cranberry orange scones this morning. Of course, I'd have to deal with Ruby. She always worked Sunday mornings. The after-church crowd was one of her busiest times. Hopefully, she'd be too busy to give me too much shit.

When Beau shut the truck door, then linked our hands together, I about swooned. Here he was, holding hands with me in front of everybody. Tedious Ted didn't believe in PDAs, so Beau was freaking me out. But as we continued down the sidewalk toward the coffee shop, I enjoyed holding his hand more and more.

He let go to open the door for me, then he guided me in with his hand on my lower back. I did a full body shiver. Mr. Marine better be buying some condoms today.

Just as I suspected, the place was packed and the line was long. Beau and I were one of the few who were in jeans. Everybody else was dressed in their Sunday best. When we got in line, Beau slipped his arm around my waist.

"What's good here?" he asked.

"Everything," the pre-teen girl behind us said. She was probably about twelve years old. Maybe three or four years older than Bella.

"What'd I tell you about listening to other people's conversations?" her mother admonished as she gave Beau and me a strained look.

"I was just filling them in," the girl grumbled.

"Beau, she's right. Everything is great here," I said.

The girl grinned at me, and I winked at her.

We were finally near the front of the line. We just had to wait for a cute high school couple to place their order. They were both staring at the pastry case like it held the answers to their next biology test.

"If they stare much longer, Ruby can file for a restraining order," Beau whispered in my ear.

I covered my mouth to hold back a laugh. Beau was right.

Ruby was at the cash register, and I could see she was getting perturbed and heading toward pissed. I looked behind us. There were at least ten more people.

"Do you like chocolate?" Ruby asked the couple.

"Shea does," the young man answered.

"You're in luck. You're my two-hundredth

customer this morning. You get a free muffin. The one caveat is that it has to be chocolate. Sorry I can't let you choose. With the chocolate muffin, I recommend the honey vanilla cappuccino and the vanilla chai. How does that sound?"

The couple grinned at one another. "I'll have the cappuccino," the young man said.

"I'll have the vanilla chai," the girl named Shea said.

"Great. I'll get the muffin warmed up and your drinks ready for you in a jiffy. Just wait at the end of the counter."

They walked away, holding hands. It made me even more aware of Beau's hand at my waist and how much I liked it.

As we stepped up to the register, Ruby took a step back and crossed her arms over her chest.

"Well, well, well," she drawled. "If it isn't Little Miss I-Don't-Date and the new town heartthrob, all snuggled up together. In public." She gave me a piercing look. "Care to explain, Missy?"

I felt my face go crimson. Beau? He just grinned.

"Morning, Ruby. Damn shame we weren't the two-hundredth customer. Since we weren't, you got anything special you might recommend?" Beau asked smoothly.

"Not anything as special as Miss Maddie's love life."

She was talking loud enough that I was sure everybody in the coffee shop could hear.

"Ruby! Dial it back." It was both a plea and an order.

She winked at me. "If you can't stand the heat, stay out of the..." Her eyes got wide. "Now, where *were* you last night?"

"I swear to God—"

"Relax, babe," Ruby laughed. "You're glowing. It's adorable. I hate it. I'm jealous as hell. Now, I know you're having a chai tea with whipped cream and either a blueberry muffin or an orange and cranberry scone. So, which is it?"

"The scone," I sighed.

"What about you, big guy?"

"I'll take a coffee black. Large. And a bacon-cheddar scone."

"Your order will be up in no time. There's a seat in the back corner. I'll have T.J. bus it. Go grab it before it's gone. T.J. will bring your food."

"Fancy service today." I smiled. "I'm liking it."

Ruby leaned over the counter and motioned with her finger for me to come closer. "I figure he wore you out last night, so you might need to sit down."

Damn, I was blushing again.

Beau was already at the table, and T.J. was wiping it down by the time I got there. Beau had my chair already pushed back for me, and he was kicked back in his. I noticed that he'd taken the one with his back to the wall. Drake had once told me he always liked to see if someone was coming at him. It must be a military thing.

By the time I sat down, T.J. was setting down our warmed pastries.

"Alice is backed up. Your drinks will take longer. Sorry."

"No problem, T.J." I smiled at him. He blushed. T.J. was a high school student who always blushed if an older woman smiled at him. Therefore, working for Ruby, he was perpetually lit up like sunrise.

Beau broke off a piece of his scone and popped it into his mouth.

"Damn, this is really good." He looked surprised.

"Told you."

He broke off another piece and ate that, too. Then he gave me a long look.

"How come social work? You always had a dream of being an interpreter. I remember how you worked so hard studying French in high school, and all those Pell grants and scholarships you applied for so you could attend ETSU.

"Go Buccaneers," I said, raising my hand.

Beau chuckled. "Did you go to many football games?"

"Of course I did. I was a student, wasn't I?"

"So, you got the scholarships?"

I nodded. "And the Pell grants. I didn't have to take out many student loans. I paid those off in two years. I was lucky."

"What happened to the dream of being an interpreter for the United Nations?"

"My roommate was studying to become a social worker. Some classes she was taking really resonated with me. Especially the one called Human Behavior in the Social Environment. When I read her text, I decided to take the class."

"Yeah, but interpreter to social worker is quite the shift," Beau said as T.J. set down our drinks. The kid left before I could even thank him, so I turned my attention back to Beau.

"It was, but I thought about how different my family's life would have been if a good social worker would have become involved. How they could have helped us, and maybe Piper wouldn't have been hurt so badly by our father."

Beau winced and set down his coffee that he was about to drink. "I forgot about that."

"Yeah, Drake tried to shield all of us from that. He told Trenda and Evie what really happened, but I heard. That's why he had to join the Navy. At least our dad had to go to prison."

Beau reached out and covered my hand and squeezed. It wasn't much, but it helped me as I thought about that horrible time in our family's life.

I needed to change the subject. "What about you? Why did you join the Marines? Why didn't you tell me you were just going to up and leave?"

Beau didn't let go of my hand. He looked me dead in the eye.

"You know that I never even considered college. It always seemed so unattainable for me. I barely scraped by enough to graduate. I wasn't the sharpest tool in the shed."

I turned my hand over and tangled my fingers with his, squeezing him hard.

"For God's sake, Beau, you could barely attend high school, not when you were taking care of your mom."

"Yeah, but even when I did, I struggled."

"Again, how were you supposed to succeed when you missed so many classes?"

Beau gave me a sad smile and released my hand and took a sip of his coffee. "You always were my biggest fan. As for the Marines. I talked to the recruiter, and he convinced me that there I could succeed. There I could find a family."

"But I was your family."

He gave me a long look. "Maddie, I wanted something different from you than just friendship. Something you weren't ready for. I needed to leave."

I wanted to cry. Beau must have seen it.

"Hey. I found a home. It was a good thing for me. Really good. I don't regret it one bit... Well, maybe a little."

"What do you regret?"

"Sometimes I wish I could have done more." He

picked up his scone and took a bite. I looked down at mine and realized I hadn't eaten any. I took a bite, then washed it down with my drink. I waited for Beau to say something more. He didn't, so I prodded.

"What do you mean you wished you could have done more?"

"My team was in Chad once. A small village outside of N'Djamena. We weren't even on an actual mission, just recon and recovery. There were kids in the village with bloated bellies and hollow eyes. One little boy came up to me and asked if I had rice. Just rice. Not candy. Not toys. Rice. It broke my heart. It broke all our hearts." His face was suffused with pain. "I work with the best men imaginable. I couldn't forget him. Still can't."

He looked down at his coffee like it held the memory.

"We gave the kid and the others everything we had. Our MREs, protein bars, raisins, granola. Everything. We knew we were going to be picked up in two days. We were going to be good." His eyes met mine, soft and shining. "It felt like we were trying to dig them out of a sandstorm with our bare hands."

He was still the Beau I remembered. I told him so.

"That's why I have to figure this out. This is more than a maybe. This seems solid. Almost like it's meant to be, Maddie. Do you feel it?"

I nodded.

But to me, it felt like everything.
It was going to kill me when he left.

Chapter Thirteen

I walked into Maverick's Bar and Grill just after ten in the morning.

The place was still half-asleep, which was perfect. The kitchen was banging around behind the closed service window, and the scent of grilled onions was starting to mix with stale beer and coffee. Bon Jovi hummed low through the speakers and only three other tables were occupied. Just as I'd hoped, Kai and I would have plenty of privacy.

When I spotted Kai, he was tucked into a back corner booth, and of course, the bastard had taken the seat that faced the bar.

Asshole.

I raised my eyebrow as I slid into the booth.

He smirked. "You're late. First one here picks their seat."

"I'm not late. You're early."

"That makes me the smart brother."

I grunted and flagged the waitress down with a nod. When she arrived, I ordered strong coffee, black.

Kai lifted his glass of water. "You look like shit."

"Didn't get much sleep," I admitted.

"Maddie keep you up all night with one of her TED Talks on social justice."

"Fuck off."

He chuckled. "Kidding. Kind of. Besides the bags under your eyes, you're looking good. I even saw you smile at the waitress... when you were through grunting out your order."

"Yeah?"

"Yeah. Not just good, it's almost like you're... I don't know. Settled?"

The waitress dropped off my coffee. I took a long sip before speaking. "Do you miss it? The teams, I mean."

Kai didn't answer for a moment. "I knew what you meant." He looked off in the distance for a while, before looking back at me. "I miss Clay. You'd like him. I miss the action. The adrenaline."

"What about the brotherhood? The purpose. The fact that you always knew somebody had your back?" I asked.

"I have those things with Onyx."

"Really?"

"Maybe not totally, but that's just because we haven't worked together that long. But Roan and

Simon? They are worthy men. I would go into battle with them in a heartbeat."

"Well, I should hope so. After all, Roan was a Marine Raider." I grinned.

"I had my doubts about Simon being a SEAL and Roan being a Raider, but despite their bad decisions, they've proved themselves."

I laughed.

"Seriously, Kai, how does it feel? Living here, I mean. Doing what you're doing now?"

"I'd been away from my team for a year working on my recovery. I think that makes a difference. Because of that, it was easier for me to transition."

"What about moving from North Carolina to Jasper Creek? Was that tough?"

"Nope, Marlowe's here. That changed everything. She's my home now. Jasper Creek? It's where my feet landed because she's here."

I nodded slowly. "I get that. I liked what I heard about Onyx the other night. It sounded like actual work."

"That was just one case. Trust me, there are others that are like our missions. Action-packed, purpose-driven, only without the red tape and orders from men who've never worn a uniform."

Kai paused and looked me in the eye.

"So, are you thinking about it?"

I sighed and took another sip of my now lukewarm coffee.

"I would be, under different circumstances. I want to get my twenty years. I want the retirement benefits. What's more, I can't leave my team now. We've been through hell together. We all promised one another we would do our twenty together. You know how it is."

Kai nodded. "I do. But sometimes you have to give up that sense of obligation when there is something more important."

Now it was my turn to look off into the distance. "I'm in love with her. I mean, down to my bones, in love with her. I can't stop myself from thinking what it would feel like to build a life with her."

"Then do it."

"I don't know how to walk away."

"You don't have to. Not yet. But think about what it would be like if you walked toward her. Toward a life with her."

I leaned back in the booth, this time staring up at the crooked ceiling fan above us. I leaned back to look at my brother. My twin. "You think I'd like working for Onyx?"

Kai gave me a knowing grin. "Yeah, you'll like it. We don't do boring. We do good work. We protect the people who matter. It's not so different from what we did before, just a different battlefield."

"Yeah," I muttered, but my thoughts were already back with Maddie. With her smile. Her strength. Her kindness. Her bossiness.

"You okay?"

"No, but I'm closer than I have been in years."

"One more thing."

I raised my eyebrow.

"If she's everything you say she is, she'll support you one hundred percent on working through your next five years. But what if she insists on you quitting the teams?"

Now that was something to think about.

That afternoon, Maddie texted me to call her. When I did, she said she was taking a mental health break.

"What does that mean?"

"I left work at four o'clock"

"So, you left work on time is what you're telling me?" I knew I sounded exasperated, but I didn't care.

"Stop it Mr. Judgy Pants. I was calling you to see if you wanted to come over. But if you're going to be like that, I'm changing my mind."

"No, don't change your mind. How soon?"

"Now."

"Done." I grinned.

I was at her place in twenty minutes. With her favorite root beer in hand.

I knocked on her door, but there was no answer. I tried again. When I tried the knob, it was unlocked.

"Goddammit."

I let myself inside and called out for her. No

answer. I put the root beer in the fridge and went to the sliding glass door to her backyard. Yep. That's where she was. Ass up, probably weeding. I took just a moment to admire her ass in cute-as-fuck cut-off jeans. They were so short I got to see a little bit of butt cheek.

She better not wear those out in public.

I slid open the door and before I could call out her name, she turned around.

"Hey, Beau." She smiled at me.

"What in the hell are you doing leaving your door unlocked?" I demanded to know.

She shrugged. "You were coming over and I knew I wouldn't hear you if you knocked or rang the doorbell. It seemed expedient."

"If you didn't answer, I would have texted you."

"Why did you turn the knob?"

"Habit." I answered. "It was a damn foolish thing to do, Maddie."

"Quit sounding like my brother," she huffed.

Well, I sure as hell didn't want to remind her of her brother. "Cute shorts," I smiled.

"They're my gardening shorts."

"Why did you call me?" I asked.

"Free labor." Her eyes were twinkling.

"Why don't you take a break, then we can get back to it," I suggested.

She wiped her brow with her wrist. Then took off her gardening gloves. "Sounds good." She got off her mat and stood up. When she turned around, I noted the Wonder Woman t-shirt that said, *Busy Saving the World*. I thought it was pretty damned appropriate.

"You gonna keep staring, or are you going to open the door?"

"Depends. What do you have to eat inside?"

"What about the words free labor did you not understand?" she teased.

"All of it." I opened the sliding glass door and motioned for her to enter in front of me.

She beelined for the kitchen and opened a cookie jar in the shape of a koala bear. The smell of oatmeal wafted out. My favorite. Unless she'd made them with raisins. Then we had a problem.

She must have been able to read my mind, because she immediately pursed her lips. "Of course I made them with chocolate chips and pecans."

Thank God.

She grabbed two plates. She put three cookies on one and she put eight on the other. The perfect amount. She pulled down two glasses and set them on the counter, then went to the fridge. She looked over her shoulder at me.

"Thanks for the root beer."

"You're welcome."

"But milk to go with the cookies, right?"

"Damn straight," I replied.

She took out the milk and proceeded to pour two full glasses and put them in front of our plates. She sat beside me at her kitchen island. I knew I should say something, but the lure of fresh-baked cookies won. After three, I could finally get my head around talking.

"Thanks for inviting me over."

"Well, I didn't bake your favorite cookies for them to go stale."

I shook my head at her sass. "I wanted to talk to you about something," I said.

"Shoot."

I rubbed the back of my neck. Opened my mouth. Then stopped. Shit, what was I thinking? Was I really going to ask if she would be okay, pulling up stakes? When we hadn't even established we were in a relationship?

God, I was stupid.

I turned around in my seat and spun her bar chair around. This way I could get a good look at her whole face, not just her profile.

Maddie frowned. "What's going on?"

I looked straight into her eyes. "I'm trying to think of the right words."

"Just say what's in your heart."

"It might seem like it's been only nine days, but really it's been all my life. You know? How does it feel to you?"

She bit her lower lip, then lowered her head.

"Baby?"

She looked up. "Same," she said softly.

It felt like a boulder was lifted off my shoulders. "I'm crazy about you, Maddie. I want to spend the rest of the time I have here in Jasper Creek with you. I want to take the time to see where this will go."

Suddenly, she looked like she was going to cry. "But you're only going to be here for eleven more days."

"That's true. But let's savor this time together and then figure out where we go when the eleven days are over. Okay?"

"Are you saying there might be a future for us? A real lasting future?"

"I'm not sure, but what I do know is, if we don't grab hold of this time together, we'll never know, now will we?"

Her eyes were bright with tears. "No, we won't."

"Trust me?" I asked.

Outside, a wind chime danced in the breeze. Inside, there was nothing but the smell of cookies, the faint tick of the clock, and the quiet hum of something real beginning to settle between us.

She reached out and placed her hand over my heart. "I trust you with every beat of my heart."

Chapter Fourteen

I released my seatbelt, reached behind me for my satchel, and grabbed my travel cup of coffee before opening the passenger door.

"Thanks for the ride." I smiled at Beau.

"Aren't you forgetting something?"

"What?" I asked.

"My kiss for driving you to work."

I looked around the parking lot. People were still getting out of their cars and walking to the building.

"I can't kiss you. People will see."

He grinned. "I never knew you were a fraidy cat."

"Take that back," I barked.

"Meow."

I put my coffee back in the holder. I grabbed Beau's cheeks in my hands and pulled his face down for a quick kiss. His hands immediately cradled my head and tilted it. His lips parted mine, and electricity sparked.

Oh God, I was doomed.

His tongue thrust into my mouth, and soon I was sucking it, desperate for him. Desperate to take off his shirt and touch his shoulders. His back. His chest.

I let go of his cheeks. My hands dipped under his t-shirt collar and kneaded his neck, glorying in the feel of his hot, supple skin over his taut muscles. Our kiss turned passionate.

Bam-bam-bam.

We broke apart.

I looked over Beau's shoulder and saw my co-worker Irene grinning like a fool through the driver's side window.

"I-I-I've got to go."

I tried to open the truck door and failed. I tried again but couldn't do it.

"Maddie, calm down. Let me open your door and help you down from the truck. You're wearing heels, and at this rate you'll fall down and break your neck."

"No, I can do it," I protested.

He gave me the look. The Mr. Marine Alpha look, so I just nodded. He opened his door, then closed it. I could hear Irene introducing herself.

Kill me now.

Beau continued to stand there and listen to Irene as she told him how long we'd worked together and how everybody loved me.

Seriously, kill me now.

Finally, she walked away.

Yay!

Beau walked around to my side of the truck, opened the door, and offered me his hand. I took it and landed on my feet just fine. Then he reached in and got my satchel and coffee.

"Do I deserve a kiss for getting your coffee and briefcase?" he asked with a grin.

"You deserve a knee to the nuts, is what you deserve," I growled.

"You wouldn't do that. I wouldn't be able to perform tonight."

He had a point.

I started to walk away in a huff.

"What time should I pick you up?"

"Probably about seven. I'll call you," I called over my shoulder.

"Gotcha."

I marched into the building. By the time I got to my cubicle, I found Irene sitting in my chair. I wasn't surprised.

"It seems like you've been keeping secrets." She smirked.

"Have not. Beau and I are kind of recent."

"How recent?"

"Almost a week and a half."

"And he's driving you to work and making out with you in the parking lot? Hell, you never did that with Tedious Ted, and you were engaged to him for almost three years. What gives?"

I looked at her with wide eyes. "Are you serious? Did you not *see* him?"

"Fine, he's hot as hell. Hotter than hell. Model worthy. But I know you, Maddie. You're kind of a prude. I don't care if he's an underwear model. You would not be devouring some guy in your work parking lot unless you were in deep. Explain to me how you're in deep after a little over a week?"

Fuck. Yet another perceptive woman in my life.

"He's the guy who was my best friend from grade school to high school."

"The guy who joined the military when he was eighteen, and you never heard from again?"

"The very same."

"But that guy is an a-hole, with a capital 'A'."

"No, he's not. He's still Beau. He's still my best friend."

"Ah, darn it. You're in love with him."

I dropped my head. "Maybe," I mumbled.

"Don't look so sad. He's back, and he looks as into you as you are into him."

"Yeah, but he's still in the Marines. He has to go back in ten days."

"Ah. That sucks."

I gave a big sigh. "Tell me about it. Now get out of my chair."

Irene got up. "So, what are you going to do?"

"I'm taking it one day at a time."

She squeezed my shoulder. "If you need someone to talk to, you call me. Okay?"

I nodded, then sat down. I really wished we hadn't talked. I had been doing really well before our conversation. Actually, I'd been flying high after making love to Beau this morning. Now I was depressed.

Get over it, Avery!

I squeezed my eyes shut for a few seconds and forced myself to smile. Then I opened my eyes, took my files from my satchel, and started to get to work.

It was just after lunch when one of the assistant district attorneys called me.

"Maddie?"

"Yeah, it's me."

"It's Oliver, from the D.A.'s office."

I frowned. "I take it this is not good news."

"Nope, it isn't. Bruce Forrester made bail."

I frowned again, trying to place who Bruce Forrester was. Then I remembered. "He's the asshole who came at me with a frying pan, right? He was beating on his girlfriend and her six-year-old son."

"One and the same," Oliver confirmed.

"What was the judge thinking, offering him bail?"

"Bruce said all the beatings on the boy were from his mom. As for threatening you with a frying pan, he said it was in self-defense because you had a baseball bat."

"Softball bat," I corrected.

"Whatever. That was his story, so the judge gave him a fifteen-thousand-dollar bail, and some bail bondsman took it when he put up fifteen hundred."

"Dammit!"

Tomorrow was my day to do home inspections. I had called into the Pattersons and had heard nothing but good things about how well Eli was doing, but I intended to see for myself tomorrow. There were other situations that didn't sound nearly as good, that I would have to check out, so I saved that for last. End the day on a high note.

"Do you know how Colleen is doing?" I asked the A.D.A.

"Colleen?"

"She's the girlfriend and Eli's mom. I'm pretty sure she went into rehab...again."

"Oh yeah. I had an associate go to get her statement. You're right, she is in rehab, and can barely string two sentences together. When she did manage to, she insisted that Bruce never laid a hand on her, or her son. The good news is, she's in no shape for Bruce's public defender to put her up on the stand."

"You're kidding me," I squawked.

"Nope. And what's worse, our perp is saying that he never touched the kid. He's saying that it was the mom."

"Dammit!"

"Yeah, that's what I say."

"Any priors?"

"Only for beating up girlfriends, nothing for child abuse," the A.D.A. explained.

"Did those other women have kids?"

"None that were in the reports."

Shit, nothing was going my way.

"Thanks, Oliver. Do you have a court date for this creep?"

"Next month, on the twenty-fourth. You'll get an official summons."

"Okay. Again, thanks for the heads-up. In the meantime, I'll see if I can get something from Eli."

"That would be much appreciated. Gotta go."

"Bye." I hung up the phone.

This meant that visiting Eli tomorrow would not be as fun as I'd hoped. *Dammit.*

I called Evie. It would be nice to hear an uplifting voice. Who would also say some nasty things about assholes.

The phone only rang once when I dialed her number.

"I hope you're going to tell me all about Beau," she answered.

"Nope. Right now, I want to bitch about my job," I whispered. I didn't want Richard, the nosy bastard in the cubicle next to me, to hear my conversation.

"Go for it," Evie responded.

"An abuser, who I'm positive was beating up a six-year-old boy, just got out on bail. He's blaming it on his girlfriend, who is the mom. She's a junkie and refuses to lay blame on the boyfriend. He did try to come at me with a frying pan, so I'll have to testify. Hopefully, I can get him put away, but it isn't likely since he didn't hurt me."

"Maddie, I'm really sorry. Will he go after the kid?"

"I don't think so. Unless I can get the little boy to talk, he's going to go scott-free is my take, and his lawyer probably told him."

"Do you think you can get the kid to talk?"

"It's a crap shoot."

"I'm sorry, Mads. I always hate it when you have to deal with stuff like this. I know you're making a difference, but I just hate it when it gets you down. Truly, I don't know how you manage to do your job. I couldn't. The first week, I'd be up on assault charges."

I giggled. It was true. Evie would have taken the bat to Bruce before Beau had had a chance to get into the house.

"Have I told you lately how much I love you?" I asked my sister.

"Not since our last telephone conversation," she said with a smile in her voice.

"Well, I do."

"I love you, too. Do you love your Raider?"

I sat up straight in my chair. What a question.

"Come on, answer the question. This is Beau we're talking about. It's not a hard question."

I still didn't say anything.

"Maddie, you there?"

"Oh my God, Evie. I do. I really do love him. I'm head over fucking heels in love with him. He means everything to me."

"Is he going to leave the teams?"

"Huh?"

"He's special operations. A Marine Raider. Is he going to skip his retirement and move to Jasper Creek?"

"I don't know," I wailed.

Richard peeked over my cube, and I glared at him. He sat back down.

"It isn't the end of the world if he doesn't. You can do like I did. Move to California and wait til he retires. That's what I've done with Aiden."

"Evie, he hasn't even said he loves me." I choked out the words.

"He loves you," she assured me.

"How do you know? Are you reading tea leaves these days?"

"Don't have to. I've talked to Trenda and Drake. They both said Beau's crazy about you."

"They did?" I winced at the hope in my voice.

"Yep."

My shoulders slumped. "They don't know him all that well."

"Well, I know somebody who does," Evie responded.

"Who?

"You. You know him that well, Mads. Sounds to me like it's time for you to have a heart-to-heart talk with him."

I sighed. She was right.

"I heard that sigh. You're going to have to pull up a pair of big girl panties. Probably cotton granny panties. Knowing you, you have a pair. Go dig 'em out and put 'em on. Then talk to the man."

"Fine," I muttered.

"Then I want a full transcript of the conversation. Got it?"

"Do you want me to record it?" I asked sarcastically.

"That would be great!" She sounded far too excited.

"Dream on, big sister. Dream on."

"I've got to go. Holden just climbed up on the counter. He's reaching for the top shelf where I keep the doggy treats. Last time, he fed Rufus all of them, and I had an ungodly mess to clean up."

"Bye, Evie. Love you."

"Love you too. Now tell Beau that."

"Yes, ma'am."

I didn't know if I'd get the words right, but I had to try. Because loving Beau felt too important to keep quiet about.

Chapter Fifteen

"What are you doing here? You want to hop up your rental?" Roan asked as he sauntered out of the first garage bay, wiping his hand on a blue cloth.

I chuckled and went over to him and shook his hand. "I don't think souping up the Camry is worth the money. Do you believe this piece of shit the rental place gave me?"

"You're right about that. What happened?"

I was still disgusted that the rental place couldn't give me a better replacement for the truck than a Camry. They better get the truck fixed damned quick!

"The alternator conked out. They towed it away, after I specifically ordered an F-250 for this trip. Then they said this was all they had, unless I wanted to wait for something from Nashville."

"Why didn't you just have me tow it and fix it?"

"Because I'm an idiot," I admitted.

Roan laughed. "You look good riding around in a white Camry."

"Fuck you. So, why'd you tell me to meet you here? Why are you working as a mechanic in your father's garage? I thought you worked for Onyx."

"It's not my father's garage anymore. He retired. Lisa runs it."

"Who's Lisa?"

"She's my fiancée. I'll come pitch in when things get overloaded."

"And she's your boss?" I asked.

"It's a long story. You want to go get a beer? I can tell you about it."

"Does your boss let you leave early?"

"Fuck you," Roan said without heat. "Let me just tell her I'm heading out. As a matter of fact, why don't you come and meet her?"

I followed Roan into the office and found a beautiful blonde in jeans and a tank top on the phone ripping someone a new one.

Roan got a shit-eating grin on his face. "One of our vendors. He's been late with the last two orders, and he keeps upping his price. Lisa is done. And I mean done. I wouldn't want to be in his shoes."

"I'll make sure every auto body and repair shop in Sevier, Cocke, Jefferson, Knox and Blount County know about your double-dealing incompetence by the end of the day if you don't get me my parts at the rate you originally quoted."

She looked up and blew Roan a kiss.

"Hell no, I'm not going to call them. I said by the end of the day. I have every single one of them on an e-mail list. We trade information on vendors so we know who to and who not to work with. Now, do you want to be on the naughty or nice list, Al?"

She rolled her eyes. "I don't give a shit where you have to get the parts. I want them in my hands tonight. We'll be closed, but you can drop them off at Roan's place. I'll give you the address. That means before midnight. Got it?"

She listened, then rolled her eyes again. "Midnight, Al. Otherwise, you're going to move up to the shit list. You don't want that, because you'll be blackballed. You got that?"

I could see he was still talking.

"Again, I don't care. You could have returned my two calls last week. You're damn lucky I'm giving you this chance. Gotta go."

I could still hear the man talking as she hung up.

"My woman, the ball-buster."

"I can't believe that asshole. Can you?"

"Sure, I can. I bet you a coke that he never pulled that shit with Dad, but he thought because you were a woman, he could get away with it."

"I should have made him sell it to us at below the rate he quoted," she muttered. Then she got up and smiled. "Who's this?" she asked, nodding at me.

"This is Beau, the man I told you about."

She walked around the counter and gave me a big hug. "Roan's had nothing but good things to say about you."

"Thanks. I think. You know, sometimes he lies."

She threw back her head and let out a husky laugh. "Trust me, I know. But only for the greater good."

"I have the Vette taken care of, so I'm going to take off. If anything else comes up, it can wait until tomorrow," Roan said.

"Sounds good."

"What time do you think you'll be home? I'm making stir-fry."

"Well, if you're cooking, I'll be home by six." She reached up and gave Roan a kiss.

It was four o'clock now. It would be nice to be spending time with Maddie, but she'd already texted and told me that tonight was going to be a late one and so I'd need to pick her up then.

"Come on, Beau, you're driving me home," Roan said.

I nodded. "It was nice to meet you, Lisa." I smiled at her.

"You too, Beau. You'll be there for dinner, won't you?"

"I've got something planned for Maddie."

"Understood." Roan nodded.

"It was nice meeting you, Lisa." I waved as I followed Roan out the door.

By the time we made it to his house, he'd made at

least eight disparaging remarks about the Camry. He was definitely a car snob. It was a really hot day, so we settled down with our beers in the living room with the air conditioning.

"You good with the information I got you on that sleazebag, Bruce Forrester?" Roan asked me.

"I wouldn't say, good. But I thank you for asking around. It sounds like he's scared of messing up a good thing."

"If I felt he needed a little more persuasion to stay away from Maddie, I would have given it to him, but his lawyer has assured him he's going to get away with this, so he's going to behave like a choir boy until his court date."

"As long as he doesn't come after Maddie or Eli, I'm good."

Roan nodded, then smiled. "So, I never saw you when you first came to town. How was it, finding your long-lost twin?"

I smiled. Now this topic of conversation was a welcome one. "Surreal. Good. Fantastic. Took me a bit of time to get my head around it, though. But now, we're really aligned. Both special forces. I mean, our growing-up years were different, since he had to grow up with our sadistic bastard of a father, but still, down at the core, we're really similar."

I liked Roan. Not only were we both Marine Raiders, but he and I had grown up together in Jasper Creek. He was a grade ahead of me, but we played on the same football team. He knew my story. He got me. He listened.

"I can't say the same about me and my brothers. The twin thing must be a whole different animal."

"I imagine it is," I told him.

We were quiet for a bit as we drank our beers.

"How does it feel being out of the teams?" I asked Roan.

"I told you at Simon's party. But what really makes it okay is Lisa. She's my touchstone. I don't know what I would do without her. We're so solid we're trying for a kid."

I chuckled. "Before the wedding?"

Roan laughed. "Dad broke his leg when he was deep sea fishing off the coast of Florida. He doesn't want to be wearing the cast for the wedding pictures, so we agreed to put off the wedding for another six weeks. It's going to be here in Jasper Creek."

"What about Lisa's family?"

"She's an only child. She has her dad and grandpa who raised her, and she has aunts and uncles and cousins. So, there will be plenty of people on her side of the aisle. I'm pretty sure that all the guys in the shop are going to sit on her side of the aisle and not mine."

I grinned. I could totally see that.

"So, kids, huh?"

"Yep. At least three."

"Sounds nice."

"What about you and Maddie?"

I rubbed the back of my neck. "I don't want to leave the teams. I want to get my twenty in." I blurted out.

"So? What's the problem?"

"Maddie lives and works here. Here's where her family is."

"Have you talked to her about moving to SoCal?"

"I don't think we're at that point yet," I admitted.

"The way I hear it, you definitely are."

I frowned. "How would you hear anything?"

"I work with the man who's married to Maddie's big sister. Sisters talk."

I took another sip of my beer. I'd forgotten how close the Avery sisters were. I was kind of an idiot. Of course, Roan would be in the know.

I leaned over and put my elbows on my knees, twirling my bottle of beer between my hands. "I'm in love with her."

"I'm not surprised. Simon's told me about her. A social worker. That takes grit."

I chuckled. "I gotta tell you, seeing her holding that softball bat while a guy almost twice her size was coming at her with a cast-iron skillet, was something to behold. She didn't flinch."

Roan laughed softly. "Lisa would have been pissed if I had taken away her chance to use the bat. I'd hear about it for a year."

"Maddie's not that bloodthirsty. She was defending someone. She's not normally the violent type. I think it goes along with her social worker nature."

"She sure doesn't take after her sister Evie."

We both started laughing at that thought.

"So, you say you're in love with Maddie and you want to get five more years in. What's your problem? Talk to the woman."

"I told her last weekend that we needed to take each day as it came. I was working up to telling her I loved her."

Roan looked at me from across the room like I was the world's biggest idiot. Hell, maybe I was. "What the fuck is wrong with you?"

I rubbed the back of my neck and set down my beer. It'd gotten warm. "I'm worried that I might be moving too fast."

"You're acting like a pussy. That's what's wrong. But the boy I knew and the man I know isn't a pussy. So, what else is it?"

I pushed up off the couch and started pacing. Roan was right. Something was stopping me from talking to Maddie, but what the hell was it? I'd loved her when I left Jasper Creek. I'd done my best to put her out of my mind when I was in the Marines, but that didn't always work. Then all that had to happen was seeing her at Maverick's and I was done.

Bam. My heart broke open.

I could think of nothing better than loving Maddie

Avery. Even so, there was something stopping me from making a commitment.

I stopped pacing.

I just stood there in the middle of Roan's living room.

"Do you have it?" Roan asked.

"Yeah," I said slowly. "I think I'm scared to really commit... not because I don't want Maddie, but because I know what it's like to lose people you love. My mom was ripped away, Brady—I mean Kai—too. I think deep down I figured if I didn't hold on too tight, it wouldn't hurt as bad if it all went to hell."

Roan nodded once, his eyes serious. "That's not being a pussy, Beau. That's being human."

Chapter Sixteen

I jolted awake, and then noticed the smell of oregano, basil, garlic, cheese, and fresh bread.

What the hell?

I stretched then threw back the covers.

I was still wearing my bra and panties that I'd worn to work. Beau had taken one look at me when he'd picked me up and insisted, I take a nap when we got home. Hell, I was so tired I hadn't even give him too much shit about the teeny, tiny little car he was now driving. I threw on one of the few truly frivolous purchases I'd ever made, a yellow-and-red silk kimono-style robe, and wandered into the living room. He was waiting for me. The man had the hearing of a bat.

Ahhh, the smell of cheese and bread. I was in carbohydrate heaven.

"What did you make?"

"Five-cheese vegetable ziti, with cheesy garlic bread."

The man knew exactly how I liked my vegetables. Smothered in cheese.

"Do I get a kiss for all my efforts?"

"Damn right you do."

He sauntered over to me with a gleam in his eye. He grabbed my left hand and walked me over to the counter that separated the dining room from the kitchen, then lifted me up on top of it. We were now eye to eye.

"Oh, so this is going to be a serious kiss."

He looked over my shoulder, then back at me. "There is still nine minutes until the timer rings. Let's see what I can accomplish, shall we?"

"On the counter?" I squeaked.

"The curtains are closed." This time I peeked over *his* shoulder and saw that he was right.

"You planned this. How'd you know I was going to wake up when I did?"

"I might have slammed the front door shut," he smirked.

"Oh, so there was a reason I woke up."

"I told you. Part of my job is planning. And Baby, I excel at my job."

I thrust my fingers into his hair and moved my face closer to his. "That's for me to judge."

His eyes twinkled. "Feel free." He slanted his head and softly met his lips to mine. With slow tantalizing swipes, he tempted me to follow him, and I did, tasting beer, bread and Beau. Soon it was a conflagration of heat and fire. I couldn't get enough of this man.

I was so caught up in the kiss, in the wild burn, that it wasn't until I was shivering that I noticed he'd untied my robe.

I wrenched away from his mouth for just a moment to ask. "Seriously? The counter?"

He didn't bother to answer. He pulled my head back and soon I was dizzy with lust as our kiss deepened even more. How it was possible, I didn't know. Teeth, tongues, lips and bites. My breasts were heaving and my panties were soaked.

When I felt his calloused hands cupping my breasts, I jolted. So good. It was just so good. Beau pulled my hands out of his hair, and slowly divested me from my bra and pulled down my robe, but as he laid me down on the granite countertop, I realized I was resting on soft wool. My body shook for just a second as I choked back a sob. The sneak had placed the wool throw from the couch somewhere handy so I wouldn't be lying on hard granite. I had never felt so cherished in all my life, as I did by that one little act of kindness by the man I loved.

"Maddie, are you okay?" Of course, Beau picked up on my feelings. We were back to how we always had been.

"I'm fine, baby," I choked out my answer. He

paused and gave me an intent look. I must have passed muster, because he smiled.

"You definitely *are* fine," he agreed with a wicked grin. Beau could do wicked so well.

"This has to go both ways. I want you to take off your shirt, too," I demanded.

He looked up, and I knew he was looking at the timer on the stove. "No can do, Chickie. We now only have seven minutes left on the clock." With that, he lifted me up and pulled the robe out from under me.

"Like the panties. You look good in yellow."

I waited.

He tugged them downwards. Then he chuckled. "Especially in damp yellow panties."

Yep, I knew he was going to go there.

I leaned up on my elbows. "No oral sex, you bastard. You've bought two boxes of condoms, so there is no excuse for you doing something for me when I can't return the favor."

His face got serious.

Oh shit.

A lecture.

"We don't have time for one of your lectures."

"Apparently we have to make time, sweet cheeks."

"And don't call me sweet cheeks!"

"Our sex life is not about quid pro quo. It's about enjoyment. Fun. Connection. Communication." Then he leaned in close, so that he was practically on top of me, his nose almost pressed against mine. "And in my case, it's about love. It is definitely not about keeping score. Am I making myself clear?"

His blue eyes had turned the color of molten silver. My heart was the consistency of mush. "I love you, too, Beau."

"And we're not keeping score? You're not just saying that because I said it?" he prompted.

I grabbed him by his ear and twisted.

"Ow!"

"I would never fuck around with saying the love word. Of course I love you, you big oaf. I adore you. You broke my heart fifteen years ago, and I know loving you now comes with risk, but I've never been surer of anything. Loving you right now is more important than thinking about the future. I want to be in the now with you. You are my soulmate."

"Maddie, I will not break your heart. I promise."

"You can't make that promise." Thank God I wasn't crying. In fact, I was filled with joy. Beau loved me. "Beau, however it comes down we have today and tomorrow. I feel blessed."

"But Maddie—"

"How much time is on the clock?"

"But—"

"How much time?" I asked louder.

"Four minutes."

"Use those minutes wisely. I'm getting cold here under the A.C."

Beau looked down at me and gifted me with the

most beautiful smile I'd ever seen. He could make a rainbow burst from the sky with that smile.

"Give me your hand."

I frowned. "What?"

"Give me your hand."

I rolled and put my weight on my left side, with my legs on either side of Beau, and reached out with my right hand. He gripped my hand, then sucked my fore and middle fingers into his mouth, swirling his tongue around them.

"What are you doing?" I gasped.

He pulled them out with a popping sound. Then he placed them at the top of my mound, right over my clitoris. I trembled.

"I want you to caress yourself, Maddie, while I thrust inside you. Can you do that, Maddie? I want to watch you play with your wet and swollen clit while I stroke in and out of your tight, hot heat. Can you do that for me?"

He pulled a condom out of his pocket and soon smoothed it over his erection and placed it against the mouth of my vagina. And didn't do one thing more. Just stopped right there, the bastard.

"Beau?" His eyes were back to light blue, and his smile was sinful.

"You're not doing what I asked. There's three minutes on the clock, gorgeous. I'm not doing anything until you start the show."

I was confused until his hand touched mine and

started moving my fingers over my sensitized clit and I shuddered.

"Again, baby." He continued to guide my fingers and soon I wasn't paying attention to anything else but the spiraling pleasure in my body. His warm hand over mine magnified the pleasure, and I trembled.

"Ahhhh!" The feel of Beau entering me was sublime. I opened my eyes to see an expression that had to mirror mine. As he powered inward, his hand never left my hand, but now he wasn't guiding me, he was following me, as I applied just the right tempo, the right pressure, the right everything to take me where I needed to go. But I lost focus as he pushed so deep inside me, I felt him everywhere. This time, Beau was exactly where I needed him to be.

I couldn't breathe and I didn't care. All I cared about was this surreal connection with the man of my dreams.

"Faster, Maddie. Come on, Baby, get there."

"You too, Beau," I gasped.

His hand pressed down on mine, and I lifted my hips to take his cock deeper, wrapping my legs around his hips.

"God yes. You're perfect. So tight. Squeeze me again."

I watched as sweat beaded on his brow as he drove harder and faster, making me moan. I couldn't keep up the rhythm as I circled my clit. I couldn't do anything but feel. Feel myself spinning out of control.

"Bea—"

I couldn't talk. "Ahhh," I screamed and shoved myself against his pelvis as hard as I could. An explosion of color and pleasure burst through me as I reached a state of bliss I'd never known before. I wanted to savor this moment in time forever, when Beau burst out laughing.

"What? Stop laughing! You are totally ruining the mood, you jerk." Then I heard the buzzer.

Beau dropped his head, snuggling his cheek against my neck, still laughing. Finally, he said, "We beat the clock."

Chapter Seventeen

Maddie looked beautiful sitting at the table. She was flushed and smiling. I was still feeling pretty happy with myself that I'd surprised her with the whole counter idea, but the kitchen timer had been a happy accident. It worked so well that I was thinking that maybe I should set my phone alarm in the bedroom sometime.

It was definitely something to think about.

She took one bite of the ziti and moaned.

"Shit, Maddie, don't do that. You'll get me all worked up again."

She swallowed her bite, took a sip of water, and winked. "That's a pretty impressive recovery time for a man over thirty. I'm thinking I lucked out."

I did my best not to smirk.

"I take it you like the ziti."

"Let's just say that if you ever want to get me into

bed again, just start with this." She picked up a piece of cheesy garlic bread, bit into it and started chewing. This time, she didn't moan, she hummed.

"Seriously, Maddie, you need to cut it out."

"It's the cheese and carbs. But if you really want to see me get worked up, let me ogle you with your shirt off while I'm eating chunky monkey ice cream. You might end up dead from overuse."

I shut up and started eating my food, trying to keep myself under control. It was tough. After hearing her say she loved me, I wanted nothing more than to take her into the bedroom and hold her and make love to her for the rest of the night. All of her moaning, humming and groaning was not helping.

"Would you have your shirt off, too?" I asked.

Her eyes twinkled. "If that's what you wanted. I might even drip some ice cream on my breasts and you'd be forced to lick it off me."

"Stop already!" I kept my seat.

Barely.

"You started it," she teased.

"Bullshit. Now be quiet and eat."

She giggled, then proceeded to eat a few bites in silence.

"Tell me how your day was," I said when my dick wasn't as hard as a post.

Maddie picked up her napkin and wiped nothing off her mouth, then sighed. "Less than stellar."

I frowned. "Why, honey?"

"Oh, there was the normal crap, don't get me wrong. Two more cases landed on my desk, which means I'm now seven over caseload cap."

"What does that mean?"

"I'm supposed to have only twenty cases, and our office is usually pretty good at allotting only that many, but during the summer months, with all the tourism in Pigeon Forge, we have more transient workers. The amount of child neglect reports increase some, so we have to go out on more calls."

"So, working so late isn't normal? It's just during the tourist season?"

She nodded.

"I've got to say, that makes me feel better."

"Yeah, I was able to close three cases today, which was really good." She picked up her bread, then put it down again.

"Hey. That has warm cheese on it. Tell me what's really wrong?"

"Eli."

My gut clenched when I thought about the little boy who had huddled under the steps. "What about him?"

"That son-of-a-bitch got bail because his public defender was able to make his case look good."

"He's out on bail?" I shouted.

"Yeah." Maddie sounded dejected as she looked down at her half-eaten meal.

"Jesus, Maddie. I need to be driving you around

the clock until he's back in jail. He could come after you."

"Didn't you hear me? The D.A. told me the case is looking pretty good that he'll get off. Colleen is in no condition to testify. According to the hospital she's in, she can barely string two sentences together, which is sad and great. Great, because Eli might just be adopted, instead of fostered, sad for her."

"But why can't he be locked up? I don't get it. He came after you with a frying pan."

She picked up her plate and headed to the kitchen. I followed her.

She got out a plastic container and put her uneaten ziti into it, then put it in the fridge and turned to me.

"He didn't touch me, Beau, so the D.A. doesn't feel he has a case to make against him since it was his house."

"That's utter bullshit. So, it would have been better if you let him bash your brains in?"

Her shoulders slumped. "Stop it, Beau. You know what I mean."

"What about Eli testifying?"

She sucked in a deep breath. "I talked to Fran Patterson today. She's been trying to see if she could get him to talk about Bruce, but he clams up, and she doesn't want to push it. Fran's been having him go to a psychologist."

I was trembling with rage, just thinking about it.

"I left a message with Oliver. He called before he

left for vacation. I've been sitting with it since Monday. I promised to update him on my conversations with Eli."

"I'm confused. Is Oliver the D.A.?"

Maddie nodded.

"How could he be on vacation if he called to tell you Bruce was out on bail?"

"He told me that three days ago."

"Fuck! Maddie, why didn't you tell me three days ago?" I yelled.

She jolted. I ran my fingers through my hair, staring at her.

She rolled forward on her feet and glared at me. "Don't you fucking *dare* yell at me, Beaumont! This is not my first rodeo, and it won't be my last. Do you know how many fathers, husbands, assholes, and perverts I've run across in my job? Do you? I sure don't need some over-protective alpha demanding that I run everything by him." She shoved her hand into my chest. Hard.

"Maddie—"

"I'm not done. When you followed me, it was not the first time I've been threatened by some meathead. I'm careful about what I do. I've taken extra training in de-escalation techniques, domestic violence intervention, and mental health crisis response. This. Is. My. Job."

"Then why in the hell are you marching around in the middle of the night to your car all alone?"

"I have my pepper spray."

I was going to lose my mind. "You should have a gun."

"That is not who I am. You joined the military, my brother did, my brother-in-law did. I didn't. I'm a social worker. I believe in a different way."

"A taser then. For God's sake, Maddie. Let me get you a taser."

"Beau—"

"I'm dying here, Maddie. You're killing me," I whispered. "Please."

"I probably couldn't hit anybody to save my life."

I stepped up to her and curled my hands around her head, bringing it to my chest. "I'll teach you, baby. Just please do this for me."

"Okay," was her muffled reply.

"Thank you," I whispered into her hair. "I love you. Love you so much."

Chunky Monkey. I'd never tried it before, but Ben & Jerry sure knew how to blend some damn fine ice cream. And my Maddie sure knew how to de-escalate a situation. I grinned in the darkness as I looked down at her, sleeping in my arms.

Carefully, I untangled myself from our embrace so I could go out to the living room, taking my cell phone with me.

"Beau?" she asked before I got to the bedroom door.

"Just getting some water."

"'kay." I watched as she rolled over, then went out the door and shut it.

It was still fairly early. Only nine-thirty. Chunky Monkey had worn Maddie out. I would have been out cold, too, if that nasty piece of work hadn't been lurking in the back of my mind. It was funny that even though I had just visited Roan, and he was part owner of Onyx security, my first inclination was to call my brother.

"Yeah, Beau, what's up?" Kai answered.

"I hope I'm not calling too late."

"If it was too late, I still would have answered. Do you want to chat, or is this about something in particular?"

I smiled at Kai's answer. I felt the exact same way. Now that I had him in my life, I was going to hold on with both hands.

"It's about something. Remember that domestic dispute where Maddie went inside, looking for the kid?"

"How could I forget? The motherfucker was coming at Maddie with a frying pan, right?"

"Yeah. Well, he made bail. Maddie's positive he won't bother her."

"But you want to make sure."

"Brother, it's almost like you can read my mind," I laughed.

"What's his name? What was the address where he was arrested? You get me that and I'll give you everything you need to know by the end of day tomorrow."

"I appreciate it." I rattled off Bruce's last name and the address.

"So, you and Maddie?" Kai asked.

"Yeah, we're solid."

"Have you figured out your future?"

I rubbed the back of my neck. "After training her to shoot a taser, that's next on my to-do list."

"Anything you need, brother. I'm here for you."

"Thanks, Kai. That means the world."

I hung up and went to the kitchen. I poured myself some water and drank it. I didn't want to lie to her. I went back to the bedroom and climbed into bed, loving how she snuggled right back into my arms. I held her close and kissed the top of her head.

I thought about showing her the Pacific Ocean. She'd look good in a bikini on the beach. I knew she loved it here in Jasper Creek, but couldn't we build something strong and real? A life? A future? In California?

She shifted even closer, as if she could hear my roiling thoughts, and wanted to comfort me.

Yes. This was definitely possible.

I fell asleep with a smile on my face.

Chapter Eighteen

It was definitely time for a big sister talk. Trenda could tell by the tone of my voice when I'd called that I needed her. She knew it was serious the second I called. But when I said I'd take a half day off work? That sealed it.

So here I was rummaging around in her fridge like I owned the place while she took baby Drake and picked Bella up from school and then took her to a friend's house for a play date. I had the best sister in Tennessee.

I paused when I saw a Tupperware container near the back.

Homemade potato salad!

Scratch that, I had the best sister in the *world*!

I laughed. If Drake had still been in town, there's no way there would have been any potato salad left in Trenda's fridge.

I rummaged further and found all the cold cuts I

needed. Plus—bless her heart in the good way—horseradish and sauerkraut for the bestest roast beef sandwich to go along with the potato salad. I made sure to leave enough for Simon to have two sandwiches when he came home, because I saw that there was turkey for Bella and Trenda. I salivated as I created a masterpiece of a sandwich.

I happily trotted my tushie to the living room. I set down my treasure on the coffee table and curled into the corner of the sofa. I picked up the remote and grinned when I found Trenda had recorded one of the Real Housewives episodes. I wondered if she made Simon watch it with her. I turned it on. I picked up my bowl of potato salad, then took my first bite and closed my eyes as I savored the perfectly spiced goodness.

The room exploded.

My bowl dropped out of my hands as I covered my ears, trying to drown out the sound of gunfire?

Gunfire!

The glass patio door was almost gone. It had a man-sized, jagged hole in it, and a man in leathers with a bandana over his face was reaching through the hole to the door handle.

Run!

I lurched off the couch and started for the front door, but somebody caught my ponytail, and my head was yanked backward. It felt like my neck was going to snap.

I fell to the ground and cut my elbow on a long

piece of glass. It burned. But it didn't hurt as badly as my neck.

"Bitch, you ain't going nowhere."

"You got her?" someone yelled from the back deck.

"Yep. We're all ready for the trade," the guy who was pulling my hair said.

"Owww!" I screamed as I was dragged through broken glass toward the shattered patio door. My jeans and boots gave me some protection, but my shirt was short-sleeved—and riding up. My back and arms were getting shredded.

Oh God, he dragged me over a huge piece of glass, I felt it stab me. Deep.

I was crying like a fucking baby and now was not the time to cry. I needed to keep my shit together.

"We need to leave a message," the voice from outside yelled.

A message? God, what kind of message?

The monster stopped dragging me. He literally lifted me to my feet by my ponytail. I screamed in pain.

He yanked down his bandana and said, "Quit your sniveling, bitch, or else I'll really give you something to cry about."

That stopped my tears. He'd said the exact words that my dad used to say, and I'd stopped crying in front of him when I was eight years old.

I stood on my tiptoes to relieve the pressure on my scalp. The man who was staring at me had a long gray beard and cold, dead eyes. "Your old man made a bad mistake," he said quietly. "He never should have taken our brother."

Dad? Dad was still in jail.

That was when I noticed he was wearing a biker's vest. Not one from around here, though. I knew all the motorcycle clubs and gangs in Tennessee. It was part of the job.

I opened my mouth to say something, but nothing came out. I was too scared. I cleared my throat.

"I think y-you made a m-mistake," I stuttered. "Dad's in jail. He couldn't have taken your brother."

He scowled. "Don't try to be cute. Your *man*. Simon Clark."

I clamped my mouth shut.

Simon?

Shit, of course, Simon. I was in his house. He thought I was Trenda. What had I been thinking? Well, the last thing I wanted to do was tell this bastard that he had the wrong sister. What I needed to do was get him and his buddy out of the house as fast as possible. Before Trenda got home with her son. Was there something else I could say?

Think, Maddie!

"Simon doesn't have your brother," I wheezed out.

I didn't have a chance to brace before his fist slammed into my stomach.

"Bitch, don't lie. We know what went down. We know you're Simon Clark's old lady. He'll do a trade.

He might have been a SEAL, but he's old and he's gone soft."

"What do you want me to do?" I needed to do something to get them out of here before Trenda got back.

"You're coming with us. If you know what's good for you, you'll keep your trap shut."

"Leave a message, Grizz." I turned my head just a little and saw an even scarier looking guy with a scar down half his face yelling from outside. "Do it fast. We need to leave."

Grizz looked down at me. Then he swiped his finger through the blood on my side and pulled me over to the sofa. He leaned over it and wrote on the back wall with my blood.

Each time he ran out of blood, he would swipe more from the cuts on my body.

WE WANT A TRADE
    YOUR WIFE
    FOR OUR BROTHER

He yanked me by my ponytail again, but this time I was ready and I managed to stay upright. He pulled me out the patio door and I opened my mouth to scream.

His fist hit the side of my head just as I screamed. The last thing I saw was the sky... spinning.

Then nothing.

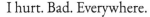

I hurt. Bad. Everywhere.

I opened my eyes.

I can't see!

My heart started racing. Why couldn't I see? I groaned, but I couldn't hear it. I tried to move my lips, but they didn't work. I tried again and felt something sticky.

Duct tape.

Everything came rushing back. I sucked in a deep breath through my nose. Good, my nose was free. No duct tape there. I tried to move. I rolled, but my arms and legs weren't working. I was tied up.

Probably more duct tape.

I took stock of my body. The duct tape had been wrapped around my upper arms, down to my wrists. Then on my legs, I was taped just around my knees. So, I could move a little bit.

I kept my eyes open, trying to acclimate to the dark. Yeah, I hurt, but now was not the time to be a wimp.

I felt myself breathing too fast.

Keep it together, Avery. Don't have a panic attack! Not now. You can have one after you're safe.

I blinked. My eyes began to sting.

No! No crying.

You don't get to cry, and you don't get to panic.

I could feel my eyes watering.

No. No. No!

What would Drake do?

What would Evie do?

What would Beau do?

They wouldn't fucking cry. They'd fight. So that's what I'll do. No panic. No tears. Just survive. Just like Beau would.

My shoulders slumped.

My eyes had finally acclimated, and I saw I was next to a water heater. Then I saw an electrical panel on the wall. The room smelled of motor oil and was drafty. I might not be able to do much with my arms, but I could at least move my lower legs. I bent my knees, and slowly spun around on my side. I saw a garage door.

I was in a garage.

I slowly rolled over, and the room began to spin. My head felt like somebody had shoved a spike through my temple.

I was lying on a cement floor.

When I no longer felt like I had taken some kind of magic mushroom, I saw a workbench with some tools hung up above it. But not many. I blinked to clear my head. Then I realized most of the tools were strewn all over the bench. Wait a minute, there were belt buckles hung up, too. That didn't make any sense.

I closed my eyes, trying to think, to focus on what was important.

I opened them again and saw an open toolbox on the floor beside the chair in front of the workbench. Maybe there was something in there I could eventually use.

I looked around the room a little more, but I couldn't see the door. I needed to roll some more to find out where Grizz would come from. There was no way I wanted to be taken by surprise. Not again.

I began to roll.

Ahh, God.

I felt like someone had just stuck me with a burning, metal spike in the side of my belly.

If I could have, I would have screamed.

I realized that there was still that piece of glass embedded in my side, right above my jeans. I felt blood oozing out of the cut. My rolling around probably made it worse.

My breath was coming in short bursts. I needed to get myself under control.

I still needed to find out where Grizz would come from. There had to be another door, some place. I curled up as best I could, so that I could start moving like a worm on my other side. Maybe if I got close to the workbench, I could lean up against it and see the whole garage.

I started moving. Pushing myself forward with my sneakers, then pushing forward with my butt and shoulder on my uninjured side.

It felt like I'd been going forever.

I looked over to see how close I was to the workbench, and I wanted to cry. It looked just as far away as when I started.

I started again, but then my sneaker lost its grip, and my butt slid through something wet.

Ah God, it was blood.

My blood.

The room started to spin again.

I slumped over onto my stomach, jarring the piece of glass.

The scorching pain was unbearable.

When I felt myself slipping away, I gratefully grabbed at unconsciousness.

Chapter Nineteen

"Beau, get over to Simon's house right now."

"Roan? What's going on?" I said into my phone.

"Just get here *now*."

He hung up.

I had a really bad feeling. Kai's phone was ringing and as soon as he answered it, his eyes got hard. He stood up from his half-eaten meal we'd been having at the Down Home Diner. He shoved his phone in his pocket and pulled out his wallet. He threw down more than enough money to cover our meals and tips.

"Let's go. You're riding with me," he commanded.

I followed him toward the front of the diner.

"Boys, you take care of yourselves. I'll say a prayer." Little Grandma said from her perch beside the hostess stand.

I looked over my shoulder at her as we were exiting. Kai grabbed my shirt and pulled me out the door. As soon as we were on the sidewalk, he started running toward his truck.

This is bad. Really bad.

I had a premonition.

As soon as we were in Kai's truck, I took out my cell phone.

"Call Maddie," I said, giving the voice command to my phone.

"Don't bother, she won't answer." Kai told me. I looked over at him. He had that look on his face. The look that all special operators got when they were going into hostile territory. It was his game face.

It displayed nothing except focus and determination.

"Tell me," I demanded.

"I know nothing more than Maddie's been taken and we need to get over to Simon's house."

"It's a fifteen-minute drive. Tell me who I can call for answers before we get there." My voice was harsh.

"I got my call from Simon. He was clear he'd tell me when I got there."

"Well, Roan can damn well tell me something now, if this is about Maddie." I was already pressing in his number.

"I told you to get here," Roan growled when he answered.

"Kai's driving. You're on speaker. Give us the rundown while we're in the car to save time when we get there."

"I'll conference in Jase. He's on his way."

I waited for what seemed like hours, but it was less than a minute.

"Okay, here's the sit rep," Roan started. "The Blood Ravens, do you remember them, Beau?"

"Yeah, they're the biker gang, the one-percenters, out of Chicago. You planned to snatch one of their brothers. Did you do that?"

"Yep, the operation went down perfectly. They had no idea who took him, or so we thought," Roan answered.

"Wait a minute, I was in on that job," Kai interrupted. "We were clean as a whistle. We followed through on that embezzlement job and got him, because we knew they wouldn't know who we were."

"The woman, the embezzler, she knew that her company used Onyx Security," Roan interrupted.

"So? Who was she going to tell? Her brother was already with the C.P.D. and the company and the D.A. were happy." Kai sounded confused as he pressed down on the accelerator, sending us twenty miles over the speed limit.

"Her ex-husband is a member of the Blood Ravens. That's who she told," Roan explained.

I couldn't stand it a minute longer. "I don't get it. What does this have to do with Maddie?"

"They kidnapped Maddie. They want to exchange her for Bishop, the one who's in jail awaiting trial," Roan answered.

I felt bile rise in my throat, but I pushed it down. "Why Maddie?" I kept my voice even.

"Maddie took some time off and was meeting Trenda at her and Simon's house. Trenda left the key under the mat for her so she could get in while she picked up Bella at school. Maddie was at the house alone when the Blood Ravens busted in and mistook her for Trenda. They left a message saying they wanted to trade. We need everyone here to see if we can find anything that might give us a lead as to where they might have taken her."

"Did you get it on film?" Kai asked.

"Simon said that he only got film on the outside," Roan answered. "Apparently he doesn't film inside the house, even after the alarm goes off."

"Do you know the license plate of the vehicle they took her in?" I asked.

"It was covered with mud. I've had Nash put an APB out on the make, model, and color. He's agreed not to come to the scene for the first hour." I'd met the sheriff, so I knew who Roan was talking about.

"How's Trenda?" Jase asked.

"Not good," was Roan's curt response. "But Simon's with her."

"We'll be there in five," Kai said. "Is there anything else?"

"Nope. Just get here."

～

I looked down at the glass shards covered in blood. I swallowed, then swallowed again. I hadn't been sick on a mission since my second. But this was close. This was Maddie's blood. Some bastard had dragged Maddie over broken glass.

"You, okay?" Kai whispered the question.

I nodded. It was all I could do.

I'd already seen the message written in Maddie's blood.

I stomped out of the living room, my boots crunching on the broken glass, hoping that the shards would slice through the tough leather and cut me as well.

When I got to the deck, I grabbed at the railing for dear life as I looked out over the empty land in front of me. I sucked down the fresh air, praying it would save me. Taking solace in the fact that somewhere out in this big, wide world, Maddie was breathing the same air as I was.

I knew deep in my gut she was still alive. Not just because the gang needed her for a trade, but because she was my soulmate, and I knew the moment she stopped breathing, so would I.

"Come inside," Roan said. "Simon has the video of the outside perimeter loaded so it can play on the TV."

I nodded and again walked through the glass and joined everybody else who was standing in front of the family TV set.

Trenda had taken the baby when she'd gone to pick

up Bella and take her over to Renzo and Millie Drako's farm. Renzo, Jase's brother, had previously worked in the government and was more than capable of protecting the women if necessary.

Before Simon started the video, he turned to me. "Brace, Beau. This isn't good."

I sucked in a deep breath. "Start it," I commanded.

The video started when two men dressed in leathers, wearing Blood Raven cuts, were holding guns and had obviously just shot through the patio door. That must have been what triggered the outside camera to start filming.

One man with a bandana over part of his face reached in and opened the door. He went inside. There was no sound on the video, but there was a clock running in the bottom corner of the video. After a minute and twenty seconds, the one who remained outside shouted something. I imagined Maddie inside being dragged through the glass. According to the clock on the bottom of the video, another fifty seconds went by, and the man shouted something again. This time, over three minutes went by, then the first man came out, holding Maddie upright by her ponytail. She was covered in blood. She opened her mouth to scream.

No! Don't do it! I shouted in my mind.

The bastard holding her slammed his fist into the side of her head. I watched in horror as he let go of her and she dropped in a heap at his feet. She wasn't moving, not a bit. Both men looked down at her coldly.

The one who had done the yelling turned and reached into a duffle bag that was lying beside him. On the back of his cut was the name Bishop. He pulled out a roll of duct tape and tossed it to Maddie's attacker.

The man I planned to kill.

The name on his cut was Grizz.

Grizz put duct tape over Maddie's mouth, taped up her arms behind her back, and then wrapped the tape around her knees. I took two steps closer to the TV and crouched down in front of it, looking to see if Maddie made any movement.

"There! Did you see it? She moved her legs." I pointed to the screen.

"I saw it," Kai said.

The other guy pulled a blanket out of the duffel bag and shook it out. A second blanket fell onto the deck.

"Motherfucker," Simon whispered.

I frowned.

He handed Grizz the blanket then picked up the other one and shoved it into his bag.

Shit! No wonder Simon was pissed. The second blanket had been for Bella.

Grizz wrapped Maddie in the blanket, then tossed her over his shoulder. He and Bishop walked back into the house to get to the front door, where it would be easier to get to their car.

The screen went black.

"Hold on," Simon said tightly. "I'll switch it to the next video feed."

It took a moment, but then we saw Grizz coming out the front with Maddie still over his shoulder. Her blanketed body looked so small against his big shoulder. Nobody would guess that he was carrying a woman.

Bishop popped the trunk of the Buick and Grizz dumped her in the trunk like she was a sack of potatoes.

I was now going to make his death five minutes longer than I had originally planned.

He slammed the trunk shut and got into the passenger side. Bishop made a three-point turn in front of the house, then drove down the long driveway and took a right turn, heading for the highway.

"That's all there is," Simon growled.

"Maybe Nash will find something," Jase said.

"He's going to find that car on the side of the road somewhere. Empty. For sure, they have another car waiting for them," Roan said.

My friend was right. I might not be into civilian investigation, but if I was in their shoes, that's what I would figure.

"They're going to want to be on their home turf, aren't they?" I asked Simon.

Simon nodded.

"So, Chicago?" I asked.

"Yeah. They know their man, Skid, is locked up in Chicago. So, I'm sure that's where they're going to make the trade," Simon confirmed. "Beau, how solid are you? Can you keep it together if we take you with us?"

"I dare you not to." I glared at the older man. I knew he thought he could act like my commander, but only my captain gave me orders, so Simon better back the fuck off. Simon must have seen my determination, because he just nodded.

"Roan, you stay here. I need you to coordinate things along with Nolan. Once that's done, get to the office and start the normal searches. Jase and Kai, you'll fly up to Chicago and get us situated. Roan will have something figured out by the time you land. Beau and I will drive to Chicago now. If we get any sightings, we can stop them on the way."

"They're going to be mostly on I-65 and I-75 if they want to make good time," Kai pointed out.

My stomach lurched. Maddie could die in that trunk with tape over her mouth if she threw up.

"We've got to find her before she leaves Tennessee," I said hoarsely. "She can't survive a trip that long in a trunk."

Kai put his hand on my shoulder. "They need her in good shape for proof of life, bro. When they switch cars, they'll get her out of the trunk."

I looked into eyes that were identical to mine, except they had confidence shining in them. Kai nodded. "I'm not lying to you, Beau. They're going to keep her alive. We've got time."

I nodded. Time was a luxury I didn't believe in anymore. But I'd take every second I could get for her. I had no other choice but to believe him. Anything else would kill me.

Chapter Twenty

I screamed.

"Did you want to eat or not?"

I blinked fast, trying to adjust to the bright light and the woman's voice, all while coping with the fact that my lips had been torn raw along with the duct tape.

I tasted blood.

"Well, are you going to eat? I don't have all day, you know."

She moved so she was no longer standing between the ceiling light and me. I could make out her over made-up face and bad bleach job.

I started to reach up to staunch the blood on my lips, and let out a cry. My shoulder burned with pain as I tried to move my arm. So did my side where the glass was still embedded.

"I'm not going to stand here all day, and I'm sure as

hell not going to feed you. You either eat now, or I'm taking it away."

"Where am I?"

"In the garage."

I looked around a little more and realized I was in a one stall garage. I saw there was one little window on the garage door.

"I meant whose house?"

"My grandpa's house." She sat down in the chair at the workbench.

"Where is it?"

"Bitch, I'm not answering any more of your damn questions, just eat your damn food." She stretched out her leg and toed the plate with a sandwich on it. There was no way I was going to be able to lift that to my mouth. Not with the way my shoulders were cramped up.

"My name is Maddie," I said, hoping to establish a connection.

"I don't care what your damn name is. I'm just supposed to feed you and take you to the bathroom. Shit like that. You've got one night here before you're on the road again."

"Can I have water?"

The blonde heaved out a long breath. She looked around the workroom as if expecting water to magically appear.

"Wait here." She heaved herself out of the chair. Then she stomped to the door in her motorcycle boots and flung it open. She was wearing really tight jeans and a tank top that didn't quite cover her left breast. She wasn't wearing a bra. She left the door open and I heard voices.

I sucked in a deep breath, trying to will away the pain that suffused my body. It hurt like a son-of-a-bitch, but I was able to lift my shirt to see if I could yank out the piece of glass, but it wasn't jutting out.

This was not good.

"Yeah, she's awake," the woman hollered. "I wouldn't be out here getting water for her, otherwise, now would I?"

I heard the grumble of a male voice, but I couldn't make out what he was saying. His voice was too low of a register, but the woman? Her screechy voice I could hear just fine.

"Fuck yeah, I cut her loose. I wasn't going to spoon feed her, for God's sake."

I heard the sound of flesh meeting flesh.

"Ow, that hurt!" she squealed.

More mumbling.

"How long are you going to stay this time, Grizz?" I couldn't stand the whine in her voice.

There was a long silence.

"Can't you take me with you? You're going to need help with her, ain't you?"

"Lana, shut up already!" Grizz shouted.

"All right. All right."

I heard her heels on the wood floor before I saw her

in the doorway. I could see the red hand mark on her face.

"I hope you're happy," she muttered as she threw the bottle of water at me. It bounced off my chest. I grabbed at it before it rolled away. As I did, my side howled in agony. Dammit, if the bleeding didn't stop, or the glass shifted deeper, I wasn't just stuck. I was screwed.

Shut it, Avery. Focus.

At least my arms were somewhat working, so I could move and eat and hopefully try to do something to get myself out of this mess.

"Thank you," I whispered.

"Don't be expecting me to do you any more favors. You ain't worth it."

Lana was now leaning against the wall beside the door, scrolling through her phone.

I uncapped the bottle and took a sip, then I grabbed the soggy sandwich and bit in. Of course, it was bologna and Wonder Bread. My life had truly turned to shit. I tried to pretend it was the roast beef sandwich that I had been about to eat at Trenda's house, but my imagination wasn't that good.

There had to be something around here I could think about besides shitty food and crappy companionship. I turned and looked at the workbench again. In the light, I could clearly see that the belt buckles were for rodeo events.

I choked down bite after bite, finishing off each

one with a sip of water. I needed to keep my strength up if I wanted to get the hell out of here. I didn't think for one moment that I could get away from Grizz and the other guy, but maybe I could get some kind of message to someone, and Lana's phone was my best shot.

"Okay, time's up."

Lana put her cell phone in her back pocket, then walked over and picked up the plate and bottle of water and went back inside. This time I didn't hear any kind of conversation. She came back holding a roll of duct tape.

"Wait," I said as she started ripping off a piece.

"What?"

"I need to use the bathroom."

"You can wait."

She ripped off a long strip of tape and bent toward me.

"Please," I said. It wasn't hard for me to work up some tears. The idea of lying around in pee-stained jeans all night was just another level up in this horror show.

Lana looked me over, and my tears must have paid off, because she set the roll of tape on the work bench and pressed the ripped tape on the side of the bench. "Can you stand up?" she asked.

I shook my head.

"Shit," she groused. She stepped over me again to pull a pair of clippers off the workbench, then she clipped through the duct tape holding my knees together. "There. Now you can walk. Get up, and I'll take you to the bathroom."

"Thank you." I gave her the most pathetically grateful smile I could conjure. I pushed up against the cement floor with my shaky arms and tried to get my legs under me so I could stand up. Like I figured, they wouldn't work. I fell back down.

"Oh, for God's sake. Get up already," Lana huffed.

"I'm trying. My legs have gone to sleep."

"Try harder."

I needed to time things right. I knew that if I made her wait for over two minutes, she'd play with her phone, which would mean when I got my hands on it, it would be unlocked.

"Can you give me five minutes? Just let me rub them, okay?"

Lana rolled her eyes. "Fine." She flounced to her spot by the door, leaned against it and grabbed her phone out of her back pocket. I watched as she started to scroll. I rubbed my legs and felt them tingle.

I attempted to get up and made a big deal of falling down. It wasn't hard. I looked over at Lana. She just rolled her eyes again. That seemed to be her go-to expression. I tried two more times, each time I landed back on my ass.

"If you could just lend me a hand, I know if I could just get on my feet, I'll be fine."

Lana shook her head in disgust, but put her phone

in her back pocket, then walked over and reached out with both of her hands and braced. It was perfect. I grabbed her hands and pulled hard. She fell on top of me. I made sure my hands were all over her as I apologized profusely.

"You dumb bitch," she screeched.

"I'm sorry."

"Get off me!"

"I'm trying."

She elbowed me in my ribs, luckily on my uninjured side, and I rolled to my back. "I'm so sorry," I sobbed. "My legs won't work. They need time to wake up."

"I should just let you piss yourself," she said as she climbed to her feet and dusted off the front of her jeans.

"Please don't. Please give me ten minutes. I'll be able to walk by then."

"You damn well better be."

"I'm sorry I ripped your tank top," I murmured.

She looked down at her tank top, then back up at me. "You bitch!" She slapped me across my face. "This was my best tank." I watched as she hustled out of the room. This time she closed the door behind her, and I hated that. I'd really hoped I'd have some kind of advance warning when she was coming back, but with the door closed, I was flying blind.

I pulled her phone out from underneath my butt. It was still unlocked. I swiped over it to keep it unlocked, then pushed up to my knees and pulled myself up, using the work bench. When I was leaning against it, I leaned in and read the one belt buckle I could make out. Champion Bronc Rider, 1972, Memphis, Tennessee. It had to be her granddad, right?

Resting my elbows on the work bench, I started a new text. The only numbers I knew by heart were my sisters. Trenda and Evie would know what to do, but the twins? Piper? They're not used to—

What if Trenda and Evie didn't see it quick enough? Fuck it, I'd send the text to all five of them.

IT'S MADS. BEEN KIDNAPPED. NO JOKE. DON'T TEXT BACK. AT HOUSE WITH 1972 CHAMP BRONC RIDER, MEMPHIS TENN. TELL SIMON.

I pressed send and deleted the entire message conversation, then dropped to the floor, flinging the cell phone over towards the water heater.

I rolled back over to where I was, doing my best not to roll onto the embedded glass in my side. I touched it and found that it was oozing blood. This was so not good. Three or four minutes went by. Where was she?

The door flung open. Lana stepped in, then

slammed the door shut. She looked furious as she paced around the room. Then her gaze centered on me.

"Did you take my phone?"

"Huh?"

"My phone? Did you take it?" She stood over me. I braced for another hit.

"I don't know what you're talking about."

There was a ding. I recognized that sound. It was the sound of an incoming text. Oh please, say it wasn't one of my younger sisters replying to my text. I should have only sent it to Trenda and Evie.

Dammit Beau. I really did love you.

Chapter Twenty-One

I shoved down my irritation as I saw Trenda's name pop up on Simon's truck display. We didn't have time for wifey shit.

He pressed the connect button so she could be heard through his car speakers.

"Hi Trenda. How—"

"I got a text from Maddie."

I sat up straight. "That's not possible. We have her purse, and her phone was in it," I said.

"No, it wasn't from her phone number. It was from a phone with an Indiana area code. I looked it up."

"Then how can—"

Simon cut me off. "Trenda, what did the text say?"

"It said. *It's Mads. Been kidnapped. No joke. Don't text back. At a house with 1972 Champ Bronc Rider, Memphis, Tenn.* It was the abbreviation for Tennessee, four letters, T.E.N.N. I don't know if that makes a difference. Then the text said to tell Simon. Everybody else has been texting and calling me."

"What do you mean, everybody else?" Simon asked.

"All the girls. It was a group text for all five of us. So, it's real, Simon. Maddie is alive!"

I was trying to keep up. "All five of who?" I asked.

"Me, Evie, the twins, and Piper. I'm betting ours are the only phone numbers she has memorized." I could hear that she was laughing and sobbing at the same time.

"Not Drake?" I asked.

Simon glanced over at me, giving me a look that said I was stupid. He was right, I needed to focus on finding Maddie now. It was a stupid question.

"After Drake left, we had to learn how to take care of one another," Trenda answered my question. "So, it was us girls against the world. She wouldn't have thought to include Drake on the text."

"Honey, you did good," Simon said. He looked over at me. "Did you get the info?"

I nodded.

"Trenda, can you text Roan with the phone number the text came from, and what the text said?"

"I'll do it as soon as I hang up," she promised.

"Love you," Simon said as he pressed disconnect.

He kept his eyes on the highway but spoke to me. "What's your take?"

"Sounds like Maddie wasn't in a position to get any names or addresses of where she was currently being held, but somehow she found out that whoever the owner was, he was a Bronc Riding Champ."

"That's my take," Simon nodded.

Roan's name popped up on the display, and Simon took it. Before Simon could say anything, Roan was already talking.

"The phone belongs to Lana Fletcher. She's in the system. Drugs and prostitution. Last known address was in Chicago, but according to her parole officer, she's no longer there."

"Do you know anything about the Bronc Rider Champion?" I asked.

"I have Clint's wife Lydia doing a search. It's kind of odd, don't you think?" Roan asked. "I mean, where would Maddie have come up with that?"

I started to get mad. "What does it matter? She thought it was pertinent, and she sure as hell wouldn't have wasted her time texting that information if it wasn't critical." I kept my voice low, but I was fucking pissed that Roan had even asked the question.

"Calm down, Beau. We're following up as fast as possible."

I looked down at my watch. Kai and Jase should have landed by now. "Have Kai and Jase talk to the parole officer. Maybe he or she didn't do a real search on Lana. They must have a huge caseload."

"Good call," Simon agreed.

"Will do," Roan said. "I'll call back as soon as I have info on the Bronc Rider. I see you're in Kentucky. It looks like you're making good time."

"I didn't realize that SEALs had lead feet," I said with a semblance of a grin.

"When necessary," Simon nodded. "Push Lydia, Roan. We need this information as fast as we can get it."

"She knows," Roan assured Simon. "You might want to call your wife back. She's really worried."

"She'll be busy keeping her sisters calm. I'll call her when I know something. Thanks, Roan. Call me when *you* have something."

The call disconnected. I flexed my fingers that I'd balled into tight fists.

Simon glanced sideways at me. "Your girl is smart."

"Yeah."

"We're going to find her. We're going to bring her home."

"Yeah."

It was the only way I could think. If I thought any other way, I'd go insane.

It was dark. It made things more ominous. We'd stopped in Louisville, Kentucky. It was an hour after we'd heard from Trenda. We figured that Jase and Kai had boots on the ground in Chicago. Therefore we should stop on the halfway mark between Chicago and Jasper Creek.

Since Maddie had texted from Lana's cell phone, it seemed logical that Grizz and Bishop had stopped some place, so staying midway between Jasper Creek and Chicago made sense.

But now I was pissed that Simon and I hadn't taken two vehicles, because then he could have been in Indianapolis, while I was in Louisville.

Fuck!

This was taking way too long.

As if Roan had heard me, his name popped up on Simon's dash.

"What?" Simon answered.

"Got the name of the man who won the Bronc Riding Championship in Memphis back in '72. It was Roy Fletcher. Wanna guess who his granddaughter is?"

Roan sounded cocky, which was pissing me off. We didn't have time for cocky.

"Got it. His granddaughter is Lana. Now tell me where he's located." I demanded.

"Harrodsburg, Kentucky. Seventy-eight miles southeast of where you're located. Lydia still can't get a lock on Lana's phone, so we don't know if that's the location where the text came from or not."

"It's the best we have, and Maddie wouldn't have given us this info, if it wasn't pertinent," I ground out.

"I hope you're right," Roan said.

"Of course, I'm right," I practically yelled. "She wouldn't have said it if it didn't matter," I muttered.

"Easy," Simon said soothingly. "I know Maddie. She's an Avery. You're right, Beau." Simon was pulling out of the Wal-Mart parking lot. "Text us the address, Roan, and see if there are any blueprints on the house."

"Lydia is already on it, and I've already sent you the address."

"Thanks."

Simon disconnected, and I saw the text come in on the dash. I pulled it up and logged the address into Simon's navigation system. It was going to take us an hour and thirteen minutes to get there.

"Wanna call in the cops?" I asked.

Simon shook his head. "We don't know if we're right, and I've been on a couple of ops since starting Onyx where things went wrong. In the back, I have everything we need. Comm system, night vision, weapons. We're covered."

I used my phone to check Google Earth to see what I could make out for the property now that we had an address. It was a bust. There were too many trees surrounding the house. I told Simon.

"It was a good thought," he muttered.

We were forty-five minutes into the drive when Roan called back.

"Yeah?" Simon answered.

"There are no plans on the house. The property was a farm back in nineteen-forty-nine, and it was parceled out into four sixty-acre lots. Chances are that's when the houses were built. But Lydia found a permit for a new stable back in nineteen-eighty. Building plans were submitted with the permits. She has those, and I e-mailed them to you."

"Tell Lydia, good work."

"Already did."

Simon disconnected the call. He handed me his cell phone and told me his passcode. I went to his e-mail and downloaded what Roan had sent. I pulled up the attachment.

Excitement roared through me as I looked it over. "We scored, Simon. With the stable, it also shows where the house is in relation to it, as well as the paddock, the fencing, and the road."

"Hot damn." He sounded as jazzed as I felt. I looked. We'd left Jasper Creek at four-thirty. We were going to get to the house at nine-thirty. Not the best time for an assault, but it was fine for reconnaissance.

I looked down at what I was wearing. Not ideal. Looking at Simon's grey T-shirt, I realized his wasn't any better.

"You got a change-out kit back there?" I pointed my thumb toward the back of his truck. "We're gonna need blacks, comms, paint, everything."

"I've got you covered every which way to Sunday."

I nodded, trying to get my head around anything else we might need. "Med-kit?"

"Yep." He nodded. "But Beau, there wasn't that much blood. It's probably all superficial."

Rage hit hard. "You can't know that!" I sucked in a deep breath. "Neither of us can know that," I said in a lower tone of voice.

"She was doing well enough to send that text. Your woman is strong. She's an Avery," he said again.

The amount of pride in his voice went a tiny way toward placating me. "I can accept that."

I looked at my watch, then looked at the time the navigation system was showing until we got to the Fletcher place. Twenty-one minutes. I needed to do something to occupy my mind besides counting down the minutes and thinking about the blood I'd seen on the carpet at Simon's house.

"I've met all the sisters except for Piper and Chloe. Can you tell me about them? Well, of course I've met them, just not since they've become adults."

"Chloe's going through a real rough patch," Simon said. "Has Maddie told you?"

"Yeah. She mentioned that she just suffered a second miscarriage. She moved into an apartment in Gatlinburg?"

"Yeah. Her husband Zarek is wrecked. He wanted her to stay at their house in Jasper Creek, but she said she needed to leave to clear her head. He offered to buy a new house. Anything." He glanced over at me. "I can't imagine if Trenda had miscarried when she was pregnant with Drake. It would have killed. But it would be a hundred times, no, a thousand times worse if she shut me out. If I couldn't hold her when her heart was broken. Zarek is going through hell."

"Is she seeing someone?" I heard how that sounded and winced. "I mean, is she getting professional help?"

"I know she was. Trenda's not sure right now. All the sisters are broken up. Except for Piper. She's out in California, and I know everyone is trying to shield her from this. I think that's a mistake, but that's the girls' decision."

"How do you think it's going to turn out for Zarek and Chloe?"

"I really don't know, Beau. It doesn't look good."

I thought about that for a few miles. Even when you thought you had the world by the tail, it could still fall to shit. I shivered and looked at the navigation system. Eight more minutes.

"Where do you think we should park?" Simon asked.

"We'll take a left onto the road to the property. From what I can determine on the permits, it looks to be about four miles from the highway to the property. We'll kill the lights at the highway turnoff, gear up just off the road. Then roll slow for two miles and go the rest on foot. Then we can do the recon."

"Sounds good."

Chapter Twenty-Two

"I told you to check in with your parole officer, you dumb bitch! You can't keep avoiding his texts and phone calls."

Grizz was standing over a cowering Lana as he was looking at something on her phone.

"He only texted me once."

I tried to keep up with the conversation, but I was coming in and out of consciousness. I could feel the blood oozing out of my side. Plus, my head was pounding like the damn bongos from that stupid band that Zoe had dragged me to that one time.

Zoe. Focus on Zoe. Remember that barely there dress she was wearing and how she started a brawl that night?

Stay the fuck awake!

I watched as Grizz back-handed Lana and she fell to the floor. "Just how stupid do you think I am? This is the fourth time he's texted you in twelve hours! Something's up, and we don't need your shit stinking up our business. Call him back!"

Lana got up off the floor and grabbed Grizz's arm. "I don't care about him. If you'd just let me stay at the Blood Ravens compound with you, it wouldn't matter if I didn't check in."

I watched as Grizz shoved Lana away from him and she landed on the floor. "Fine. You want to stay at the compound? Then we put you to work with the other whores. Is that what you want? But you'd probably be too stupid to even be any good. Why? Because you can't fucking check in with your parole officer! Text him back, Lana!"

Grizz threw her phone at her head. It bounced off it onto the cement floor. She started to cry. Then he turned to me. "And you! Get up off the floor. Bishop and I want some dinner. Since Lana is busy sniveling, you need to cook for us."

Shit, I didn't even know if I could make it up off the floor, let alone walk. And he wanted me to cook? This was not going to be good.

He stomped over to me and grabbed my ponytail.

"Wait! I'll get up. I promise. Don't hurt me. I'll get up and cook. My side is bleeding. It's just going to take a minute."

"Jesus Christ, another snatch with fucking excuses. You have three minutes to get into the kitchen and start cooking. You better give us something good, otherwise we'll take something else from you. You understand me?"

I looked up into his glittering eyes, and I understood exactly what he meant.

"I understand."

"Good."

Please say my text got through.

He turned to leave, but he took the time to prod Lana with the toe of his boot. "After you send the text, Bishop has a hankering for you in the living room. Get your ass up and wipe the snot off your face. You hear me?"

Lana sat up and nodded. She used the bottom of her tank top to wipe her nose, exposing her breasts. I swallowed back the bile that was rising up.

When Grizz left, she looked over at me with wounded eyes. "Why won't he take me to live at the compound?"

"You want to be a prostitute?" I couldn't believe my ears.

"I love him," she whispered.

God save me.

"Lana, text your parole officer and tell him where we are. Tell him we need help."

In an instant, her expression changed to maniacal rage. "You fucking cunt! I would never rat out my man. I hope they do fuck you over. I hope they kill you!" She shoved to her feet, and I watched as she furiously texted. Then she went to the door and yelled in a sing-song voice, "Bishop, honey. I'm coming."

I had to be losing my mind. None of this could be real. I sat up and touched my side.

"Owww," I moaned. My fingers came away sticky with fresh blood. I grabbed at the work bench and pulled myself up into a standing position, then left the workroom for the first time. Every step was agony.

"Well, there she is, Miss America," Grizz laughed.

The living room, dining room, and kitchen were all one long room, separated by a kitchen counter. Grizz and Bishop were sitting on the couch, side by side, watching television. Lana was kneeling between Bishop's knees, doing something I didn't want to even think about.

I averted my eyes.

"Oh, are you modest?" Grizz laughed.

I ignored him and went into the kitchen and opened the fridge. In one of the chiller drawers, I found some ground beef, but underneath that were rib-eye steaks. Even better. How could they bitch about steaks?

Somebody turned up the TV, blotting out all the other sounds coming from the living room, and I could have wept with relief. I pulled out the steaks and looked around some more. Eventually I found a box of mashed potato mix, butter, some bread and Cheez

Whiz. All the makings for a motorcycle gang feast as far as I was concerned.

"What's taking you so long?" Grizz roared from the living room.

"I'm making you steaks. I want to get them right." I kept my eyes on the stove, which faced away from the living room. "How do you like yours cooked?" I yelled back.

"I can't hear you," he yelled at me.

"How do you like your steak cooked?" I screamed.

"Turn around."

Asshole!

I turned around and pain shot through my side. I hissed.

Lana was still at it.

"Excuse me, sirs. How do you like your steaks cooked, sirs?"

Bishop and Grizz burst out laughing.

"How do you like that? She called us sir." Grizz howled.

"I like mine medium rare," Bishop said.

"I like mine burned," Grizz answered.

"Okay. Dinner will be up in fifteen minutes."

They continued to laugh as I turned back to the stove. I carefully crouched down to find a skillet, a pot to mix the potatoes and a broiling pan. I figured I could toast the bread and melt the Cheez Whiz on it, kind of like the garlic bread that Beau had made for me.

Beau.

Just the thought of him and that night had me on my ass in front of the cabinets as I covered my mouth.

Don't cry. Don't cry. Don't cry.

I wanted Beau. I wanted him right now. I couldn't stand the pain, and I couldn't stand one more second of this horror show.

"Bitch, where are you?" Grizz hollered.

I pulled out the skillet and the pot and stood up. I held them over my head. "Got them."

"Stay where I can see you," he hollered again.

I nodded. I wiped the tears off my face, then went to the sink and filled the pot with some water. It looked about right. I put the skillet and the pot on the electric stove and watched them heat up. Soon the water was boiling, and I stirred in the potato flakes. The pain was a constant burn.

I listened to some kind of ultimate fighting cage match blaring from the front room, praying it would continue for hours and hours.

I didn't even bother to rinse off the steaks when I took them out of the packaging. Maybe they would get sick. Maybe I should spit on them. Maybe I should wipe them in my blood. I threw them into the skillet and watched them sizzle in the butter.

I'd already turned on the oven and set it to broil, so I got the bread and put it under so that it could toast the bread a little before I melted the cheese. I'd found some garlic powder that looked like it had been purchased when the house had been built. Again, I hoped it would kill these motherfuckers.

I turned Bishop's steak and left Grizz's on to burn. I opened the fridge and found beer and ketchup. Something told me that Grizz would like ketchup to go with his steak. I threw butter into the potatoes.

"What's taking you so long?" Bishop hollered.

Why was he yelling?

I turned around without thinking.

Iccckkk!

Lana was now kneeling between Grizz's legs.

I needed bleach for my eyes.

"Yours is ready. I'm still burning Grizz's steak," I hollered back.

"Bring it to me," Bishop commanded.

God no! Come on. I buy girl scout cookies. I donate to the food bank. No! Shit, I'd known I was in trouble for never returning that library book. Now, this was my punishment.

I plated Bishop's food. Grabbed utensils, beer, and everything else I could think of because I only wanted to make one fucking trip. I walked around the counter and kept my eyes down. I concentrated on the sounds coming from the TV.

The crowd is electric.

Did you see that?

Both fighters are taking a beating.

He's got a good chin, he's taking those hits like a champ.

"Move it, bitch. I'm hungry," Bishop growled.

I set the food on the coffee table to the left of Bishop. I'd successfully not looked at anyone on the couch.

"Hey, this looks good."

"I'm glad you like it," I mumbled.

I turned around and almost fell from the pain, but caught myself. I scurried back to the kitchen as fast as I could.

I looked in the skillet, and Grizz's steak was definitely looking burned. I plated his food and waited for him to holler.

I felt like I was going to fall over. I gripped the edge of the counter in front of the sink, careful not to look out of the corner of my eye into the living room. Instead, I concentrated on the trees outside the kitchen window.

I probably should've eaten something to keep up my strength, but I would just throw up.

Drink water.

It was Trenda's voice bossing me around.

I went to the fridge to see if there were any more bottles of water, but there weren't. I grabbed a glass from the cupboard and examined it to see if it was clean. It looked clean, but I washed it anyway. My head jerked up when I heard a noise against the window.

I looked. It was weird, but it looked like there was a head. I squinted.

It is a head!

I looked over at the living room. Damn, Lana still wasn't done. There were windows above the couch. The curtains weren't closed. I looked back at the head in the kitchen window.

Oh thank you Jesus, it's Beau!

He was pointing toward the ground.

I immediately dropped down to the kitchen floor.

Chapter Twenty-Three

The house was a fairly small, U-shaped rambler. Three bedrooms along one side of the U, then this living room, dining room, and a kitchen along the back, with the garage forming the other side of the U. The only places that were occupied were the living room and kitchen.

Simon and I kept watch. Him on the living room, me on the kitchen. We didn't want to waste any time. This looked like an ideal time to strike.

"What do you think?" Simon's voice came over the comm.

"I see one gun on the couch, and one gun on the coffee table," I said. "Both of the men are occupied, one more than the other."

"Agreed," Simon concurred.

"I want to keep Maddie in the clear. The garage door connects to the kitchen. If I go in through the kitchen window, she should be able to slip into the garage while you and I engage Grizz and Bishop."

"Got it. You want me coming in from the bedrooms?" Simon asked.

"Yeah. Use the rear corner bedroom window if you can, then come down the hall to the living room. Once you're in position, I'll breach through the kitchen, ensure Maddie made it to the garage. You take the guy eating. Neutralize him fast. I'll cover the woman and the other one."

"Copy that. Minimal force?"

"Only if they make us. Fast, quiet, and clean."

We hadn't really talked about it, but it just came about naturally that I was leading the op. Simon knew I needed to. He was a good man.

It was less than two minutes when Simon told me he was in position. I tapped on the kitchen window, where Maddie was staring out at the trees. She jerked.

I stood still, and I watched as she squinted. I wasn't wearing night vision, since the house was lit up like a roman candle, so I knew she could make out my head, if not my face. At least not to begin with. I waited. I knew the exact moment she knew who I was.

Her relief was obvious.

I pointed down, and she immediately dropped out of sight. Damn, she was smart.

I jimmied off the window screen, then tried opening the window.

It was unlocked. Smiling, I opened it up and quickly slipped inside. I dropped down beside her.

She was trembling. Gray. Locked in place. Staring at me, her eyes huge.

Her arms were cut to hell, but from what I could see it was all superficial. I winced when I realized she was wearing one of the crop tops she loved so much. I desperately wanted to pull her into my arms. Turn her around and examine her back to see how much damage was done when she had been dragged through the glass, but we didn't have time for any of this.

I put my mouth right to her ear.

"You good?" I whispered.

She nodded.

I pointed to the garage door six feet away. There wouldn't be any cover when she ran from the kitchen to the garage door. "On my command, you run low to the garage. Get in there and close the door until I come for you. You got that?"

I saw her struggle to ask questions, but she didn't, she just nodded.

"Good." I smiled in appreciation.

"I'm in position," Simon said through the comm.

I pointed at my ear, so that Maddie would know someone was talking to me.

"I'm ready," I responded. "On my count."

I mouthed to Maddie, "You ready?"

She bit her lip and nodded again.

I held up three fingers. As I counted down, I closed my fingers. "Three. Two. One. Go."

Maddie fled toward the garage. Not nearly as fast as I would have thought she could. Something was definitely wrong, but I didn't have time to worry about that. I had a job to do. I burst around the corner and in four long strides, I had my gun pointed at Grizz's head as Simon tapped Bishop with a sharp elbow to the throat. It was brutal and fast.

Bishop lunged for the pistol again, so Simon slammed the heel of his boot down on the man's wrist with a sickening crunch. Bishop screamed, but Simon didn't let up. He flipped the man over with a knee to the ribs and wrenched his good arm behind his back, zip-tying him face-down in mashed potatoes.

The blonde's head stopped bobbing and Grizz looked up at me with eyes that glittered dangerously. He reached for the gun beside him, but I'd already retrieved it and had it in my left hand.

Grizz turned his head slowly to his right and saw that his partner was incapacitated, and he slowly raised his hands.

Suddenly the blonde whipped around, her hair flying. I couldn't see her face, only the glint of a knife as it came toward my thigh. I kicked out, and she slammed against the low coffee table in front of the TV. Grizz reared off the sofa toward me, his hands outstretched. Flicking my safety off, I aimed for his shoulder and shot. Blood sprayed as he jerked back, but he stayed standing, then he lunged again.

I sidestepped his lunge, drove my elbow into the back of his neck, and brought him down hard onto the coffee table, splintering the wood beneath his bulk. He rolled and tried to stand, so I wrapped my arm around his throat in a modified rear naked choke and yanked back. He flailed, grabbing at anything, everything.

The man was strong, but I'd spent fifteen years fighting stronger.

With a grunt, I shifted my weight and brought my knee into his side...once, twice, until he went slack. His breath came in wheezes, and his limbs twitched as I shoved him face-down and yanked his arm behind his back.

"Stay down, you hairy fuck," I growled, zip-tying his wrists before checking his pulse. Alive. Barely.

"Watch out!" Maddie yelled.

I'd already seen the blonde coming at me again, but Simon yanked her back by the hair and subdued her with the contact stun to the side of her throat. She went down in a second.

"Get to the fucking garage!" I yelled at Maddie. If I'd had the time to be pissed, I would have been lava hot.

"These two are contained," Simon said.

"On your knees," I growled at Grizz. "Hands on your head."

"Can't," he gasped. "My arm won't work."

"I've got this. Go get Maddie," Simon ordered.

What sweet words.

I nodded and ran to the garage. When I got there, Maddie was leaning against a work bench. Scratch that, she wasn't leaning. She was hunched over and trembling. That's when I saw blood trickling down her side, and the side of her jeans had a dark patch of blood that went from her waist all the way to her knee. How much actual blood had she lost?

"Maddie," I whispered as I went to her. I went slow, not wanting to scare her.

"Beau," she moaned, not looking up. Instead, her head fell to the bench.

I was there in an instant, picking her up, then dropping to the floor and holding her close. Every instinct, every atom of my being demanded that I squeeze her tight, wrap her so close that we were one being, but I couldn't. I didn't want to cause her pain.

She thrust her head between my shoulder and jaw and shuddered.

"You came," she whispered. "You saved me."

"Always, Maddie. I'll always be here for you, from now on. For the rest of our lives."

I took out my phone and pressed in Roan's number.

"You good?" he asked.

"I need a medevac chopper to this address. Maddie's lost a lot of blood."

There was a half-second pause. "On it. I'll call back with status, ASAP." He hung up.

She wasn't talking anymore, but I felt her warm breath against my neck.

"Maddie?"

Nothing.

"Maddie, wake up, baby."

Nothing. I shook her gently.

"Beau?"

"Stay with me, baby."

"Always. Loves youz," her words were slurred.

My phone rang. It was Roan.

"The chopper will be there in fifteen."

"Good."

"Anything else I can do?" he asked.

"Pray."

Chapter Twenty-Four

I liked the feel of the wind through my hair. I hugged Beau even closer as he pushed his Harley even faster. I felt safe holding onto him. I knew that no matter where he took me, he would always keep me safe. I rested my cheek on his leather-covered back.

No, that wasn't right. He wasn't wearing a leather jacket. Why wasn't he? My cheek was resting against his skin. I could smell him, practically taste him.

Nothing made sense.

"Maddie? Can you wake up now? Come on baby, I want to see your pretty brown eyes."

How could I hear Beau so clearly if we were riding on his Harley?

Wait a minute. He didn't have a Harley. Grizz had a Harley. Grizz was the biker.

I whimpered.

Grizz.

I hurt. My skin felt like it was on fire.

"Honey, are you in pain? Let me help you."

Beau. He's here. I opened my mouth, but nothing came out. I tried to open my eyes, but I was too tired. I felt his hand touch my face, his thumb traced my bottom lip. It was Beau's touch.

"Where?" I finally got out the one word.

"You're in the hospital. You're in the ICU."

He wasn't making any sense.

I wanted to cry. Nothing made sense and I hurt.

"It's okay, honey, I've just pressed the button for more pain medication. You're going to be feeling better in just a minute or two."

Beau stopped touching me, and I whimpered again. Then I felt his breath against my lips, and he kissed me. I sighed. He made my pain go away. His kisses always made my pain go away.

"I promise you, Trenda. She was awake a few hours ago. The doctor said it was good she was sleeping. Her body needs to heal."

Beau was talking.

Who needed to rest?

"Chloe, you should go down to the cafeteria. Being here isn't good for you. You hate being in hospitals."

That was Trenda, always the big sister.

I tried to hear what Chloe said, but I couldn't.

Then I felt warm breath next to my ear, and I knew it was Beau. "Can you open your eyes, Sleeping Beauty? Your sisters need to see that you're getting better. They're girly girls and might cry. They don't kick ass like you do."

Did I just choke out a laugh?

"That's right, Maddie. Open your eyes. Save me from their tears."

I concentrated with all my might, and then I felt my eyelids lift. I slammed them back shut when the light slammed into my brain.

"Ow," I hissed.

"What's wrong, baby?"

"The light," I whispered.

"Hey, Simon, can you turn off the light? It's hurting Maddie."

"Yeah. I'll open the door, to let in just a little."

"Good call." Beau lightly squeezed my hand and kissed my cheek. "The light's off," he whispered. "You can open your eyes now."

I found him staring at me as I opened my eyes. He hadn't shaved, and he looked exhausted. There was still some black paint smeared on his face from when he rescued me at the house.

"I'm in the hospital? How long have I been here?" I croaked out the question.

"You're in the ICU. The piece of glass nicked your spleen. They had to operate. It's been fifty-hours and thirty-seven minutes since you've gotten out of surgery."

I licked my dry lips. "Not that you were counting."

He laughed.

Good, I hated to see the worry and tension on his face.

I looked over his shoulder and saw Chloe, Trenda, and Simon. I was shocked.

"Chloe's here," I whispered.

He looked over his shoulder. "Only two visitors allowed, Simon. I'm staying. Figure it out."

I watched Simon grab Trenda's elbow. "You can come back after Chloe's visited with Maddie."

I noted the look of indecision on Trenda's face, but after a moment's hesitation, she nodded. After they left, Chloe stood silently in the middle of the room. I turned my attention back to Beau. "Is Chloe okay?"

"God, I love you," he said as he lifted my hand and kissed my palm. "Here you are in ICU and you're worried about your sister. No, I don't think she is," Beau answered my question.

I nodded. "Tell her to come here."

Beau hesitated, then picked up my hand and placed a kiss in the center of my palm. He got up from the side of my bed, careful not to let the mattress move too much. He went over and said something to Chloe. Somehow, he made her smile. Of course he did. He was Beau.

Chloe came over and sat in the same place that

Beau had vacated. She picked up my hand and held it to her cheek.

"You scared me."

A tear dripped down her face.

"You shouldn't have come," I admonished. "You should have waited to visit me when I got home." I started to cough. Then I coughed some more.

Fuck, that hurt.

I felt my eyes water.

"Mads, don't talk. Do you need a sip of water?" Chloe asked.

I nodded the best I could.

Suddenly, there was a cup with a straw in front of me. Chloe was lifting my head so I could sip from the straw.

"Not too much. You've been out of it for over two days. Your tummy can't handle too much." Chloe set the cup back on the stand beside my bed, then she stroked my hair from my brow.

"It's greasy, right?"

Her lips twitched. "You've had better hair days," she admitted.

"Beau's acting like I almost died. It's freaking me out," I whispered. I knew he had bat-like hearing, so I whispered really soft.

Chloe kept stroking my hair. "You lost a lot of blood. Apparently, you were in hypovolemic shock by the time they got you into the OR. The piece of glass that was embedded inside you nicked your spleen.

They had to take you into emergency surgery as soon as you arrived. It was bad, Maddie. Simon told Trenda that if they hadn't had found you, in another couple of hours you would have died."

I winced. "Poor Beau."

"How can you say that? Poor all of us! Losing you would have killed us, Maddie. I should know. I don't think I could survive if I lost you, too."

She had my hand in a death grip. She was grinding my knuckles together so hard that for the first time, the rest of my body didn't hurt. "Chloe, I'm not leaving you. I'm not, sweetheart."

I watched as tears trickled down her face.

I tried to reach up to pull her down so I could hug her, but I was connected to an IV. "Chloe, I need a hug." And I did. I needed to comfort my little sister.

Chloe reached down and wrapped her arms around my neck. I gathered her close as best I could, with my one free hand.

My sister sobbed for a long time, and I stroked her hair for a change. I said a bunch of nonsensical words, just trying to soothe her. I blocked out my pain and concentrated on her. Her sobs came to a shuddering stop and lifted her head.

She looked like she had the weight of the world on her shoulders, and that it was killing her.

"Sweetheart, you need help. You have to know that."

She touched my cheek and shook her head. "I'm

handling this. I just need more time. I was able to come here, wasn't I?" One side of her mouth curled up, offering the saddest excuse of a smile humanly possible.

"Yes. Yes, you were, Chloe. And I adore you for it. You're not driving back to Gatlinburg tonight, are you?"

"It's only five p.m."

"Still. Promise me you'll stay with Trenda or Zoe."

She sighed. "I promise." She bent over and kissed my temple. "I love you, Mads."

"Love you more." I smiled.

I watched her walk out of the room, and Beau came back to my side. "How much of that did you hear?" I asked.

He gently sat down on the bed and I pushed my body against his warmth.

"I heard all of it," he replied. "And yeah, you so easily could have died, Maddie."

"I'm sorry."

He barked out a half-hearted laugh. "Baby, you have nothing to be sorry for."

Things were becoming clearer. "Oh. Yeah. What about Grizz and Bishop?"

"They're in real trouble. You were kidnapped and taken across state lines. They're going down."

Beau looked savage. I could see a vein in his forehead pulsing. I needed to stop this.

"What about Lana?"

"This is her third strike, and it's a big one. The

D.A. told Roan that she's going to be behind bars for at least twenty years, unless she takes a plea and turns state's evidence."

I winced.

"Do you need more pain medicine?" Beau immediately asked.

"No. It's not that. I feel sorry for Lana. She was so mixed up. She was so in love with Grizz that she was willing to work as a prostitute just to stay with him." I wondered if she had it in her to testify against Grizz. What a mess.

Beau gave me a funny look. "Do you want some water?"

I nodded.

He held the straw for me as I took four long sips. I leaned back against my pillows. The water helped clear my head.

"Hey, wait a second," I cried out. I didn't give a shit that it hurt my head. "That bitch tried to kill you! She should get life in prison."

Fuck! I twisted my shoulders, trying to relieve the pain I'd just caused. Note to self, no more yelling.

Beau's lips twitched.

"The doctor said you might not remember everything that happened the night we rescued you."

"Oh, I remember everything now just fine," I assured him. I opened my mouth to thank him. To tell him just how damn much he meant to me, but instead I yawned. Then yawned again.

"Maddie, you need to sleep," he murmured.

"Don't want to."

"It will help you heal faster."

I felt sleep pulling me under.

"Are you going to be here when I wake up?"

"You can count on it." The gentle kiss he whispered across my lips was sublime. When I closed my eyes, I drifted off to sleep and found myself in a meadow. Beau was there with me. Then I realized something.

Beau was always going to be there.

Chapter Twenty-Five

"Seriously, Maddie. I don't think this is a good idea. The doctors said for you to take it easy." Maddie was in one of her sleep shirts, covered in giraffes. Standing in the middle of her bedroom, she held a bright blue folded towel against her chest as we discussed the merits of her taking a shower.

"It's just a shower."

I winced. I recognized that tone of voice. After three days back at her house, that fake calm tone became very familiar. She was so close to ripping my head off, it wasn't even funny. Okay, it was a little bit funny.

"Fine, we'll shower together. How does that sound?" I waggled my eyebrows.

Her eyes widened in alarm. "I want to shower alone," she said through gritted teeth. So much for calm.

I mentally counted to ten. "At least let me check your bandage. Make sure that it really is watertight."

"I've already checked."

Yep, calm had left the building.

I changed tactics. "Please, Maddie? For me?" I asked softly. "I know I'm driving you crazy, but I'm still waking up nights covered in sweat, remembering that helicopter ride to the hospital. Won't you please let me check your bandage?"

She dropped the folded towel, walked to me, and put her hands on my chest. "I should have thought of that. I'm sorry, Beau. I was selfish to just be looking at things from my point of view."

I covered her hands and kept them tight against my chest, not wanting to lose our connection. "You have nothing to be sorry for. Nothing."

"How about for being a raging bitch?"

"Damn, Maddie, if that's what you consider being a raging bitch, I've fallen into a bucket of shit and come out smelling like a rose. Seriously, you are one of the kindest, most even-tempered people I know."

She dropped her head on my chest. "I don't deserve you."

"Does that mean I get to shower with you?"

She looked up at me from under her lashes. "Don't press your luck."

I laughed. "Lift your shirt so I can check your bandage."

"Yes, doctor," she sighed.

I knelt down in front of her, and she lifted her sleep shirt the bare minimum amount to let me see her wound. She was wearing cotton panties with bunny rabbits. Who knew bunnies could be so sexy?

Cool it, Beaumont.

"Is today your animal day?" I teased.

"Huh?"

"Bunnies and giraffes?"

She giggled. "Tomorrow is flowers."

I checked her bandage and saw that she had applied the watertight covering exactly right. I stood up. "You're good to go."

"Told ya," she said as she quickly dropped the hem of her sleep shirt.

"Just go slow. Lean against the shower walls if you need to. If you need me, I'll be right outside the door, so don't think twice about hollering for help. Okay?"

She stroked my chest. "Okay."

She went into the bathroom and left the door mostly open. I went and leaned against the wall next to the bathroom door. For some reason, she didn't want me to see her naked, hence not having the door all the way open. I didn't know why, but I respected it. I'd get to the bottom of it when she was feeling better.

It was a houseful. Evie and her two boys. Trenda with her daughter Bella and her infant son, then

Zoe, were all visiting. I suppose I could have made myself scarce while they visited Maddie, but I was too antsy to leave her alone. She'd only been out of the hospital for five days. So, in order to horn in on this little soirée, I was making food for all of them.

"Me and Zephyr want french fries," Holden said as he walked into the kitchen.

I looked down at the little boy and smiled. He looked nothing like his mother. He was blonde and blue-eyed and was soon to turn five years old.

"How about a mini hot dog instead?"

"A hot dog?" he asked suspiciously.

"Yeah, but really small. That way you might get two."

A big smile brightened his face. "Mom never lets me have two. I throwed up the last time I ate two hot dogs."

"Your mom is a smart woman."

"That's what Dad always says. But he says we're smarter because we know to tell her she's always right, even if she isn't."

I threw back my head and laughed. Something told me I would like Aiden O'Malley.

"When can I have my hot dogs?"

"Soon. I'll make sure to save you some. But let's not tell her, okay?" I held out my hand so he could shake it. Instead he held out his fist, and I bumped mine against his.

"Don't forget Zephyr," he said, referring to his little brother.

"I won't."

He ran out of the kitchen. "Mom, I get two hot dogs! Mr. Beau said so!"

"Little rat," I muttered, grinning.

I went into the fridge and pulled out the crab dip that I'd made up and took off the plastic wrap. I grabbed some of the cut-up pieces of bread that I had in a bowl and swiped it through the dip for a taste test.

Not bad. Bonus, it shouldn't poison anyone.

Out of the corner of my eye, I saw Zoe walking in.

"We need more wine. And no, we're not opening the cheap bottles that Trenda brought. She's got to get over that. She's not a single mom anymore."

"Some habits die hard," I said. "What did you drink when you were in college?"

"I drank when I was invited to parties and they had a keg. I also ate a lot of ramen noodles. It's just that we were dirt poor for so long growing up that I don't want Trenda to be raising Bella to think that she has to squeeze every penny."

"Are you kidding?" I asked. "Bella is squeezing all of us for every dollar. From what Maddie's told me, both Trenda and Simon spoil her from time to time, just not every time they go to the store, like some parents do."

Zoe tilted her head. "Yeah, I guess you're right. I

know you're not an uncle or anything, but are you a godparent or something?"

"A couple of the men on my team have kids. I've been around them a lot when we're on a training cycle. Teams tend to end up being family," I explained.

"Makes sense," Zoe nodded.

I went to the fridge and pulled out one bottle of Chardonnay that Evie had brought. I opened it up and handed it to Zoe.

"Thanks." She smiled and sauntered out of the kitchen. I followed her with the dip and bread. All the women were sitting around the dining room table.

"Whatcha got there?" Evie asked as I set the food down.

"My famous crab dip that I made for the first time."

The ladies chuckled. I took a good look at Maddie, who was sitting close to Trenda. She was drinking water, since her meds and wine didn't mix. She looked at ease, surrounded by her sisters. She really belonged here. How the hell was I supposed to ask her to leave this behind for Southern California?

"Rumor has it you're going to give my kid two hotdogs. Just know that you're on puke duty," Evie told me.

"Huh?"

"Two hot dogs? Holden throws up. Sound familiar?" Her eyes twinkled the same way Maddie's did.

"I'll keep that in mind," I smiled. "I've got a few more things to bring out. Don't fill up on the crab dip."

Bella sidled up next to her mom. "Can I have a taste?"

"You don't like shellfish, honey," Trenda said.

"But that's dip. I like dip. Especially with bread."

I chuckled as I made my way back to the kitchen. I felt someone following me. The kitchen timer went off.

"What's in the oven?" Evie asked.

"Little smokies, or hot dogs for your son."

"You're sneaky." She opened the fridge and took out a bottle of water. "And don't think I don't know why you volunteered to do all the cooking."

"What are you talking about?" I asked as I used a spatula to put the pastry-wrapped smokies onto a platter.

"You couldn't stand the idea of leaving Maddie, even with three of her sisters. You're so tightly wound that you're going to have an aneurysm."

"I'm not going to have an aneurysm," I protested.

"Fine, how about this? You're wound so tight, I bet you could crack a walnut between your butt cheeks."

I started laughing. "Did Aiden tell you that one?"

"Hell no, that'd be Drake." Evie grinned.

"Figures."

"She's fine, you know. She might be a little sore. But she's fine."

I was done with the smokies, so I turned, leaned

back against the stove, and crossed my arms. "I mostly know that. But I'm the one who found her. I'm the one who was with her on the Medevac flight. I just need a little more time to deal. Okay?"

"You're going to have to speed up the process. You're driving my sister up the wall."

"Evie, she's stronger than you realize. She can handle me hovering, for now..."

Evie looked at me thoughtfully. "Actually, you're probably right."

"I know I am."

Chapter Twenty-Six

"Freedom," I sang, tapping the dashboard of Beau's truck like it was a drum.

"Freedom," I sang a little louder, keeping the beat with my fingers.

"Freedom," I sang really loud, stretching the word out in an off-key falsetto, drumming like I was Travis Barker.

Beau looked over at me. "You do realize there are other words to that song, right? It starts with 'I won't let you down, I won't give you up.' Pretty solid lyrics, Maddie."

Naturally, I ignored him.

"Freedom," I sang with even more conviction, like George Michael himself had taken over my body... minus the talent.

Beau started to laugh. I liked that about him. He

thought I was funny, and he didn't tell me I sounded like a sack full of cats yowling, like my family did.

"Happy to get out of your house, huh?" he teased.

"So much happier than you can ever imagine. I'm freeee!"

He laughed some more.

"What are you going to do after you drop me off at Down Home Diner?" I asked.

"I'm going to go for a run with Kai. Then I've got a few calls to make to my team."

I shifted in my seat so I could see him clearly. "Damn, Beau. I didn't even think about it. You're late going back to Camp Pendleton. Isn't your boss, I mean your captain, mad?"

"Down girl, I'm not AWOL. I have his permission to be here. He gave me extra time after the whole 'my girlfriend was kidnapped' thing."

I bit my lip and turned all my attention to him. "Yeah, but for how long?"

He let out a long breath. "Why don't we save that conversation for when I get you home?"

"Beau, I don't think I can wait that long. It's kind of like I have the Sword of Damocles hanging over my head. I'd prefer to know when it's going to drop."

He reached over and grabbed my hand.

"It's going to be okay, Maddie. We'll figure something out. I promise."

How could he sound so calm?

How could I be such an idiot? It was like I'd had my head in the sand since I'd woken up in the hospital.

"Maddie?" He squeezed my hand.

"Hmmm?"

"We're going to work something out. I promise."

"You can't make that promise," I whispered.

"Yes, I can. Now we have ten more minutes until we reach the diner. Why don't you pick up my phone out of the console? I've got the Bluetooth set up with the SUV. Download "Freedom" from iTunes and you can sing along to it. Isn't it good that they upgraded me to this Escalade after I bitched about the Camry? The sound system is fantastic."

"Are you trying to placate me?"

"Absolutely."

Soon George Michael's voice filled the SUV. As I sang along with the chorus, I started to feel a little better.

As I was walking up to the diner, I got a text from Ruby telling me she was going to be half an hour late. The supplier for Java Jolt arrived late, and she needed to make sure they got their entire order.

It was one o'clock, and the diner closed at three. I hated that our time was going to be cut short. There was no one in line when I entered, which had been my plan. I had hoped to miss the lunch crowd.

"Maddie!" Little Grandma cried out. "Come give me some sugar."

I grinned. Little Grandma slipped off her stool by the hostess stand and held out her arms for me. I bent down and gave her a big hug. I didn't hold her too tight, because she was over a hundred years old. But she grabbed onto me pretty good.

"I prayed they'd find you, Maddie Girl."

I frowned. "But how did you know I was taken?"

"I knew."

I shook my head. Nobody ever questioned Little Grandma.

"Ruby was supposed to meet me now—"

Little Grandma patted my hand. "I know, honey, that dratted supplier was late to our place here, and Java Jolt was his next stop. Lettie!" she called out to her granddaughter.

"We have a four-top ready for you by the window," Lettie called back from across the restaurant. That didn't bother any of the residents of Jasper Creek who were finishing up their lunches.

I matched Little Grandma's steps as we walked to the table near the window. She sat down slowly, and Lettie came over putting a cup of tea in front of her before asking me what I would like to drink.

"Lemonade please."

"Coming right up."

"I am so glad we get this time to talk, Maddie," Little Grandma said, starting off the conversation.

"I am, too. I always love our talks." And I did. We had our granny, but she lived a couple of hours outside of Jasper Creek. Little Grandma was always a constant in our lives when we were growing up. For me especially. I was often lost in my books, and I seemed to take things harder than a lot of the older kids in my family. The yelling, the screaming, the abuse. I never showed it on the outside, but Little Grandma knew. She found me in the library, and would take me into the stacks and sit there with me and put her arm around me. Giving me quiet solace.

"I hear tell that you were unimaginably brave during your captivity."

I laughed. "Someone has been feeding you tall tales. I was scared to death. A little bit pissed-off, but most of the time, petrified."

"You were somehow able to text all of your sisters, weren't you?"

"I guess."

Lettie plopped a lemonade in front of me, along with a BLT. She put a perfectly baked biscuit with butter and marmalade in front of Little Grandma.

"Mom put extra mayo and bacon on your sandwich, Maddie, just the way you like it."

"That was fast."

"She gave you Harvey's. He's going to have to wait a little bit longer," Lettie whispered. The three of us giggled.

"Poor Harvey. Is there a cinnamon roll left over from breakfast?" Little Grandma asked.

"I'm sure there's a couple, but I was hoping to give them to Maddie so she could take them home to Beau."

"Oh. That's a grand idea," Little Grandma complimented her granddaughter. "Give Harvey a free side of macaroni salad. He'll like that."

"Will do," Lettie smiled and walked away.

Little Grandma took a sip of her tea while I took a bite of my sandwich. Why did everything taste better here than when I made it at home? While I chewed, Little Grandma started talking.

"You know, Maddie Girl, being humble is a good thing, but you don't always need to hide your light under a bushel. You are a remarkable young woman. Beau is right to be ass over teakettle in love with you."

I felt myself blushing. "Did you just say ass?" I teased.

"Don't try to waylay me, Missy. You get my point, now, don't you?"

My shoulders slumped. "Yes, ma'am."

"Now tell me, do you need to talk to a professional about what happened to you?"

That was another thing I loved about this woman. She might be over one-hundred years old, but she was definitely up with the times.

"I'm one-hundred percent fine. The doctor gave me a clean bill of health. I feel great."

"So emotionally you're okay?" she asked me, as she raised one white eyebrow.

"Absolutely." I smiled. I took a bite of my sandwich.

"Well, you'd know. In a sense, you are the professional, being a social worker and all." She broke off a piece of her biscuit and buttered it. "I'm glad to hear there are no residual effects."

Shit.

I thought about how I wasn't letting Beau see me naked.

Little Grandma must have seen me hesitate.

"Is there something on your mind?" she asked gently.

"Normally it's Trenda I'd talk to..."

"But?"

"She feels so guilty because they mistook me for her. I can't tell her anything about what happened."

"Honey, can you tell me?" the older woman asked quietly.

I looked around the room, and I realized there were no occupied tables close to us. I slowly nodded.

"It's really no big deal. I mean, nothing terrible happened to me."

"You were dragged away from Trenda's house. You needed emergency surgery. You almost died. Bad things happened to you, Maddie."

"I mean, they didn't really abuse me, you know?"

"Define abuse, Sweetpea."

God, she's talking to me like I talk to the kids that I deal with in my job.

Shit! I'm sounding like them too!

My eyes went wide.

Little Grandma gave me a wry grin. "Had an epiphany, did you?"

"I was punched and slapped. Not so much different from the stuff that happened if you weren't quick enough to get out of the way of dear old Dad."

The smile on Little Grandma's face was wiped clean. "That man needs to rot in hell."

"I won't disagree with you, especially after what he did to Piper."

"Do you want to talk about what else happened?" she asked in a solemn voice.

I nodded. "I think I need to." I bit my lower lip. My hands were clenched in my lap. "You know my job, right?"

She nodded.

"So, I've seen some really bad things, but I also know that sometimes even small things can mess with you. So, I guess I'm messed up."

"You never have to apologize for your emotions, Maddie. We've discussed this. How you feel is how you feel. You're entitled to your feelings."

I let out a breath, and some of the knots in my stomach seemed to ease.

"There were two of us in the house where the two men were. I mean two women," I explained, looking down at my sandwich. "Only, Lana wasn't a captive. She was kind of one of the men's girlfriend."

Little Grandma nodded. Encouraging me to go on.

"She was out of her mind. I don't know if it was drugs or what. She begged her boyfriend. He was a biker. She begged him to let her live at his motorcycle compound. He said he would make her a prostitute, but she didn't care."

Little Grandma sucked in a deep breath, but when I looked up at her, her face looked calm.

"I asked her to help me, and we'd both escape. She said vile things and said she wouldn't. She said she loved Grizz." I looked down at my sandwich again. "It was sick. She was sick." I stopped talking.

"And then what happened?"

"Grizz threatened to rape me."

"Aw, Maddie Girl."

"But he didn't. Not even close," I rushed to assure her.

"Yes, Sweetpea, but you had to be scared."

"I really was scared when they forced me to cook dinner. I saw what they were doing to Lana out in the open." I felt a tear dripping down my face. "I decided not to think about it. So, I didn't. But deep down, in my heart, and in my gut. I was scared."

"Give me your hands." Little Grandma put her hands on the table, palms up. I clutched them.

"And now, Maddie?"

"It's stupid," I whispered.

"We agreed. Nothing's stupid, remember?"

"I've been feeling dirty. Like somehow this did touch me."

She squeezed my hands, and we stared at one another. Suddenly, my stomach growled. Loudly.

I giggled. Then Little Grandma giggled.

"How are you feeling now, besides hungry?"

My eyes widened, and my shoulders totally relaxed. I wasn't feeling dirty anymore.

Beau was in for one wild night.

"I'm feeling better," I said slowly. "I'm feeling lighter." I grinned. "You should bottle your wisdom and sell it as Little Grandma's Cure-All Elixir."

"Enough with your sass. Eat your lunch."

Chapter Twenty-Seven

"Did you have fun with Ruby?" I asked as I opened the car door for Maddie's.

"Ruby couldn't make it. I had lunch with Little Grandma instead." She put a pink box in the foot well in front of her.

"You'll have to tell me about it." I closed her door and went around the nose of the Escalade to the driver's side and got in.

"Have I told you lately that I love you?" Maddie asked with a smile as soon as my door was closed.

"What's bringing this on?"

"Just answer the question."

"You tell me in a lot of different ways, honey," I said as I started the engine.

"Well, I love you. I think you're wonderful. And I'm so glad you came back into my life."

Maddie was wearing her heart on her sleeve. I leaned over the console, cupped her cheeks, and closed my mouth over hers. She parted her lush lips just a bit. Not too much. My girl didn't want to make a scene here in the town square. I continued to caress her cheeks with my thumbs as I lifted my head. "I love and adore you, Maddie. You have given my life new meaning."

I saw her eyes start to glisten. "Take me home," she whispered.

"Yes, ma'am."

I pulled out of our parking spot and headed toward her house. My house was nice, but her house felt like a home.

"Why couldn't Ruby make it?" I asked.

"There was a problem with a delivery. Not only were they late, but they also tried to short her. Apparently, it was a mess. Ruby had to stick to her guns and go head-to-head with the supplier."

My lips quirked. Ruby wasn't like Maddie's sister, Evie, but she was no slouch when it came to getting what she wanted. I chalked it up to Ruby's red hair.

I held her hand as we drove through the picturesque street of Maddie's neighborhood. I parked out in the street in front of her house. Her Jeep and this Escalade would not fit under her carport. She handed me the Down Home Diner box as I helped her out of the big SUV.

"Leftovers?" I asked.

"Yeah, and something for you. Those ladies adore you." Her eyes were twinkling.

"Well, I think they're pretty wonderful."

We walked up to her house. I unlocked her door, and we went inside. She immediately turned on the A/C and took off her sandals, then went to settle down on the couch. I frowned.

"You pushed it, didn't you?"

"Maybe an eensie little bit," she admitted. "But it was fun." She yawned.

"Bedtime?"

"It's not even four o'clock," she protested.

"Sorry. Should I have said nap time?"

"Probably," she agreed, as she yawned again.

"Let's get you to bed."

"'kay."

I held out my hand and she took it. I pulled her off the couch and when she swayed, I swept her into my arms and walked toward the bedroom.

"I could have walked... but I do like it when you carry me." She nuzzled her face into my neck.

"Then this works out, since I enjoy carrying you."

I set her down so that she was sitting on the side of the bed. She pulled off her blouse, then went to work on her bra. I turned away and went to her dresser to get a set of pajamas. I still didn't know why she felt uncomfortable being naked around me, but that was one thing I intended to get to the bottom of today.

When I turned around with the pajamas in my

hand, she was standing up just in her panties. She waved her hand at me. "I don't need those." She gave me a weary smile. "When you're here, panties or naked is good for me."

I was happy as hell, but I didn't understand. "What changed?"

She slipped under the covers. I went over and made sure they were adjusted the way she liked them.

"I'll tell you what changed after my nap, 'kay?"

Her pretty brown eyes were barely open. "Okay, love." I brushed a soft kiss against her lips. "Sleep tight."

She chuckled. "I won't let the bedbugs bite."

"Nut." I kissed her again.

As I was turning off the light in her room, I heard her whisper. "Yeah, but I'm *your* nut."

"That's the captain for you," Pete said. "He definitely understands family issues."

"Yeah, Phillips is a good guy," I agreed.

"So, are you thinking of leaving the Marines early?" Pete asked.

I was out in Maddie's backyard. I'd weeded the whole thing before finally calling my best friend on my team. I knew he would ask the hard questions.

"I don't want to. It's not just because I want to wait for my twenty and early retirement. It's also because I'm not ready to leave the team. You know?" I admitted. "But for her, I'd do anything."

"Yeah, that's how I feel about Darla," Pete agreed. "She and my daughter have me wrapped around their little fingers."

I laughed. "I knew that the day I came over and caught you wearing a tiara for Amy's tea party."

Pete started laughing, too. "I put up a mirror right beside the front door after that fiasco, so I could check for tiaras and the like. Also helps Darla makes one quick check to see how badly I've fucked up her lipstick."

I heard the back door open and looked over my shoulder. Maddie was standing there, wearing one of my T-shirts, and probably just that pair of panties she'd slept in. "I've got to go, Maddie's awake. It was good talking to you, Pete."

"You, too."

Maddie put her hand on my shoulder. "Was that your teammate? The man who you caught wearing a tiara?"

"The one and the same."

"I loved that story."

I got up off the ground from where I had finished weeding. "Yeah, Pete's a good guy."

"Wanna come in and eat some ice cream?" Her voice was laced with temptation.

I put my arm around her shoulders and hugged her

close as we both walked back into the house. "Chunky Monkey?"

"What else? Somebody has been loading up my freezer with the stuff every time he goes to the supermarket."

"Sounds like a smart man," I teased. I steered her toward the couch. "Why don't we sit down and talk first?"

"That sounds ominous." Her brows pleated as she sat down.

I cuddled her close. "Nothing bad at all. I just wondered about your talk with Little Grandma. It seems to have done you a world of good."

She looked up from where her head had been resting on my chest. "It did." She let out a deep breath. "You know I've had a couple of hang-ups since you rescued me. I mean, it's been kind of obvious."

"Yeah, but you told me you weren't sexually assaulted or touched that way..."

"No, I wasn't," she assured me. "But I'd gotten mixed up after the stuff with Grizz..."

"Okay, what stuff, honey?" I waited for her to continue. It was tough, but I kept myself relaxed with a calm look on my face. I knew I wasn't going to like this.

She looked me straight in the eye. "Grizz threatened me. That he and Bishop would..." She looked down, then up again. "Then somehow seeing Lana doing...*that* with the men. It got mixed up in my head and I ended up feeling dirty."

I didn't quite understand how she ended up feeling dirty, but I definitely had friends who had PTSD, and I knew the mind was tricky. The ultimate trickster, in fact.

"Honey, do you need to talk to someone? A professional, maybe?"

She gave a little laugh. "I did one better. I talked to Little Grandma. I don't know how but just talking it through with her unlocked and unloaded it. Just like it sometimes does with the kids I work with." Her hands moved, and I felt her fingers lifting the hem of my shirt.

"Maddie," I protested. "Are you absolutely sure about this?"

She looked up at me with sparkling eyes. "Stay here, stud. I'm going to get the ice cream."

I caught her before she could get up off the couch. I wasn't in the mood to play. I was in the mood to make love with Maddie. Make slow, tender, gentle love with the woman I adored. And I was going to start with a kiss.

I pulled her onto my lap and smoothed back her hair, pulling out the scrunchie that kept her hair in a ponytail. Then I threaded my fingers through her dark, silky hair.

"Mmm," she murmured. "I like that."

"I'm glad."

I kissed her temple and jaw. The bruise was gone, but I remembered the green and yellow colors that had marred her flesh. Even now, the thought of it made me hurt. I kissed down until I finally reached Maddie's irresistible lips. I licked along her bottom lip, tasting a hint of lemon. I took my time, licking and tasting, while she slowly opened for a deeper kiss. I dipped my tongue into the honeyed cavern of her mouth and dueled with her tongue. We caressed one another in a sensuous slide that seemed to go on forever. Our strokes matched my fingers that were sliding through the thick curls of her hair.

Maddie whimpered, and inside, I smiled.

She writhed against me, but I chose not to move my hands, even though she was now caressing my abs. She was killing me in the most incredible way possible, but she didn't understand. This was all about her. She might have said she was feeling all right, but it was my job—it was my duty and my pleasure—to ensure that she felt only joy as we came together.

I changed my methods just a little. Instead of just stroking through her hair, I began to massage her scalp in soft circles. As I did, her hands relaxed. She was no longer frantically trying to unbutton my jeans. Instead, she went back to stroking my abs. I broke into a sweat.

This woman was going to be the death of me.

I pushed up off the couch with Maddie in my arms and carried her into the bedroom. Before setting her on the bed, I pulled back the duvet and sheet, then laid her down. I gathered all the pillows and put them behind her head so that she was in a reclining position.

Maddie's eyes were almost black, and her lips were swollen. She held out her arms for me to join her.

I shook my head. I needed a moment.

Finally, I looked up at her and I gave her a semblance of a smile as I fingered the T-shirt she was wearing. "Can I take off this shirt?" I asked hesitantly.

She frowned. "Of course you can. Beau, are you okay? I'm not fragile, you know."

I sat down on the side of the bed and dipped down for a long, languorous kiss. When I finally sat back up, I spoke. "I know you're not fragile, Maddie. You're an Amazon, a Valkyrie, a warrior princess. But right now, you're Maddie, my woman, my lover, the woman I love. I have this need to lavish you with love and care."

She searched my face.

How could I explain this, except for... "I need this," I choked out.

She cupped my right cheek. "Whatever you need, Beau. Always."

I gathered her close, my face buried into her neck, then felt myself convulse.

What the hell?

But I couldn't stop my emotions from storming through me.

I'd had so many nightmares, thinking about that moment when I saw all that blood, when she wasn't responding, and I didn't know if the chopper would make it in time.

"I'm here, Beau," she whispered into my hair. "You saved me."

She spent forever massaging my back, crooning soothing words until I could finally feel her with me.

Safe.

Whole.

Mine.

This time when I kissed her, it was hungry and needy. I held nothing back and Maddie met me kiss for kiss. When we broke apart, I pulled her sleep shirt over her head, kissing every fading cut along her arms. She was no longer wearing a bandage, but her surgery scar was still angry and red. I brushed it with gentle kisses.

Then I took my time teasing her naval with my tongue. Something I had found drove my woman insane, and today was no exception.

"Beau, stop that," she said as she squirmed.

"Make me."

She grabbed at my hair, and I redoubled my efforts. I pulled off her panties and put her legs over my shoulders. I teased the lips of her sex with kisses.

She stopped pulling my hair and dropped back against the pillows.

"You don't have to stop doing that," she admitted with a sigh.

"Good to know."

She was already wet, but I was feeling greedy. I wanted more. I gently latched onto her clit with my teeth and Maddie whined my name. I swept my tongue against her swollen nub as I eased two fingers into her sex, intent on finding that spot that would drive her crazy. I didn't have long to wait.

"S-so good. P-please, I need more."

So did I. But first, I was going to give her the orgasm of her life. I nibbled at her clit as I rubbed my fingers inside her sheath.

"F-fuck. Beau!" she yelled.

Her muscles locked tight around my fingers as she released more honey for me to taste. She was right, it was so good. Maddie continued to tremble for long moments, then her body relaxed back into the pillows, her breathing beginning to even out.

I pulled my fingers out of her sex and drove my tongue inside her.

"Beau?" she shouted.

I began circling her clit with my thumb, slow and steady.

"Beau!"

I lifted my head. "You're strong. You can take it. I want another orgasm."

I bent down and went back to the best job of my life, driving Maddie Avery crazy.

Chapter Twenty-Eight

I woke up with my stomach rumbling, and I was also more than a little grumpy. I snuggled into Beau's embrace a little more. God, it felt good waking up in his arms. He smelled so good, and I felt so safe. But seriously, my guy had a really strong competitive streak, and that was the reason I was grumpy. Capital 'G' grumpy.

I turned my head so I could get a good look at him. He looked more relaxed than I'd seen him since I'd come home from the hospital, but there were still dark circles under his eyes. After feeling him break down earlier, I could have kicked my own ass for not realizing just how much me being kidnapped had wrecked him. I was just so hyper-focused on him being the big, bad Marine Raider and my hero that I never considered just how scared he'd been for me.

I was a total dumbshit.

Then there was the fact that Mr. Hero felt the need to give more than take this afternoon. He'd been waiting on me hand and foot since I'd come home, not letting me lift a finger. I'd started to assert myself, but I'd figure things would work their way out over time. But here in the bedroom? No way. This needed to be equal. I needed to nip this bullshit in the bud! Plus, I liked doing for him.

Strike that, I *loved* doing for him.

I moved out of his arms and got off the bed.

"Maddie?" he asked sleepily.

"Bathroom," I answered. "Go back to sleep."

I waited until his breathing evened out, then bent down, picked up the T-shirt I'd been wearing, and put it on before going out to the kitchen.

I had a plan. It would handle both of my issues at the same time. I got the ice cream out of the freezer and put it in the microwave for fifteen seconds. It was easier to deal with when it was slightly melted.

As soon as I got the Chunky Monkey out of the microwave, I ate a couple of good-sized bites. It was damn good. Not orgasm good, but pretty damn good. I went back into the bedroom.

When I got in there, I couldn't have asked for a better situation. Beau was sprawled on his back, and he had kicked off the covers. I looked between his thighs and spotted my target. However, painting his dick with ice cream while he was asleep would not be the sexy wake-up call I was going for.

But I had ideas.

I scooped out a mouthful of gooey goodness and sucked it off the spoon, then I put the carton of ice cream down on the nightstand. Beau still hadn't stirred. It really made me realize just how tired and wrecked he'd been about my kidnapping. Normally, I wouldn't wake him up because he really needed his sleep, but he could go back to his nap after I was through torturing him. After all, he'd be relaxed when I was done.

If my mouth wasn't full, I would have giggled.

I moved closer and admired the bounty in front of me. Lucky me, my playground was on full display. I swallowed the last of the ice cream, then crawled up the end of the bed toward my man.

His eyes opened just as I closed my cold mouth over the head of his cock, and he jerked.

"Jesus! That's cold! What the hell, Maddie?"

I gently cupped his balls as my cold tongue curled around his soft cock. It took no time at all for Beau's body to get with the program. Soon I had much more than a mouthful to contend with.

I swirled my tongue around the head of his erection, loving the feel of all that strength enveloped by such rich, velvety skin. After a minute or two, Beau started moving with my strokes.

"Maddie. Yeah. Just like that," he rumbled.

I breathed in through my nose and caught that mix of spice, heat, and male that never failed to make me a little crazy. We'd showered together after our marathon sex, but still there was a musk that was all Beau, and I wanted to roll around in it like a cat with catnip.

Now that he was fully engaged in my little project, I had to use one hand to hold him as I sucked him deep. I relished the way his length stroked along my tongue, in and out, in a mind-numbing rhythm. I made sure to tease the underside of his cock with the tip of my tongue each time I allowed him to slip upwards.

"My God, woman, don't ever stop."

I smiled around my prize.

In and out. Up and down. I squeezed his balls gently, and Beau groaned loudly.

Again, I smiled.

He was so close. His heels were digging into the sheets, his body trembling.

"Let up, Maddie. I'm close." His voice sounded like whiskey over gravel, and it made me ache.

Made me yearn.

This was so good.

"Maddie I told you—" He was using the commander's voice, but I was in command.

I held on and sucked him deep.

He shouted his release, and I welcomed it, still smiling.

Minutes later, we were both resting against the headboard. Beau was done recovering, and I was salvaging my melted ice cream. Beau looked over at me. "You're looking mighty smug over there."

"Who, me?"

I scooped out the some of the last of the ice cream and held out the spoon to him. He took his time sucking the treat off the spoon. Damn, I was getting achy again.

"Give me another bite, Maddie," he whispered.

I did.

He took even longer to suck the ice cream off the spoon.

My nipples were so tight they actually hurt.

Beau yawned. "I think I need another nap."

He scooched down and pulled his pillow into his preferred position under his head and closed his eyes.

What the hell?!

Wait a second. I came here specifically to give him pleasure and make sure he got some rest. *So, cool your jets, Avery*. I put the empty carton of ice cream on the nightstand beside me, shoved the pillow down, planted my face into it, and began counting sheep.

Suddenly I was hauled into Beau's arms, one hand cupping my butt, the other tangled in my hair. He was chuckling.

"You're asleep," I protested.

"Do you want me to be?"

"No."

"Then let's play."

He didn't have to ask twice.

An hour, two orgasms, and one ripped pillowcase, later, I was seriously considering awarding myself a medal. Bonus points for Beau now sleeping like a baby.

I didn't know what tomorrow would bring, but tonight, everything was right in my world.

The next day, Ruby called and wanted to know if she could bring over homemade tamales and all the fixings for carnitas tacos. I just wanted to know who I had to kill. She explained she had enough to feed an army, so if I wanted to invite more people, I might want to consider doing so.

That was how I ended up with Kai, his fiancée Marlowe, Ruby, Beau and myself, all sitting around my backyard having margaritas after filling up on the best Mexican food I'd ever eaten. The evening was perfect, not too hot, not chilly, just a sultry Tennessee night with friends.

"How did you learn to make such good tamales?" Marlowe asked Ruby.

"Tia was one of my best friends growing up in LA. Her parents owned a Mexican restaurant. Tia and I worked there during high school and after we graduated. I worked in the kitchen,"

"With your looks, I would have thought you'd want to be a waitress for all the tips you could have made," Marlowe said.

"Tia was the pretty one. And you're right, she made bank."

"Oh, you must have been one of those late bloomers," Marlowe laughed. "I bet everybody's eyes popped at your high school reunion."

"Nope, you've got it all wrong." Ruby smiled. It was a bright, phony smile. "This has been me since I was fourteen. Nothing much has changed." She gave a short laugh and shook her head. "It's easier for a girl like me in Tennessee, but in LA, I stood out like a sore thumb. I was not up to spec, if you get my meaning."

There was an awkward silence where we could only hear my next-door neighbors' wind chimes, so I jumped in. "That was California's loss and Tennessee's gain. So, tell me, Ruby, how many more years until your ten-year high school reunion?"

"Five. Does anyone else want another margarita?" she asked as she got up with her half-full glass.

"I could use another beer," Beau said.

"So could I," Kai agreed.

"I'll take a refill on my margarita," Marlowe said.

"Why don't I come in and help you?" I scrambled up from my chair and followed Ruby into the house.

"Do you need another margarita?" Ruby asked me.

"Definitely. Yours are even better than Trenda's."

"It's the balsamic vinegar. You just add a dash, and it enhances the strawberry flavor and brings out a subtle savory note." She blended up another batch of margaritas for the three of us, and I got the beer out of the fridge for the two brothers.

"Every single time I'm around you, I learn something new. Your talents are wasted just being the barista at Java Jolt."

"Karen is going to be leaving at the end of the month," Ruby told me. "The owner has been talking to me about taking Karen's place as the manager." She poured out the margaritas.

"What do you think about that?" I asked.

"I told him it wasn't going to be easy, because Jordan has been working there for five years, and he expects to be promoted. I flat out told the owner that Jordan is going to be resentful because I'm a woman and I'm younger."

"What did he say?"

"Sam said he'd have a talk with Jordan."

Ruby bit the end of her thumb.

"Do you want to take the job?"

"I really do. I think I could kick ass. I learned a lot about managing a restaurant when I worked at Tia's parents' restaurant. And it would almost double my salary, but the hours would be a lot longer."

"For what it's worth, I think you'll do great, but I'll back you no matter what you decide."

Ruby grinned, and we walked back out into the backyard.

"How are you feeling?" Beau asked me as he rubbed my feet later.

"I am definitely not feeling any pain. Between the foot rub and the third margarita, I am floating on a cloud."

It was just about eleven o'clock on Saturday. I still had one more day off before I had to report to my first day back at work since my kidnapping. I was feeling really happy.

"Are you good enough to have a serious conversation?" Beau asked.

"Is there going to be a test afterwards?"

He dug in deeper on my arch and I moaned in pained pleasure.

"Nope, no test," he assured me.

"Then I'm all for a deep, dark conversation. Fire away."

"Speaking of that, 'firing away' I mean, tomorrow Kai and I are getting both you and Marlowe taser guns. Then we're going to take you to Simon and Trenda's house to train you how to shoot them on their land out back."

I relaxed into the foot rub. "So, is that the serious conversation? Cause that was easy." I wiggled my toes. He tickled the bottom of my foot.

"Hey! No fair."

"I wanted to make sure you were paying attention." He grinned. "Nope, that wasn't the serious part." His fingers slowed to where he was just tracing circles on the bottom of my foot. When I looked up at his face, I got concerned. He looked pensive. Not a normal look for Beau.

"What is it?"

"You love living here, don't you?"

"Absolutely. I've lived in Tennessee all my life. The only time I didn't live in Jasper Creek was when I was attending Eastern Tennessee State University and lived in the dorm, and then my apartment. But hell, that was only a two-hour drive back home. Plus, I had Zoe and Chloe with me when I was getting my masters."

He blew out a deep breath. "Did you ever think of leaving? Tennessee, I mean? Trying a new place on for size?" He was now holding my foot in a tight grip, and I'd bet anything he had no idea he was doing it.

Was he talking about me moving to California?

"Yeah, I've considered it once or twice. Why?"

"I just know how much you love it here. It's your home. It's always been your..."

"You're right. It is," I nodded. "But I'm not afraid of change."

He let out a deep breath. "That's good to know."

I frowned. "Is that it? Was that the big, dark conversation?"

He leaned forward and kissed me. "For now. It is, for now."

Chapter Twenty-Nine

I had seven more days until I had to fly back to California. The thought of leaving here was killing me. Leaving without Maddie would be like leaving half of my heart behind. I needed to make her mine.

Officially.

Hell, if I had my way, we would just fly to Vegas and get the deed done before I flew back to California, but after hearing about Drake's wedding and Evie's wedding, I knew that wasn't going to fly.

At minimum, I needed to get a ring on her finger before I left. I considered who to take with me to pick out a ring for Maddie. It was definitely going to be one of her sisters. But which one?

Chloe! Her name exploded in my head, as I remembered Maddie hugging on Chloe right after she'd been rescued.

Yeah, Chloe would realize that I'd know her

circumstances, but who in the hell cared? The important thing is she'd have an idea of what kind of ring Maddie would like.

Now all I needed was Chloe's number.

I called Simon.

"Yeah?" Simon answered. "What can I do you for?" he asked me.

"I need to go ring shopping," I told him.

"Congratulations, Beau. I couldn't be happier for you. But don't ask me to help you decide on one. It took me a whole day to find the right one. But I can tell you the name of a great jewelry store in Nashville, if that will help."

"That would be great. I'm also calling for Chloe's number. I want to take one of Maddie's sisters with me when I go shopping."

"If you can get her out of her apartment, that would be fantastic. Trenda and I were amazed when she showed up in Kentucky to visit Maddie in the hospital. She's turned into a recluse. Trenda has confronted her, but that went nowhere. I suggested an intervention."

"How'd that go?" I asked.

"Trenda isn't for it. I said my piece, now I'm staying out of it. But if you could tempt Chloe out of her cave, that would be great."

"I'm going to need her number. I'll text her first. I figure she won't answer an unknown number."

"You're right about that," Simon agreed. "I'll text

you with the name of the jewelry store, too. I don't remember it off the top of my head."

"Thanks."

After I hung up, it occurred to me I didn't even know what Chloe did for a living. All I knew was she was living as a hermit in an apartment in Gatlinburg since she'd moved out from the home she'd shared with her husband, Zarek.

Maybe she wouldn't be available on a weekday to go ring shopping.

I went into the laundry room and pulled out Maddie's delicates that I had washed. I hung up what needed to be air dried and put the rest in the dryer on low. My phone pinged, and I read Simon's texts.

I looked up the address of the jewelry store and saw that it was on the east side of the city. It was still fairly early, only nine-thirty in the morning. That meant that if we left soon, Chloe and I could get to Nashville in three-and-a-half hours, spend an hour dithering over a ring, and be back here by six, since we should miss Nashville traffic.

I winced. I suppose I shouldn't consider it dithering.

I laughed to myself. *Maybe don't be a screw-up and buy the first thing they show you. Yeah, that's it.*

I texted Chloe and asked her to call me. I hoped she would call soon. That is, if she would even bothering calling me back.

I gave a slow grin when my phone rang, and her number came up.

"Hi, Chloe, this is Beau."

"Hi. You caught my interest. So, you want to go ring shopping for my sister, huh?"

I wasn't expecting this. I was expecting shy and hesitant. Not somebody who kind of sounded like Maddie.

"Yeah. The thing is, the jewelry store that Simon is recommending is in Nashville."

Husky laughter came over the phone. "I'm not surprised."

"What do you mean?"

"What kind of ring do you want to get her?" Chloe asked.

"Something special. Not one big diamond. You know? Something colorful and pretty."

"Hmmm. You're not going to be here in town much longer, are you? Are you hoping to propose before you leave?"

"Yes."

"When are you leaving?"

I frowned. "Sunday."

"This could work. Come pick me up. I'll text you my address."

"Can you get off work?"

She laughed again. "Don't worry, I don't have a deadline."

She hung up.

Deadline?

I pulled up to a five-story building that wasn't close to anything. It looked like some kid had made a Lego apartment building and plopped it down in the middle of nowhere. When I got there, I saw Chloe's apartment was on the top floor, and the elevator wasn't working. That was fine with me, but it sure would be a problem for anybody moving in or out.

All in all, I couldn't imagine her husband being thrilled about her living here.

I jogged up the five flights of stairs, then got to her apartment and knocked on her door. Today she was dressed in leggings and another shirt that was two sizes too big for her. She had her hair in a ponytail, like most of her sisters often wore theirs. But she pulled hers back so tight, I thought it might hurt. Almost like she was trying to keep every aspect of herself tightly under control.

"What?"

"What-what?" I asked,

"You're staring at me."

"I'm just noticing how much all of you Avery girls look alike," I said as we started walking down the stairs together.

"Weird. Mostly, people only comment on Zoe and me looking alike."

"I've seen pictures of the six of you together. Yep, there is definitely an Avery girl model."

"Huh," was all she said as we made it to the parking lot. She didn't sound like the woman on the phone.

"My ride is over here," I said as I pointed to the Escalade.

"Nice," she murmured.

"There was a screw-up with my original rental. They upgraded me."

"Huh."

Uh-oh. I hoped I wasn't destined for a monosyllabic conversation for the rest of the trip. If I was, I hoped she liked the same music I did.

I opened her door and waited for her to get in before closing it and hopping into my side.

"Before we head on out of here, I want to show you my idea," Chloe said.

Hallelujah, a full sentence.

She reached into her large purse and pulled out a folder. "I called Brantley Hawkins. He said he could fit your project in, depending on the stones you want to use. He'd charge you a small rush fee, but I think he's worth it. I printed out some of his designs to see if you like them."

She handed me eight sheets of glossy printer paper with beautiful pieces of jewelry. Six of them were rings, two of them were pendants. All of them were like nothing I'd seen before. "What are these stones?" I asked.

"I'm pretty sure this is a pink sapphire, but I'm not sure about the lighter pink. Then those are diamonds. So, are those the two styles you like the best? They don't look like traditional engagement rings."

"But Brantley has made them?"

"For different clients. He's amazing. If I had my way, he would design all the rings for all my sisters. Now, he wouldn't do anything exactly the same for you. He could come up with something similar, using the stones you want. He charges fifteen percent over materials, and then he normally has a ten percent rush fee, but he would give you a three percent rush fee."

"Three percent?" I frowned. "Why so cheap?"

"You're a friend of mine, and you're in the military. His sister is in the Coast Guard. So, do you want to go over to his shop?"

"Absolutely."

"Head for downtown Gainesville. Let me get you his address so you can put him into your navigation system. I'll give him a call."

It took us less than fifteen minutes to get to Brantley's studio. I'd figured it would be in a shopping strip, but instead it was in a professional building next to a dentist's office. It had good security, and we had to be buzzed in.

I don't know what I was expecting, but it wasn't a stylish man about my age in a suit and tie.

"Chloe! When are you coming out with your next

issue? I need another hit of Seris. I need to know what comes next for her."

I watched as Chloe blushed. "Her story will come when it comes, Brantley. Can't tell you more than that."

"I forgot, you're indie. You get to decide your own deadlines." He grimaced. "Must be nice." Brantley turned to me. "You must be Maddie's guy. Chloe's told me about you. You're quite the hero. It would be an honor to work with you on an engagement ring for Maddie."

He held out his hand, and I shook it.

"Let's go have a seat in my conference room. We can look at designs, gems, and discuss prices."

We sat down, and I pulled out the printouts of the two rings that I thought would be good for Maddie.

Brantley looked at them, then tapped his finger on the two pieces of paper. "Can you tell me why you thought these would be good for her?"

I shook my head. "That's a hard question."

"Humor me."

"Well," I started slowly. "I haven't seen anything with gold in her house. It's all silver or stainless steel, so that's why I discarded these others." I motioned to the rings with gold bands.

"Makes sense," Brantley nodded. "What else?"

"She's down to earth. She doesn't wear a lot of make-up, but she always wears pink lip gloss. That's why I think she'd like the pink."

He nodded.

I was getting into this. "Neither of these are too high, like those single diamond rings are, so they won't catch on things."

"Makes sense. All of these are sensible reasons. Anything else? Anything emotional?"

"Emotional?"

Aw, shit. Woo-woo.

I looked down at the two printouts. Then I looked at his tray of gemstones. "May I?"

"Sure, look through them," he nodded.

I sorted through the stones. There were purples, blues, greens which I was pretty sure were emeralds. Diamonds, of course. I finally found one of the light pink stones, like what was in the one picture. I set that one aside. I liked that it was a rectangle cut. It looked noble. The color reminded me of the color Maddie's cheeks would get when she blushed. I kept pushing through the other stones, placing each one beside the pink one. The bright pink stones were nice, but too overwhelming, whereas the less glittery diamonds really set off the light pink stone. The pink in the middle with small square diamonds on either side looked regal.

Strong.

Like Maddie.

It took me more than a minute to explain all of that to Brantley, but I managed to. When I looked up from the tray, I saw there were tears in Chloe's eyes. She immediately looked away.

"Did that answer your question?" I asked Brantley.

"It definitely did. Can I have your e-mail? I think I can give you preliminary sketches tonight. In the meantime, let me price out the light pink sapphire, and let you know what you're in for on that. I'll be working in platinum, so I'll give a ballpark on what that will cost. I'm not sure what I'm going to design, but the ballpark should be pretty accurate. I won't know on the diamonds. But when I e-mail you the designs, I'll be able to give you pricing."

The three of us stood up. "Let's go to my office, where I have everything." Brantley smiled as he picked up his tray of gems.

"I'll leave the two of you to it," Chloe said. She pulled out a sketchpad from her tote bag. "I'm going to draw for a bit."

"See what you can do about drawing more of Oracle's Silence. I've been on the fan page, and the natives are getting restless. I'm not the only one jonesing for the next installment," Brantley said before we left the conference room.

"Yeah. Yeah." Chloe waved us away.

When we sat down in his office, I asked Brantley what he was talking about.

"Don't you know?"

"Know what?"

"Chloe writes one of the most popular manga series out there. She has a huge cult following. She hasn't released in over a year. Doesn't matter. Me and the rest of her fans will wait for years if necessary to read the next installment of Seris'."

"Huh."

I thought about one of the guys on my team who read manga. I wondered if he'd ever heard of Oracle's Silence.

"I've got to tell you, Beau. It's going to be a pleasure working on Maddie's ring. How you explained things has really inspired me."

I looked at the man in surprise.

"Seriously. I can tell you really know her. Not many men do. I hope one day I find a woman to love like that."

Chapter Thirty

I sat next to Eli in the Patterson's living room. I'd been talking to him for ten minutes, but he wasn't opening up to me. I couldn't get him to talk about his mom much, and he just froze when I mentioned Bruce's name.

Inwardly, I sighed.

Then I spotted the PlayStation setup that was connected to the TV. There were a couple of games lying on the floor beside it. Bluey and Paw Patrol. I pointed to the two games. "Do you play those games?" I asked.

For the first time since I arrived, he gave me a gap-toothed grin. "Yeah. With Mr. Patterson. He's not very good."

"Do you think you could teach me?"

He gave me a long look. "I dunno. You're old and you're a girl."

I managed not to laugh. "Please? I really want to try."

He gave a big, put-upon sigh. "All right." He wiggled off the sofa and went over to the TV and turned everything on. Then he sat cross-legged on the floor. He looked over his shoulder and stared at me. "Come on."

I took my cue and sat down next to him, cross-legged. He handed me a controller.

"Okay, now we're going to start. Are you ready?"

I shrugged. "Sure." I looked at the screen. Nothing was happening.

"You're holding it upside down. Give it to me." Eli took the controller out of my hand and flipped it over, then handed it back. "Now you can play."

Again, I had to suppress a grin. Now I was seeing the little boy I'd hoped to see. "Now what?" I asked.

He leaned over and pointed at my controller. "See this button? This is the 'X'. That one makes them jump. The stick makes them run or walk. Mostly they just walk, cause they're puppies. You know?" He turned his head sideways to look up at me.

"Makes sense," I agreed.

"Give it to me and I'll show you." He took the controller again, moved the joystick and wiggled it. One puppy ran around. "If you press the circle button he barks. Watch." The dog on the screen barked. "But don't let him bark at people. That would be bad."

"Why?"

"That's rude. We can't be rude."

"Who says? Your mom?"

He continued to fiddle with the joystick, but slower. He shook his head. "Not Mom. Mrs. Patterson. She knows a lot. She's teaching me things. So is Mr. Patterson. He's not ever mean. He doesn't even yell." Eli handed the controller back to me.

"That's really good, Eli."

"I like it here." He went silent.

I softly bumped him with my shoulder. "Show me some more," I encouraged.

He grinned at me. "Now you get to pick your puppy. Press the 'X'."

I deliberately pressed the square.

"No, you did it wrong. Give it to me."

I relinquished the controller again, and he pressed the 'X'.

"Oh wow, Eli. Look at all those puppies. I get to have one?"

"Yep." He was grinning really wide. Then, in a flash, his grin turned wobbly, and I saw his eyes fill up with tears.

"What is it, Eli?"

"What happened to Sparks?"

"Who's Sparks?" I asked.

"My dog."

I tried to think. Things were kind of a blur from that night, but after a moment I remembered Beau telling me he had called animal control.

"Sparks went someplace where they could take care of him. He was sick, honey."

"I know. Bruce was really mean to him."

"What did he do?" I asked gently.

"He hit him and whipped him, just like me. Sparks tried not to cry, but sometimes he did." Eli's voice broke. "Miss Avery, where is my dog?"

I'd never seen a child so in need of a hug, but he was sitting so stiff that I knew I couldn't hold him, at least not yet.

"Remember the man who found you under the stairs?"

Eli nodded.

"He made sure that Sparks got to a hospital. Just like you."

"I didn't see him at the hospital."

"That man made sure he went to a hospital for dogs, honey."

"Will I get to see him again?"

"I don't know."

His lower lip trembled. "Please, can't I see him? I don't want him to ever live with me again, cause I know Bruce will just hurt him again, like he did me. I want him safe. But can't I please see him?"

Eli about broke my heart.

"What did Bruce do to you?" I asked.

Eli looked away from me and started staring out the big bay window over the couch.

Fuck, I'd lost him.

"Eli? What did Bruce do to Sparks?"

"I don't remember." His whisper was so low, I had to strain to hear him.

"Honey, if you don't tell me, I can't make sure he doesn't hurt Sparks again."

He turned to look at me, his blue eyes wide and shimmering with tears. "You can do that? You can make it so he doesn't hurt Sparks again?"

I nodded. "But only if you tell me what he did."

"When Sparks was hungry, and I tried to get food for him and Bruce kicked him. Really hard. It hurt."

The way Eli said it hurt, told me that the kick had happened to him, too. "Did you try to protect Sparks?"

Eli nodded slowly.

"Did you get in the way so Sparks wouldn't get kicked?"

"Sometimes," he whispered.

"Did Bruce kick you instead of Sparks sometimes?"

Eli looked at the controller in his hand. A tear splashed down on the black plastic. "Sometimes."

"What else did he do to Sparks?"

"He had a piece of wire. It made a whizzing noise when he swung it. He would hit Sparks over and over and over again with it. Sometimes he made him bleed."

Eli wiped his nose with his sleeve.

"Did you try to protect Sparks from the wire?"

Eli nodded.

"What happened when you did?"

"It hurt. One time, he took off my pajamas and hit

me with it. I was bleeding just like Sparks, but mom made him stop that time."

I scooched closer to him so that my arm rested against his arm. After a few moments, he rested his head against my shoulder. It felt like I had won a marathon.

"What else did he do to Sparks?"

"He didn't feed him. He said he wasn't worth food. Sparks would get really hungry. Sometimes I would get up in the middle of the night and steal food from the fridge and give it to Sparks. Bruce never caught me."

Thank God for small miracles.

"I don't want Bruce to ever be around Sparks again," I said.

"That would be good," Eli mumbled. "But Mom made him go away once, but he came back, and he was madder."

"Bruce?" I asked.

Eli nodded.

"I can make it so Bruce goes away for a long, long time."

"You can?" I got another powerful hit from those blue eyes. This time, they were filled with hope.

"Yes. I can. But I'd need your help."

"I can't do anything. I'm little."

"You're teaching me how to play video games."

"You're not very good."

I chuckled. "No, I'm not. But you've helped me.

You did, Eli. So, can you help me stop Bruce from ever hurting Sparks again?"

"How?"

"I need you to tell a friend of mine the same things you told me. He's a lawyer, and he can make it so that Bruce can never hurt Sparks again."

"He can?" Eli looked amazed.

"He really can."

"Can I see Sparks? Can he come here and live with me?"

"I'm going to work really hard to find Sparks, but he might have already found another family who adopted him."

"Like Mr. and Mrs. Patterson are taking care of me?"

"Sort of. Let me see what I find out. I'll come back tomorrow. Okay?"

He nodded with a tremulous smile. "I can teach you more Paw Patrol."

"I'd like that."

Irene had volunteered to check in on some of my cases for me this week so I could spend more time with Beau since he was leaving on Sunday. But first I used that time to visit two of the animal shelters in Gatlinburg to see about Sparks, but I didn't have any luck. They suggested two additional animal shelters, so I left messages.

I also made a call to Oliver. He was excited to hear that I got Eli to talk. He told me what he planned to do with this new information, and then I got excited.

By the time I got to my house, I wasn't as early as I'd hoped to be. And I was majorly bummed when I didn't see the Escalade sitting outside my house. Oh well, I'd text him when I got inside, then take a shower. I pulled into the carport, shut off the engine, and gathered up all my crap.

By the time I made it inside, I realized how hungry I was. I dumped everything in my hands onto the dining room table and took my phone into the kitchen. I texted Beau to let him know I was home, then scrolled through to see if the two animal shelters that I hadn't visited had responded to my calls. They hadn't.

I opened my fridge and pulled out a root beer and was halfway through it when a text from Beau came in saying he would be home soon. That meant I needed to get my ass in gear and make something for dinner.

Another text came in. It was from Beau again. I grinned.

BEAU: Do you want me to pick up something from Polly's?

MADDIE: Hell yes. Want me to place the order?

> BEAU: Hell yes. I want chicken and dumplings. Is there beer in the fridge?

> MADDIE: Yes.

> BEAU: Then don't get anything to drink for me, but get a piece of cherry pie.

> MADDIE: Got it. How soon should I say you'll be there?

> BEAU: Tell her I'll be there ASAP.

> MADDIE: Great. Love you.

> BEAU: Love you too.

I finished off my root beer, called in the order, then headed for the shower. Maybe I'd surprise him and put on a sundress.

Chicken and dumplings and chicken-fried steak deserved the dining room table, so I pushed my stuff over so half of the table was cleared off, and then I set out plates and silverware. Just as I was finished, Beau was letting himself into the house. I could immediately smell the homemade goodness.

"Maddie, you look gorgeous in yellow. I love the dress."

I sauntered over and gave my man a kiss. "I love it when you supply me with food."

Beau looked over my shoulder. "We're going to eat at the dining room table, huh? Pretty fancy."

"Yep, we're going to eat our food on plates, not out of takeout containers."

"Big day." Beau snuck in another kiss.

Good man.

"Let's eat before the food gets cold," I said as I took the plastic bag from his hand. "Bring the plates back to the kitchen, and I'll plate the food. I didn't really think it through when I put the plates on the table."

I had the containers all out on the counter when Beau came in and I was just putting the vanilla ice cream that Polly had packed separately with ice cubes, into the freezer. I liked my apple pie à la mode, and I didn't have any vanilla ice cream here at the house.

"I'll leave the pie in the kitchen and we can warm it up later. The food seems to be warm enough right now," I said as I put everything on plates.

Beau carried the plates out to the table and we sat down.

I was a third of the way through with my chicken-fried steak and well into my mashed potatoes before I realized neither of us had said a word. When I looked up, I saw Beau smiling at me.

"What?"

"Nothing. I'm just enjoying watching you."

"You enjoy seeing me eat like this is my last meal?"

He frowned. "Did you eat anything today besides breakfast?"

I put down my fork and sighed. "No. My stash in the Jeep was empty. And things got away from me. But I did have a root beer as soon as I got home. That counts, right?"

"Maddie, I've cut up cantaloupe and bought raspberries and string cheese for you. It's all there right by the root beer. Those would have been better choices. I worry about you."

I felt my heart melt. "You did?"

"You saw me cut up the cantaloupe. I know that your favorite fruits are cantaloupe and raspberries. I should have put together something for your car."

"Beau, you're amazing." I said. And I meant it.

"You're not going to get out of this conversation by complimenting me. I've seen you close to hitting the wall when you haven't eaten. I'll put some protein bars in your car tomorrow. Do you promise you'll eat them for lunch from now on?"

Okay, now he was getting annoying. "I hear you, Mr. Marine. You don't have to run this into the ground. I'll eat something during the day. Okay?"

He gave me a long assessing look, then smiled. "Okay."

I looked down at his plate and saw that he was more than halfway through. "What about you? Did you eat lunch? You've sure eaten fast."

"Yes, I've eaten lunch. I'm just a growing boy." He smirked.

I rolled my eyes.

I took a bite of my mashed potatoes and gravy. Polly sure knew how to make good food.

"So how was work today?" he asked.

"It was pretty damn good. I spent time with Eli today. I got him to talking. He tried to teach me how to play Paw Patrol on his PlayStation. I sucked."

"He's liking it with the Pattersons?"

I nodded as I swallowed some steak. "Yeah. Better yet, I got him to tell me about what Bruce had done to him. First, he told me what Bruce had done to Sparks, but then Eli confessed what Bruce had done to him."

"That's good news, right? You told me how the D.A. didn't have a case against Bruce and he'd probably go free."

I nodded. "I called Oliver. He thinks that with Eli's testimony and the hospital records of how Eli had been abused, it will be a slam dunk. He's going to call Bruce's public defender and see if Bruce will just take a deal, so Eli doesn't have to testify."

"That is good news."

"What about you? How did you spend your day?"

"Went for a run with Kai, then went back to his place and we talked for a quite a while. I can't tell you how weird and great it is to have a brother after all these years."

"I'm so happy for you."

We continued to talk about different things going on in the world and in Jasper Creek as we finished our meal, then our pie. We took our plates into the kitchen and Beau loaded them into the dishwasher, then he turned to me. "Did I tell you how much I really like the sundress you're wearing?"

"You might have mentioned it."

"It's kind of early to go to bed. Should we watch some TV?" he suggested.

I shook my head.

"Wanna play pinochle?"

I shook my head.

"Scrabble?"

I shook my head.

"Wanna fuck?"

"Now that's an activity I can get behind." I grinned.

"How did I get so lucky?" Beau whispered as he took me into his arms.

"I let you win at pool," I answered with a laugh.

And wasn't that one of the smartest things I'd ever done?

Chapter Thirty-One

Brantley had come up with a design that was perfect on his first attempt. Somehow, he had listened to what I'd said and figured out a ring that totally fit Maddie. I called him back immediately to get started on it. I couldn't care less that it was going to be a significant hit to my savings account. It was totally worth it. Now I just needed to figure out a way to ask her to marry me. I'd heard how Simon had popped the question to Trenda, so I was going to have to do this up right.

Right now, though, I had bigger fish to fry. Maddie had sent me on a mission to find Sparks, if it was at all possible. She had visited two animal shelters in Gatlinburg yesterday, and they said they never received a dog with Sparks' description, and she'd been given two more shelters to check out. I was going to go about this another way.

I went back a couple of weeks ago to when we had

discovered Eli under the stairs, and I had arranged for Sparks to be picked up by animal control. I knew the date, time, and address of the pickup, so that was where I started. I explained the situation to animal control, that the little boy who had been beaten by the same man who had beaten the dog wanted to be reunited with the dog. The woman I talked to was extremely helpful. She told me which vet Sparks was taken to, so that's where I went next.

When I got there, I told the vet who was on duty the same story that I had told animal control. He was very sympathetic. I found out that Sparks had been kept there for over a week until he was healthy enough to be handed over to a no-kill shelter in Pigeon Forge. The vet told me that even though they'd sent him to a no-kill shelter, he was worried that Sparks was so aggressive, he might have to be put down if he tried to attack someone.

I thanked him for the information and headed over to Pigeon Forge. On my way over there I got a call from Roan.

"Hey," I answered. "How's it going?"

"Not so good," Roan replied.

I frowned. "What's going on?"

"You told me to monitor that fucker, Bruce. I'm guessing he was informed by his public defender today that they're going to use Eli's testimony against him."

"Okay. So, what makes this not so good?"

"Bruce's car is parked in Maddie's office parking lot."

"Fuck!" I took the first right I could into a parking lot. It was a bank. "Tell me everything."

"Do you know where Maddie is?"

"She's working at the office today. We need to call her right now and tell her she is not to go out into the parking lot, no matter what. I'm going to conference her in right now."

I pressed the add-call feature on my phone and pressed in Maddie's number.

"Hey, Beau," Maddie said, with a smile in her voice. "Any luck—"

"Maddie, I need you to listen, okay? I'm going to conference in Roan."

I pressed the button on my phone and confirmed that the three of us were on the line. "Maddie, Bruce is currently waiting for you in your office parking lot," I said.

"What? How do you know that? Are you out there?"

"I put a tracker under his wheel well on his car," Roan answered.

"Why did you— Oh, never mind. So, is he out to get me?"

"That's what I'm thinking," I said.

"No," Maddie said excitedly. "I bet he intends to follow me to Eli."

"Either that, or somehow get you alone, and get you to tell him where Eli is," I said.

"Always with the positive attitude," Roan commented.

"You've noticed that too, huh?" Maddie teased.

"Shut up, the both of you. This is not funny." I tried to keep my voice calm, but it was tough.

"Why don't we just call the police and say he's harassing me?" Maddie asked.

"Because he really hasn't harassed you," Roan answers. "Instead, let's see if we can do something that will get Bruce a longer prison sentence. Would you be up for that?"

"What the fuck are you talking about?" I demanded. "We're on this call to protect Maddie."

"Hold up, Beau," Maddie said soothingly. "Let's listen to what Roan has to say. Is there really something we could do to make sure that Bruce is put away longer?"

"If he's caught trying to break into a place where he thought Eli was, thinking he could harm the kid, then yeah. I think the D.A. would have a huge case against him."

I hate how excited Roan sounds.

I really fucking hate how right he sounds!

"Wouldn't he need to have actually kidnapped him?" Maddie asked.

"Not if he broke into the house where Eli was staying with an intent to do harm," Roan explained.

"But you'd only be able to do that if Maddie was a decoy," I spoke up. "And that is a non-starter in my book."

"Beau, that's not your decision to make," Maddie said. "Obviously, this is what Bruce has planned, and you've already fixed it so he can't do it because you had Roan plant a tracker in Bruce's car. Why not use this advantage and really put the wood to Bruce?"

She sounded so reasonable that it drove me up a wall.

"I'll tell you why we won't use this advantage. Because I already saw you in the hospital once, after you were almost killed. I refuse to let you be placed in danger for some stupid stunt," I roared over the phone.

There was dead silence on the line. Neither Roan nor Maddie said a word. They were letting me play back what I had just said.

"Come on, Roan. Admit it. We should let this drop." I prayed my friend would agree with me.

"It's Maddie's decision," he said. "What do you think?"

She sighed. "Beau, if you really can't deal with this, then we won't do it. But what's to stop Bruce from following me in the future until he pleads out and goes to prison?"

"I'll tell you what," I growled. "I'll go have a talk with the motherfucker. Trust me, he won't get within a mile of you after I'm done with him."

"What's to stop him from trying to go after Eli after you go back to California?" Maddie asked.

"Onyx Security will keep tabs on him. We have the tracker in his car, and the Pattersons' location is confidential." I kept my tone as reasonable as possible.

"Why wouldn't he just go after a different social worker?" Maddie asked.

I rubbed the back of my neck. She was killing me. "Fine. We'll come up with a plan to trick him into trying for Eli, then call in the cops."

"You're making the right decision," Roan assured me.

Roan and I had gone into Maddie's office through the front door, on the opposite side of the building from the employee parking lot. She invited us into a small office, and Roan pulled out his goodies. He had a comm system that she could wear that wouldn't show underneath her hair. We showed her how it worked, which took less than a minute. I'd also brought a large cardigan from her house so that she could wear it over a bullet-proof vest.

"Isn't this overkill?" she asked.

"No," Roan and I said simultaneously.

We continued to go over our plans.

Maddie had already talked to the Pattersons, and Mr. Patterson had stopped by with a key to their house. He was then going to join his wife and Eli over at his in-laws.

I provided the last thing. It was a good-sized teddy bear. The thought was that Bruce would assume it was a present for Eli, therefore, he wouldn't have a reason to stop Maddie and question her about Eli's whereabouts.

Maddie had her taser gun with her, along with her pepper spray. Roan and Simon would take turns following Bruce, so he wouldn't realize he was being tailed. I would go to the Pattersons' house two hours before Maddie left so I could set up cameras, and then answer the door when Maddie arrived.

"I still don't like this," I grumbled.

"I wouldn't like it if Bruce were following Lisa," Roan admitted.

"Thank God I have Drake as a big brother, and I know the workings of overprotective male minds, otherwise I'd kick both of you in the nuts." Maddie glared at both of us.

Roan gave me an amused look, and I started to laugh.

I pulled Maddie up from her seat, hauled her into my arms, and gave her a short, hard kiss. "You stay safe. You got me?"

She cupped my cheek. "I got you. I promise not to do anything but what we agreed on. I'm taking no unnecessary risks."

I glared down at her. "No. You need to promise not to take any risks at all."

"Fine, Mr. Marine. No risks at all. You happy now?"

"Closer. I'll be happy once Bruce is locked up for good."

She reached up and kissed me. "Me, too."

I picked up the bullet-proof vest. "Let's get you armored up." I hated that she needed this.

Hated it.

"Okay, honey." After I had it on her, she looked into my eyes and bit her lip. "It's going to be fine."

There she was, once again, trying to comfort me.

God, I loved her.

"She's almost there," Simon said into the comm link. "Three more blocks. Bruce is tailing a block behind her. He's really shitty at being covert."

Of course he is.

"You doing okay, Maddie?" I asked into my mic.

"For the fifth time, I'm doing fine," Maddie answered.

I heard Roan chuckle.

"I'm pulling up to the house. I'm going to park in their driveway," she told us.

I had cameras set up at the three entry points in the house, with two extras. One was inside the front door where Maddie was going to enter, the other was outside where I could watch Maddie's approach.

Roan, Simon, and I had bets as to how Bruce would decide to enter. Roan was saying through the patio door, and Simon was saying through the kitchen door. My bet was that Bruce would muscle his way in behind Maddie. The man was all brawn and no brain. That meant I wanted to have the front door open and Maddie inside before Bruce could lay a hand on her.

Maddie pulled into the driveway.

"He just passed the house," Simon explained. "I've got a visual on him. If he's smart, he'll drive on around the block."

Roan laughed. "He's not smart. He just parked three houses down."

"Maddie, get your ass into the house. Now." I commanded.

"He needs to see me walking in with the teddy bear. I'll be fine. For God's sake, I've got two Marine Raiders and one Navy SEAL protecting me."

I watched as she got out of her Jeep and then wandered around the back and opened the hatch to pull out her satchel and the teddy bear.

"He's out of his car. He's wearing a hoodie and gloves. He sure is out of shape," Roan said. "You shouldn't have interfered that last time, Beau. Maddie could have taken him out with the bat, no problem."

"Shut the hell up, Roan, and concentrate on your job. Does he have a weapon?"

"None that I see," Roan replied. "What about you, Simon? Did you see any?"

"No."

"He's crossing through the front yards. He's almost at the house," Roan said needlessly. I could see him.

"Maddie, move your fine ass," I growled. "I want you in the house *now*!"

She got to the top of the front stoop, and I opened the door. She looked calm as hell. Of course she did. That was my Maddie, strong as fuck. I forced myself not to yank her in, knowing that would give away the game.

"Get in here," I said through gritted teeth.

As soon as she walked over the threshold, I closed the door and pulled her into a fierce hug, forcing her face into my neck.

"No more. You hear me? No more of this shit. From now until you're Little Grandma's age, it's nothing but needlepoint and baking cookies. You got that?"

"Whatever you say, Beau."

I was pretty sure she was laughing, but I didn't care.

Chapter Thirty-Two

There was a polite knock on the front door. I wasn't expecting Bruce to be polite.

"Get into the kitchen, now. Open the kitchen door. Either Simon or Roan will be there," Beau told me.

"Are you going to answer the front door?" I asked. "Scratch that, of course you're not. He has to break in."

"Maddie, get into the kitchen and open the door." Beau was getting pissed.

I ran to the kitchen. As I did, I heard Bruce pounding on the front door. I didn't like leaving Beau. I

He's a Marine Raider, Maddie!

I wished that calmed me down. I immediately went to the Patterson's kitchen door. I put my hand on the deadbolt and got ready to turn it.

"Maddie, let me in."

I jumped. It was Roan's voice through the comm. I'd forgotten we were all linked.

I unbolted the door and let him in.

"Stay here," he said as he skirted around me.

"Whatcha got?" he asked into his mic.

"Bruce is still pounding on the door, but I see him getting ready to break in the glass beside the door," Beau answered.

"He's got a gun," Simon said.

He must have been at the house's front, watching Bruce.

"I see him," Beau acknowledged. "I'm good."

Roan left the kitchen with a gun in his hand.

I heard glass breaking.

"He's reaching in and turning the doorknob," Beau whispered.

I really wanted to see what was happening at the front door, but I wasn't going to look. My job was to stay put and not get myself accidentally shot like a dumbass.

"As soon as he crosses the threshold of the house with a gun, we've got him," Roan whispered.

"He's mine," Beau growled.

He sounds sexy when he's all growly.

I heard a loud noise, then a grunt, and something that sounded like a crack and a thump.

"I've got his gun. He's down!" Beau yelled.

"Hands behind your head!" Roan yelled.

"He's out. He can't move, Roan," Beau laughed.

"Can I come see?" I asked.

"Yeah, baby. You can come out now," Beau said. I could still hear the smile in his voice.

When I sprinted out into the hallway, I saw Roan putting zip-ties around Bruce's wrists.

"Is it really over?" I asked Beau.

"Oh yeah," he said as he put his arm around my shoulders and kissed my temple.

Simon walked through the front door. He was putting his phone into his back pocket. "The police will be here momentarily. Good job, everybody. He's going to go away for a long time."

I looked down at Bruce again. Lying on the floor with Roan, Simon, and Beau standing over him, he looked insignificant. I really wished Eli could see him like this, and know that he was really just a bug, and he would never hurt him again.

"We'll talk to Eli. He won't have to be afraid anymore." Beau promised me. "Plus, I have a lead on Sparks."

"You do?"

What couldn't this man accomplish?

He squeezed me tight, his eyes bright and filled with love. I couldn't wait to get him home.

∾

It wasn't until nine-thirty that we made it back to my place. First, we'd talked to the police, then I'd called Oliver. He was not happy that he hadn't been kept in the loop. After I'd tried to defend myself on my phone for over three minutes, Beau had finally taken the phone out of my hand and given Oliver a piece of his mind. He'd handed my phone back to me, and Oliver was suddenly extremely thankful for all that I'd done.

After that, we went to the animal shelter in Pigeon Forge, and they took us back to see Sparks. He was in a cage that was not near any of the other dogs. As soon as we got close, he growled. When he saw us, he started barking like crazy. He was pissed.

Beau squatted down in front of his cage.

"Hey, Sparks, do you remember me?" Beau crooned.

Sparks continued to bark as if Beau were the enemy.

Beau looked up at me. "Honey, you have your Kindle with you, don't you?"

"Yeah, why?"

"This is going to take more than a minute. Why don't you go out to your Jeep and read for a while? Sparks and I are going to get reacquainted."

"Wouldn't it be better if it were me? After all, it was a man who beat him."

"Just give me some time. I have a thing for dogs. I partnered with a dog for a while when I was overseas. I don't know if I can get through to Sparks, but there is no way we can let Eli near him when he's in this state."

I nodded. It was true.

I squeezed Beau's shoulder, then left the shelter for my Jeep. I really hoped Beau could accomplish something.

I was halfway through a new book when I heard some noise and looked up. Beau came out with two women. They were locking up. He looked tired, but he still smiled at me.

When he got into the Jeep, he leaned his head against the headrest.

"How'd it go?"

"I got him to take a treat from me. So, there was progress. But I won't be here long enough to gentle him before I leave."

"Beau, you can't fix everything."

He rolled his head and looked at me. "I want to."

"You're too soft-hearted to be a social worker," I teased.

That made him grin. "Take that back."

"Nope. Just calling it the way I see it. Now, do you want to eat out, or do you want to pick something up for dinner?"

"Let's order pizza and pick it up on the way home."

"Sounds like a plan."

After he was done ordering the pizza, he dialed another number. I gave him a quick questioning look before I turned my head back to the road.

"Kai? Yeah, it's me. How are you with dogs?"

There was a pause.

Beau laughed. "She does, huh?" He looked over at me, then put the phone on speaker.

"You're on speaker, Maddie's listening. I've got a favor to ask."

"Hi, Maddie. What's the favor, Beau?"

"One of Maddie's kids has a dog that was abused right along with the kid."

"Is this Eli?" Kai asked.

"Yep," Beau answered.

"So, what's the favor?"

"He's currently in a no-kill shelter in Pigeon Forge. He's not in good shape. Pissed at the world. I finally got him to take a treat from my hand. He's Eli's dog, but after all the abuse he took from Bruce, I don't trust him with Eli, and I just don't have the time to gentle him."

Kai laughed. "I get where you're going with this. Marlowe loves dogs. You've both met Chaos, Marlowe's Bernese Mountain dog. He's a gentle beast. Chances are, she'll do better gentling this dog than I will. But I'll check things out. I'll see what I can do about having him transferred to somewhere here in Jasper Creek. We'll work with him. We'll make sure Eli and his dog are reunited."

I could feel tears starting to well, but I blinked them back so I could concentrate on the road.

Dammit, my man really did intend to rescue the Western Hemisphere.

"Thanks Kai, I appreciate it."

If it weren't for Beau, the pizza wouldn't have even made it to the fridge. I was fine with leaving it on the counter. For some reason, I was coming apart. Seeing Sparks and how damaged he was because of Bruce and knowing that Eli had been just as damaged. Knowing that Beau was leaving me again, no matter how much we loved one another. Even the stress of what the guys were calling the 'op' even though it had worked out. It all seemed like too much, and I needed Beau's arms around me.

"Hey. What's going on?" Beau asked when we reached the bedroom.

I dropped my head to his chest and shook my head.

He put his knuckles under my chin and lifted it. I hated he could see the tears in my eyes.

"Maddie? Honey? What's wrong? You gotta tell me, so I can fix it."

"Hold me?"

"Always."

He wrapped his arms around me, and I slid mine around his waist, holding on like I'd never let go.

"I've got you, Maddie. I'll always have you."

God, I prayed that would always be true.

I don't know how long we stood there, just breathing, just being. A moment? A minute? Forever?

Then, like he could read the shift in me, Beau moved. He scooped me into his arms and laid me gently on the bed, following me down like it was the most natural thing in the world.

My emotions were still spinning out of control, and Beau was my only anchor in a world gone mad. I desperately grabbed at his shirt, trying to yank it over his head. He caught onto my need. This time there was no laughter, only quiet acquiescence in the face of my desperation.

Soon we were both naked, but it wasn't enough for me. I needed... something. I didn't even know what. Just more of him. Of us.

"It's going to be all right, Maddie. I promise you," he crooned.

"You can't know that. You can't promise that." My whisper was desperate.

His hands stroked boldly up and down my body, proving he knew me, that I was his. I arched into his touches.

"You're right, Maddie, I can't promise that. But I can promise that I will always lay down my life for you. You will always come first in my world."

"No," I wailed. "I don't want anything to ever happen to you! That's not it. I just want... I want..."

Fuck! What did I want?

His mouth captured mine. It wasn't a gentle kiss. It

was commanding. He took total control. In a flash, my desperation was gone as I melted into the man who was my world.

Beau.

Just Beau.

He continued to kiss me like his life depended on it.

His hands were everywhere. Our teeth clashed. Our tongues dueled. He bit my lip, and I bit his. He grasped my chin and kissed me harder.

Then he was trailing kisses down my jaw, licking my neck, going down further until he had my nipple in his mouth. He sucked and licked.

It was sublime.

He shoved a leg between mine, and heat blossomed in my core. I pushed up and started to ride his leg, trying to catch the perfect rhythm. I wanted to come.

He lifted his head. "No. You don't get to climax until I'm inside you. I know what you need. You need to know we're together. You need to know that it'll always be the two of us, no matter what. You need to know that, don't you, Maddie?"

Did I? Was that it?

I spread my legs and gripped his butt. "Inside me," I panted. "I need you inside me."

"I know you do," he agreed.

I heard the nightstand drawer open, and then he was pushing my legs farther apart. I couldn't help but smile; despite my desperation, he touched me between my legs to make sure I was aroused enough to take him.

"Now, Beau! No more waiting."

In one smooth thrust, he was locked deep inside me. I reveled in the connection. He waited, looking into my eyes. He must have seen what he was looking for, because he began to move, slowly at first, but then faster.

He was hitting all the right spots inside me. I wasn't going to last. I wrapped my legs around his waist as he pushed in and I squeezed him tight. I was getting so close, and I could feel the telltale tremors in his body. We were both so close.

"Now, Maddie," he shouted.

I went over the edge into a magical universe of light and color that I had only traveled with Beau. Caught in this amazing universe, I felt a level of serenity that I had never achieved before.

"Maddie?"

I smoothed my hand down Beau's back. "I'm here," I whispered. "I'm right where I've always meant to be."

And I was. I'd found my anchor. My soul had just found its home.

Chapter Thirty-Three

I was two blocks from Maddie's house, two hours early for the party at Trenda's. Maddie and I had agreed that we needed some time alone before facing all our friends and family for my big send-off.

I opened up the pink velvet box once again and ran my thumb over the most important thing I'd ever purchased. It made sense, because it went along with the most important and best decision I was ever going to make.

Sunlight streaked through the open window of the SUV, causing the two rectangle diamonds on either side of the large, light pink sapphire to quietly sparkle. But the diamonds didn't overshadow the stone in the middle. The sapphire represented everything Maddie was. Honorable. Kind. And the woman with the biggest heart I'd ever known.

I took the ring out of the box and looked at the

engraving. *We Were Always Meant To Be*. It might have taken me years to get there, but it was my truth now.

I put the ring back in the box, then shoved it into my jeans pocket, and drove the rest of the way to Maddie's house. As soon as I pulled up, Maddie threw open the door. She looked beautiful, and I couldn't get to her fast enough.

I got out of my rental and was soon in front of her, knocked out by that same yellow sundress with the red flowers that she'd worn once before. I don't know what she'd done with her hair, but it flowed around her shoulders in a way that had me itching to run my fingers through it.

"Beau," she whispered.

I looked into her big brown eyes. They were shadowed. She was in pain.

Oh God. No.

"Let me in, Baby."

She took two steps backward, and I followed her, shutting the door behind me. I scooped her up into my arms. She was soon in my lap on the couch.

"I can't do this. I thought I could play happy and say goodbye. But I can't." Her voice trembled.

I shifted her so that she was straddling my lap and we were nose-to-nose. Her eyes were glistening with tears.

"I'm not leaving you this time. I promise."

She bit her lip. "Yes, you are, and I don't blame

you, Beau. I know you're committed for five more years. I respect that." One lone tear dripped down her cheek.

"No, Maddie. Leaving without you is impossible. It would be like ripping out my heart." I wiggled as I shoved my hand into my jeans pocket. When I finally pulled out the pink velvet box, I drew her even closer. "You love me, right?"

"With everything I am." She nodded.

I held the box up in front of her. "I love you with everything I am, too. These last weeks made me realize I haven't been living a whole life. And I refuse to go another day without you permanently in my world."

I wiped the tear off her cheek.

"Marry me, Maddie." I flicked the lid open. "Make me whole."

Her eyes went to the ring. She caressed it with one finger, then she looked up at me. I felt like my whole world hinged on her next words.

"Really?"

"Of course, really. You're everything to me. I want to make a life for us in California. You can do that, can't you?"

I saw her face transform from sorrow to bliss.

Then... then... She gave me a blinding smile, full of mischief.

"Of course, I'll marry you and move to California. On one condition."

"What's that?"

"You need to beat me at a game of pool."

I threw back my head and laughed.

Her smile turned into a giggle.

I would never get enough of this woman and the joy she was going to bring to my life.

The words on her ring were true.

We were always meant to be.

To Read Ruby's Story, Pre-Order: A Tempting Seduction (Book 5)

To Read Chloe's Story, Pre-Order: Her Unending Horizon (Book 6)

About the Author

Caitlyn O'Leary is a USA Bestselling Author, #1 Amazon Bestselling Author and a Golden Quill Recipient from Book Viral in 2015. Hampered with a mild form of dyslexia she began memorizing books at an early age until her grandmother, the English teacher, took the time to teach her to read -- then she never stopped. She began re-writing alternate endings for her Trixie Belden books into happily-ever-afters with Trixie's platonic friend Jim. When she was home with pneumonia at twelve, she read the entire set of World Book Encyclopedias -- a little more challenging to end those happily.

Caitlyn loves writing about Alpha males with strong heroines who keep the men on their toes. There is plenty of action, suspense and humor in her books. She is never shy about tackling some of today's tough and relevant issues.

In addition to being an award-winning author of romantic suspense novels, she is a devoted aunt, an avid reader, a former corporate executive for a Fortune 100 company, and totally in love with her husband of soon-to-be twenty years.

She recently moved back home to the Pacific Northwest from Southern California. She is so happy to see the seasons again; rain, rain and more rain. She has a large fan group on Facebook and through her e-mail list. Caitlyn is known for telling her "Caitlyn Factors", where she relates her little and big life's screw-ups. The list is long. She loves hearing and connecting with her fans on a daily basis.

Keep up with Caitlyn O'Leary:

Website: www.caitlynoleary.com
FB Reader Group: http://bit.ly/2NUZVjF
Email: caitlyn@caitlynoleary.com
Newsletter: http://bit.ly/1WIhRup

facebook.com/Caitlyn-OLeary-Author-638771522866740

x.com/CaitlynOLearyNA

instagram.com/caitlynoleary_author

amazon.com/author/caitlynoleary

bookbub.com/authors/caitlyn-o-leary

goodreads.com/CaitlynOLeary

pinterest.com/caitlynoleary35

Also by Caitlyn O'Leary

PROTECTORS OF JASPER CREEK SERIES

His Wounded Heart (Book 1)

Her Hidden Smile (Book 2)

Their Stormy Reunion (Book 3)

Back To Our Beginning (Book 4)

A Tempting Seduction (Book 5)

Her Unending Horizon (Book 6)

OMEGA SKY SERIES

Her Selfless Warrior (Book #1)

Her Unflinching Warrior (Book #2)

Her Wild Warrior (Book #3)

Her Fearless Warrior (Book 4)

Her Defiant Warrior (Book 5)

Her Brave Warrior (Book 6)

Her Eternal Warrior (Book 7)

NIGHT STORM SERIES

Her Ruthless Protector (Book #1)

Her Tempting Protector (Book #2)

Her Chosen Protector (Book #3)

Her Intense Protector (Book #4)

Her Sensual Protector (Book #5)

Her Faithful Protector (Book #6)

Her Noble Protector (Book #7)

Her Righteous Protector (Book #8)

NIGHT STORM LEGACY SERIES

Lawson & Jill (Book 1)

BLACK DAWN SERIES

Her Steadfast Hero (Book #1)

Her Devoted Hero (Book #2)

Her Passionate Hero (Book #3)

Her Wicked Hero (Book #4)

Her Guarded Hero (Book #5)

Her Captivated Hero (Book #6)

Her Honorable Hero (Book #7)

Her Loving Hero (Book #8)

THE MIDNIGHT DELTA SERIES

Her Vigilant Seal (Book #1)

Her Loyal Seal (Book #2)

Her Adoring Seal (Book #3)

Sealed with a Kiss (Book #4)

Her Daring Seal (Book #5)

Her Fierce Seal (Book #6)

A Seals Vigilant Heart (Book #7)

Her Dominant Seal (Book #8)

Her Relentless Seal (Book #9)

Her Treasured Seal (Book #10)

Her Unbroken Seal (Book #11)

THE LONG ROAD HOME

Defending Home

Home Again

FATE HARBOR

Trusting Chance

Protecting Olivia

Isabella's Submission

Claiming Kara

Cherishing Brianna

SILVER SEALS

Seal At Sunrise

SHADOWS ALLIANCE SERIES

Declan

Made in the USA
Columbia, SC
18 June 2025

59557187R00189